*Highway to Love*

*Highway to Love*

Second City Books
2118 Plum Grove Rd., #349
Rolling Meadows, IL 60008
www.windycitypublishers.com

Published in the United States of America

First Edition: 2012

ISBN:
978-1-935766-53-7

Library of Congress Control Number:
2012939239

Cover Production by Amanda Inkinen
Cover Image: KWest/Shutterstock #13177333

# Highway to Love

*by Dani Burke*

A Division of Windy City Publishers

*For the two Marys in my life~*

*My mother, and my friend, who have been with me
from the very beginning, encouraging me to follow my dreams...*

CHAPTER 1

It was a beautiful spring day, and Alex and Stephanie were on the Kennedy Expressway heading in to work.

"Hey, Steph. This isn't bad. At least traffic is moving."

"Wow, look over there," Stephanie pointed. "Boy, this is going to be a good year for eye candy." The men she pointed to were both tall and *very* fit judging by the pecs and biceps, which could be seen bulging from their gray tees. One had dark blond locks, and the other dark brown hair, peeking from beneath their hardhats.

"Come on, boys. Take off those sunglasses so we can see those eyes," Steph coaxed.

"You *are* a trip. We need to find you a man real soon, honey. And I'm engaged, or did you forget? I don't need to be getting all hot and bothered looking at a couple of strangers," Alex countered.

"Oh, yeah. Sorry about that. Can't you just have fun and fantasize with me?"

"Okay, I'll fantasize with you, but don't embarrass me by trying to get their attention. We don't have time to flirt with a couple of construction guys."

The two men looked mid-40s, but it was hard to tell with hardhats and sunglasses obscuring the view of their faces. The two beefcakes Steph was zeroed in on were engaged in conversation over some sort of blueprint. Definitely great looking guys from what Alexis could see, as she watched the two men start laughing.

Steph was craning her neck as traffic moved because she didn't want to lose sight of them. "Wow, just look at him, will ya," she pointed to the one with darker hair. Looks like that mouth was just *made* for sin. Alex, go a little slower so I can get a better look."

"There's traffic behind me. For crying out loud. Get a grip, will ya?"

Stephanie sulked back into her seat as Alex hit the gas and left the two lookers behind. "Party pooper."

To keep her friend from being crabby for the remainder of the ride into the city, Alex made an offer. "We'll drive in again tomorrow, and hopefully you can get another look okay?" Alex and Stephanie were neighbors and generally commuted together to the LaSalle Street law firm where they were both employed. Steph shot Alex a huge grin in agreement.

That evening, shortly before six, Alex had cleaned off her desk. It had been a long day, and she was ready to head home. Hopefully traffic wouldn't be bad. Usually the construction crews that plagued Chicago's roadways during the spring and summer were long gone by that time of day, so there wouldn't be any delays.

Enroute to the firm's reception area to meet Steph, Alex ran into Richard. She had only been able to speak with him briefly at a meeting earlier in the day.

"Hi, Pumpkin. I've missed you today. You guys getting ready to call it quits?" Richard asked.

"Yup. There's Steph now." She gave him a quick peck. "I'll talk to you later, Sweetie." Then she leaned in and whispered something suggestive in his ear.

He recoiled and spoke in a low volume. "Alexis, you know I don't like it when you talk dirty."

Eyeing Stephanie making her way down the corridor, Alex mumbled her apologies in response to Richard, then masked her disappointment by pasting a smile on her face as she turned to face her friend.

"Ready to roll?" Stephanie asked. "Oh, hello, Richard." It was no secret there was no love lost between the two of them, a fact that Alex dealt with as best she could.

Giving his fiancée another quick peck on the lips, the tall, dark-haired attorney sporting an impeccable Brooks Brothers suit retreated. "Well, you girls have a nice evening. Honey, I'll talk to you later."

As the women made their way to the parking garage Stephanie commented, "I forgot to ask you. How was the theater and dinner with Richard on Saturday?"

"It was nice. Brian Dennehy was awesome in *The Iceman Cometh*. And Petterino's is always good. Love their pasta. Then we came back to my place."

"I take it he spent the night?" Steph suggested, expectantly.

Alex sighed and tried to control her temper. "You know, I'm tired of you asking me this every Monday. Yes, of course he spent the night—and yes, we made love. Does that make you happy knowing this? I suppose you want the juicy details. Well frankly there *are* no juicy details."

"No, I don't want the details." She lowered her voice. "It's just that you never seem enthused about the sex. I mean could you just for once say we had wild and crazy sex? You know if there is no zip or zing in your sex life, then you're setting your marriage up for failure."

Alex replied, "Look, our sex life is just fine. So he's a little reserved in the lovemaking department. Maybe it'll get better once we're married. I've tried spicing it up, but he doesn't seem to like that very much."

"Well, I hope for your sake things get better. You know, marriage is hard enough even if you *do* have a fantastic sex life. Anyway, I'm looking forward to the drive in tomorrow and ogling those great-looking guys. Hopefully we'll see them again."

The next morning, even though clouds were threatening rain when they left for work, Stephanie was still hopeful to see her "eye candy boys," as she referred to them.

"Boy, I sure hope the road crew doesn't get a rainout before we get there."

Alex hesitated. "Steph, I really think you should join one of those dating services. If all you can think about is good-looking construction guys, you have a huge problem, honey. Yes, they are cute, and some are very hot looking, but you know nothing about them. They're probably married anyway."

"Well, we'll just have to find out, won't we? You wait and see. I'm going to meet that hunk if it's the last thing I do."

Alex laughed, "So help me, if you embarrass me..."

They had left earlier than usual, and even with the threat of rain, the road crew was out there, and traffic was slowing to a halt.

"Oh, oh," Steph explained and pointed, "there they are! If you could slow down and just move up a bit, we'll be right by them and maybe we can catch their eyes."

"I *told* you: We move when traffic moves and stop when traffic stops. Did I tell you to not embarrass me?"

She replied in a haughty tone, "I just want to try to make eye contact with cutie boy and flirt a little. What's the harm in that? Maybe I'll be successful, okay?"

*Sure,* Alex thought. *Successful at what? Flirting with some construction guys for God's sake? AND what were the odds one or both of them were unattached? If the guys were single, they were probably hitting the bar scene and sleeping all over the place, just like every other unattached guy out there.*

Just as those thoughts were running through Alex's head, traffic edged up a bit and stopped. Her car stood directly in line with the two men.

"Okay, roll down the window and just look at them—maybe one of them will catch your eye," Steph coached.

*I'm engaged for God's sakes. Do I have to stoop to this flirting just so my best friend can get a date?* Alex groused to herself.

But she did as asked. Rolling down her window, Alex looked toward the hunky honeys. She had to admit, upon closer perusal, they were both pretty much "10s." This was saying a lot, because Alex was pretty picky. Her eyes scanned from the men's white tees covered by those reflective vest things and came to rest satisfyingly on the way their jeans showed their rear ends to best advantage.

Since rain was threatening, and the sky was getting darker, the guys didn't have on sunglasses. The women took in the dark-haired Mr. Muscle's intense eyes. He had looked hot in his aviators, but without them, he was a sapphire-eyed angel. Adonis's partner was just as tempting.

Alex glanced at the dark-haired guy and started a mental checklist. Nice body. No—*great* body. He had great teeth, arms of steel, and oh those azure eyes! Tufts of silky hair poked out beneath the edges of his hardhat. Yum!… Wait a minute! Why she was making a list, Alex had no idea. Probably because her mind had been wandering a lot with all the upcoming wedding pressure. Lately she had found herself assessing other men to see how well they compared to Richard.

While Alex was tallying his attributes, as though sensing her eyes taking inventory, the studly brunette looked up and stared right back at her. Their eyes locked, startling Alex. Breaking the spell suddenly, the man's gaze wandered over to Steph, who was practically in the driver's seat trying to get a better look at the construction guy show.

Steph flashed him her most seductive smile, and then proceeded to give him her flirty little wave. Azure eyes' expression softened as he gave her a little wave back. Then his eyes were back on Alex, studying her again. Her cheeks suddenly reddened and she could feel their heat. This guy had a very unwelcome effect on her. She suddenly found herself reveling in a fantasy about hot, sweaty sex. He looked like he'd be a perfect and willing candidate for just that very thing.

Just then, Mr. Hottie's blonde colleague walked over to him. He must have said something about the two crazies in the Lexus, because they both started laughing. The blond man looked at each of them and gave them a little salute. It was pretty obvious the guy with the lighter hair was taken with Steph because he kept checking her out.

"Why doesn't the other one look at me instead of you?" she pouted. Alex looked up. Stephanie was right. The brunette had his head tilted a bit as if he was assessing *her*. Traffic began to move.

"Okay, the fun is over so be nice and wave goodbye," Alex instructed.

Steph waved again and they waved back. Alex looked at them and shrugged her shoulders with a "don't ask me why we're doing this" look before she accelerated.

"Wow, that was fun, wasn't it?" Steph asked, though she needed no convincing.

"Fun for you, yes," Alex replied. *I can only imagine the look of horror on his face if Richard saw me staring at these guys. He'd probably give me that "I'm disappointed in you Alexis" look and tell me I'm being childish.* She loved Richard, but sometimes he could be so closed-minded.

"This is going to make the summer so much fun! Hmm… I'll have to put on my thinking cap to figure out how we can meet them," Steph schemed.

Alex chuckled. "Okay, you just do that, and let me know what grand plan you come up with."

The two men had opinions of their own. As the Lexus rolled away, Mike said, "I think I'm in love."

Joe just laughed.

"Blondie looked like one hot chick to me, don't you think? I mean, don't get me wrong, they are both do-able! But there is something about that blonde. Did you see her giving you the once-over? From the looks of her, I know she would definitely be your type. But for once, let me have the first shot at it. Okay?" Mike said.

"Whatever," Joe shrugged. "I thought the brunette was kind of cute myself.

Something in her eyes made me think she's got spunk. You know, kind of like she'd be up for any kind of challenge. Do ya think they're married and just flirting to pass the time? Or were they serious? Well, who knows about women. Besides, how do you figure you're gonna meet 'em, anyway?"

Mike curled up one side of his mouth in a questioning look. "I don't know yet. But, you've always been up for anything. I can say *that* about you, Baker. But what's up with you giving the brunette the eye? Looks-wise, she is *so* not your type. Is this celibacy thing starting to get to you? Frankly I don't know how you're doing it."

Joe replied with a sigh. "You sound like my mother. She's always harping on me to find the *right* woman. And soon. My sisters are on me, too. Well, we both know marriage isn't all it's cracked up to be."

"Yes we do, but I wouldn't mind trying it again. You know, if I found the right person. I know you would, too." Mike really wanted a relationship again. He liked being married, and even though his ex had walked out on him, he wanted that connection with someone he cared about again. He didn't totally regret what he had gone through, because that union had brought him his son, Jason, who had just graduated from Illinois State.

After Joe's divorce, he had entered into quite a few brief relationships, none of which ever became serious, at least not on his part. Recently, he decided to take a break, and he hadn't been with a woman in over a year. He'd just given up and was tired of fighting it. Sometimes he seriously doubted he would ever find the right woman again.

Mike said, "Maybe we'll see them again tomorrow. Let's keep an eye out and try to work closer to the road. Maybe we make sure traffic is a little delayed, so we give ourselves a chance to talk to them. You know, find out a little what they're like. And if they're really interested, or just passing the time. If I think she's available, maybe I can ask the blonde for drinks or a Sox game or something."

"Suit yourself," Joe replied, amused.

Unfortunately, that night the storms began just prior to midnight and continued well into the next morning, creating lightning strikes and huge downpours, putting an end to Steph and Mike's plans. Joe, on the other hand, welcomed the inclement weather. He had tons of paperwork to do and was glad to spend the day in the office catching up. For once, the weather had delayed traffic, instead of one of his crews. The thought made him chuckle. The heavy rain had caused flooding, making the trip downtown arduous. Joe felt empathy for the weary commuters who faced these kinds of delays day after day, whether it was because of the weather or road construction. Progress sucked, but roads had to be built and repaired. Fortunately for him.

Joe hadn't slept much the previous night. Was it the storm that caused him to toss and turn, or was it his constant thoughts of the brunette in the Lexus? His mind began to wander as he sat stopped, waiting for traffic to move.

Mike was probably right. This celibacy thing was stupid. Here he was having feral thoughts about a stranger who he knew nothing about, not to mention that she was not even his type, at least looks-wise. But something about her made him want to know her. *Probably married or engaged or at least somewhat attached, and probably too young for me anyway.* He had had a birthday the previous month, and these days it seemed like everyone looked younger than he did. But then Mike had guessed the ladies were probably near his and Mike's age.

The Nextel brought him back to reality. "Hey, bud. You on your way to the office?" Mike's voice wafted over the airwaves.

"Yup, stuck in traffic. How about you?"

"Stuck in traffic? We don't get stuck in traffic. We only *cause* people to get stuck. Isn't that why people hate us and give us dirty looks most days of our lives?" Mike couldn't resist joking.

"True, except for but those two chicks yesterday. They were all about it. You know, I hate to admit it, but I spent the better part of the night thinking about the brunette. How about you? Still thinking about her passenger?" His friend replied.

"You mean you're not interested in her?" Mike's voice was slightly incredulous.

"If you can figure out a way to actually meet them, then sure, you get the first shot." Joe agreed.

Joe wasn't the only tired commuter that day. Alex also started her morning feeling drowsy. She had slept poorly. All night she lay staring at the ceiling as the lightning lit up her room like fireworks. The pressure of committing to wedding plans was stressing her out, and if it hadn't been for the storm she would have been awake anyway. Her doubts about Richard were growing daily, paralleling his daily pressure to set a date. *Was marrying Richard a mistake? Maybe Stephanie was right. Maybe I should see a professional to help me with my indecision.*

Stepping into the shower, as the warm water began to pelt down, Alex started to fantasize about the dark-haired construction guy. Should she take his attentive glances as a compliment? Normally guys just ogled Steph. And Stephanie *did* seem pretty interested in him. God knows he exuded sex appeal. The other guy was no slouch, either.

The weather sucked, and she didn't want to be driving in it. It would have to be the train today. Wrapping a towel around herself, she grabbed the phone and dialed Steph's number. "Hi. Let's take the 7:20. The roads will be a mess with all the water. Probably downed trees, too."

Steph wasn't pleased. "Well, it's your call. You don't think the road crew will be out there, do you?"

"Are you crazy? There's lightning all over the place. They don't work in this kind of weather. You've got all frickin' summer to flirt with them. That road work isn't going anywhere." *And we'll be stuck in it*!

CHAPTER 2

The weather didn't improve until late Thursday. On Friday morning, the sun came scorching through hot and humid, and Alex agreed, after much pleading from Stephanie, to drive into the city.

Having planned her wardrobe the previous evening, Alex quickly slipped on her camel lace sleeveless shirt and a short black skirt. She added her new Jimmy Choo animal print sandals with the little heel, and finished the ensemble with her tiny gold bear drop earrings and matching bear necklace set. It was already eighty degrees at 7:00 a.m., with the forecast calling for a temperature near ninety by early afternoon. Adding in the steadily climbing humidity, the day was slated to become a scorcher.

Alex and Stephanie were neighbors in side-by-side brownstone townhouses, and they agreed to meet at Alex's garage for the ride in to work.

"Geez, it's awful outside. Who can stand this heat?" Steph groused.

"Well it's only supposed to get worse. Supposed to be around ninety and hot over the weekend. Richard wanted to go on a picnic tomorrow, but I'm nixing that idea and planning something nice, cool, and indoors," Alex confirmed.

The road crew had started at 6:00 a.m. that morning. They were behind schedule because of the rain and had to work quickly to make up for lost time. Everyone was already cranky and sweaty because of the humidity. Joe knew it would be a long day, so he spent time first thing that morning making sure there was plenty of drinking water on hand to keep his crew safe and sane.

He was a boss who cared about his men's health and safety. Most of his guys had been with him a long time. Mike had always respected the way he treated his employees. He ran a tight ship, and that was one reason for the company's success.

The crew had a huge pour that day along the concrete barrier edge closest to the open traffic lane, and Joe wanted to get it done before it got too hot. This was an important section of roadway and he didn't want it screwed up. Unfortunately, they would have to utilize part of one of the open lanes to get the trucks in and out quickly so the concrete would not set up too quickly in the drums.

"Okay, let's get this going. We've no time to waste," he barked out. "Here come the first few loads." The flagger had stopped traffic to get the half dozen mixers in from the remote site. Commuters weren't happy, but then they never were. It was so hot that a couple of cars had already overheated. IDOT was standing nearby ready to help.

The crew got the trucks in as quickly as they could, trying to minimize the traffic disruption. Things were moving along pretty well, at least for the moment.

"Ooh," Steph cooed. "Look ahead. They're working close to the road today. Maybe we'll be close enough to say hi if we see them. Wow, I think they're stopping ahead. Hey! Come on! Why are you turning the air off?"

Alex was losing her cool because of Stephanie's obsession with these guys.

"They tell you that in conditions like this you should keep the air off and open the windows to keep the car from overheating. I've told you that before. What do you want us to do, have a car that dies on us?" Alex chided.

Things started to open up and they were moving again. Traffic was beginning to move quickly, so she wasn't sure today was the day they would be saying "hi," as Stephanie hoped. Alex zoned in on the two guys, as did Stephanie. To her delight, both were looking up at traffic. *Are they looking for us?* Alex thought.

Fortunately the guys spotted the Lexus, and both waved to the girls. Steph leaned into Alex, yelling out the window and waving. "Hi guys!"

Alex just laughed, shaking her head. "You are such a nutcase. You know that?"

"Who cares? This is fun. Just because you can only look but not touch doesn't mean I can't. I think they're having just as much fun as we are." Traffic was moving quickly now, so their encounter was disappointingly brief. Alex stepped on the gas, and the Lexus moved off, Steph's eyes still glued to the two guys.

About fifty yards or so from where the women had passed the road crew, however, the Lexus started to sputter.

"Oh no, please don't die on me. Not here in all this traffic," Alex moaned. But within moments, steam began to appear from under the hood. Alex screamed, "No!" She knew she had to shut down or blow the engine. Exasperated, she started pounding the steering wheel. Cars started honking because they had nowhere to go. Drivers who could began to pull over onto the shoulder to get around the disabled vehicle. Alex didn't know what to do.

Mike noticed the commotion first. "Looks like a stall up ahead. Want me to check it out?"

Joe just shook his head. *What a way to start the day.* "No, I'll do it. I'll give you the sign to call IDOT if we need to." As he was making his way to the problem, he stopped dead in his tracks. He saw "her" getting out of the Lexus. It was like a slow-motion scene from a movie. Looking like she was ready to kill, the woman hiked up her skirt and threw one leg, then the other, over the concrete barrier. For the life of him, he couldn't figure out where the hell this insane female thought she was going. Before Joe could shout "*No*," she had scaled the barrier and plunked herself into wet concrete. The crew had just poured that section. It was fresh and hadn't even begun to set. Joe stared in disbelief. "She" had just ruined an entire section of fresh roadway with her flailing around.

She looked shocked once she realized what she had done, looking around in despair and then down at her feet. *My new Jimmy Choos! Oh my God!*

Alex looked back, and saw "him" running at her yelling out, "Don't move! Don't move a fuckin' inch! Do you hear me?"

Oh, Alex heard him all right. When "he" caught up to her, Mr. Construction put his hands on his hips and blasted her.

"Are you crazy? That stuff's wet. Obviously you're too dense to realize it!" he blurted out, looking none too pleased.

When Mike saw Joe start running, he knew something was up. "Mario get IDOT on its way!" he called over his shoulder, as he trotted after his buddy.

Stephanie had exited the Lexus and ran over to figure out what was going on. "Oh, my gosh!" she shrieked. "Alex, what do you think you're doing? That stuff's still wet!"

"Oh, my God! My Jimmy Choos are ruined!" She looked at Joe, pleading, "Do something, *please.* I don't know what to do, and my shoes are getting ruined."

Joe was incredulous. She had just cost the company thousands of dollars, and all she was worried about was her shoes? He couldn't help it. He turned up the volume. "I don't give a shit about your shoes lady! You just ruined a perfectly good section of roadway. So cool your jets, and stay put until I can get you out so you don't screw up any more of our stuff!"

Mike reached the trio, out of breath. "What do you want me to do?"

"Pull the service truck around in that lane up behind her car. I'll have to lift her out."

Joe looked back at this nutty chick. If he had been any closer, he probably would have wrung her neck. A look of disgust registered on Joe's face as he took off his sunglasses and hooked them on his shirt. He stood glaring at the stranded damsel in distress with his feet apart, hands back on his hips, just shaking his head.

"You know," he barked, "in all the years I've been paving, never have I encountered anything so stupid. And believe me, I've seen some pretty stupid things. What the hell possessed you to do this? Are you some kind of an f-ing nutcase?"

"No, she is not a nutcase! The car died and she got upset. What do you expect?" Steph growled in Alex's defense.

"I expect people to use their heads and think first before doing something idiotic and insane. Your friend here apparently does not *think*," he yelled back.

"Stay put!" he pointed a warning finger as Alex watched him approaching.

"Quit yelling at me. I'm sorry. What else do you want from me? I'll pay for any damage I've done," she said calmly and contritely.

"It's not money, *darlin',*" he said with a killer glare. "It's time. It's a schedule we have to keep. It's the damned weather. My guys don't need this kind of crap."

Joe's eyes were on fire and his jaw was set. Although Alex's brain was taking in the guy's anger, she couldn't stop herself from thinking *Oh, my God. He is the most handsome man I have ever met in my life. And I thought Richard was handsome.* She just stared at him. Now that he was this close, she could see his face was chiseled, his cheekbones were high, his chin had a small cleft, and when he gritted his teeth she noticed again they looked straight and very white against his tanned face. His eyes were absolutely mesmerizing. *He is hot. No, correction. He is sizzling!* Alex laughed at herself with the absurdity of the situation. She was trying to decide whether his crude language, flung at her in his Northside accent, could mar his physical appeal.

"I'd like to see you working *your* little ass off in this heat," he seethed.

Alex bit her lower lip. He was right. The sweat was rolling down her neck and cleavage. She couldn't imagine making a living this way. Before she could stop it, tears began to sting her eyes and one lone tear slipped down her cheek. She whispered, "I'm sorry." She did *not* want to cry in front of this man, but she couldn't control it, so she turned her back to him. It was baking standing here outside in the heat, which only increased her misery.

He blinked his eyes a second, hesitated, and then blared, "Can it, lady. Don't try the pout or the tears thing, because they have absolutely no affect on me. Whatsoever. Ya got that?"

Just then, Mike pulled the service truck up behind the Lexus. He pulled out the lift on the rear and turned to them. "What can I do?"

"Nothing. I'm gonna just lift her out, put her on the gate, clean her up, and get her on her damned way and out of our hair."

*He's going to lift me out? How the heck does he think he is going to do that?* Alex thought.

Joe placed himself directly behind Alex, with the tips of his boots touching the barrier, getting as close as he could for leverage. He reached out and put both hands on her hips. She turned her head as best as she could to give him one of those *don't touch me* looks, but he didn't seem to be paying attention. She knew better than to argue with a man this angry.

"Hey!" she protested. "What are you going to do?"

He lifted his eyes and they stared at each other a second. "I'm going to get you," he grunted, as he began to lift her, "out of this situation you've gotten yourself into." Suddenly, Alex felt his strong biceps lifting her up and over the barrier. Then, without hesitating, Joe put one arm under her knees and picked her up like a groom carrying a bride over a threshold, carrying her like she weighed no more than a butterfly. Before she knew it, they were at the service truck, where Joe gently sat her onto the rear lift.

*God, he has to be pretty strong to carry me. He didn't hesitate for a second, and he did it so effortlessly. Hmm, must work out a lot.* She couldn't believe the insanity of the situation: here she was with a dead car, concrete all over her beloved Jimmy Choos, and yet she was focusing on how hot and fit her rescuer was. This should be *Stephanie* making a fool of herself. Not calm, cool, engaged Alex! After all, *Steph* was the one so hell bent on meeting this hunky road warrior.

"Get me the damned hose," Joe yelled. IDOT had pulled up and was working on getting the Lexus started. "And get me some towels!" He threw his hard hat on the bed of the truck. His arms and face were wet with perspiration, as was the longish hair at the base of his neck, hair that was very dark with slight touches of gray scattered throughout. His hair was kind of wild, in a sexy way: not curly, not wavy, not spiky, either. *He definitely uses some kind of a gel,* she thought. At that moment she caught a slight scent of wet, warm male skin, which she did not find at all unpleasant. *I want some of this. I want some of him.*

Joe removed Alex's shoes and threw them to the ground. He began to hose off her feet and legs, rubbing as he rinsed.

"Don't treat my shoes like that!" she bristled. "Would you kindly rinse them off and try to save them, please. They're Jimmy Choos and they cost a fortune."

Joe stopped and looked up at her. "Well, your friend Jimmy, whoever he is, will just have to buy another pair." Alex glared at him, but then it occurred to her that she might need to use a different approach. She switched to her pouty, soft, "please" look.

It worked. Joe softened up and said patiently to Mike, shaking his head, "Get the other hose and try to see if you can bring them back to life, okay?"

"Thank you," she smiled.

Joe returned to the task of getting the stuff hosed off. When he had removed the majority of the gray ooze, he grabbed a rag and started washing off the remainder. *Women, they can make you crazy. They are so damned unpredictable.*

When he was rubbing off the last of the muck, Joe suddenly stopped. *What the heck?* He stared at her little red toe nails. He had always had a thing for red polish. He slowly looked up at her and his eyes changed from furious to something totally different. The rescuer's mouth parted and he took in a deep breath. His eyes met hers, and then moved down to her mouth, which she noticed he spent just a little too long looking at.

*What the heck is this all about?* Alex wondered.

For an instant, just an instant, Joe had the ridiculous thought that he wouldn't mind finding out what that mouth tasted like. Her lips looked soft and warm, just like her big brown puppy dog eyes. He considered the pink gloss shimmering enticingly off of her lips and imagined the delight of licking it off.

His intent gaze continued downward, stopping for a brief moment at Alex's breasts, then back down to those cute little toes. Then he rolled his eyes slowly back toward hers, and found himself staring back into hers.

*Oops!* Clearing his head and refocusing on the task at hand, Joe turned his attention back to her feet. He started rubbing again, this time a bit more gently. *Oh, yes! This is good!*

"What are you looking at?" Alex demanded, noticing his inappropriate level of interest.

He looked up and their eyes locked once again.

"Nice toes," he said, suppressing a grin.

*You've got to be kidding me! He's looking at my toes?* Alex thought. *Is he some kind of pervert with a foot fetish? There are guys like that. I remember one from one of those Bachelorette episodes.*

*Okay, Baker, get a grip here,* Joe thought. He realized he needed to turn his attention away from her adorable little feet. "Mike, how you doing on those shoes? You gonna save them for her friend, Jimmy?"

Mike looked at Alex and joked, "So, is your friend Jimmy a transvestite or something?"

Stephanie was standing nearby watching the progress. The girls looked at each other, shaking their heads in disgust. *Men are so dense. They know nothing about fashion. But what else can you expect from construction workers?* Alex thought. Richard was the only man she knew who understood the value of a good pair of Jimmy Choos. Anything expensive and timeless, he could comprehend. Jimmy Choos were the female equivalent of his Rolex watch.

Stephanie retorted on Alex's behalf. "No, he is not a transvestite! It's a brand. You know, like Goodyear is to tires, Jimmy Choo is to shoes." She shot Mike a look of disgust, but when Joe appeared confused, she turned to him and gave him her best smile and her sexiest little laugh. A guy didn't need to be hit over the head to know when Steph was interested.

Mike handed the shoes over for inspection. "Here, I don't think these look too bad. I mean, I think once they dry they're probably salvageable. Whatcha think?"

Alex took them from him and had to admit they didn't look half bad, considering what they had been through. "Thanks—I appreciate it." Wow, this Mike guy was cute. His dimples and smile lit up his face in such an endearing way, and he seemed genuinely nice. *Maybe Steph should start flirting with him instead of Mr. Hard Ass.*

Alex looked back down at Joe, who was finishing up with her feet. As if sensing her looking at the back of his head, he looked up and wiped the sweat out of his eyes on the forearm of his shirtsleeve. He again gave her a slow once-over starting from the top of her head, back down to her feet. Her face was beet red, her face and chest shiny with sweat. He figured she probably was not used to this kind of intense heat and sun, and he hoped she wouldn't succumb to heat stroke. Joe had grown thirsty, and he knew she could probably use some water. "Hey Mario, get us all some water over here, okay?" he called out.

Mario reached into the cab of the service truck and grabbed waters, handing two to Mike and Stephanie and two to Joe.

Joe screwed off the top of one bottle and thrust it toward her. "Drink," he commanded. She took it gratefully. He opened the second bottle, took a long drink, reached in his back pocket, and pulled out a clean handkerchief. He poured some water on it, lifted her bangs, and wiped her forehead. He lingered on her cheeks, and then wiped the rest of her face and neck. When Joe was finished, he poured the remainder of the bottle onto the cloth, wrung it out, and hung it around her neck, letting the ends hang down the front.

"Here, this will keep you cool until we're done and they can get your car started."

Joe glanced over to Stephanie to see if she was doing okay. Alex studied his profile while he was questioning her friend. *Oh, my God. This guy is gorgeous, even if he has been yelling at me most of the time. He did wipe down my face and give me water, so he can't be that bad can he? Not to mention he rescued my Jimmys.* Even sweaty, he exuded a masculinity that was scary. He certainly would have a big affect on any woman. And she had to admit he was having a heady affect on her.

Joe looked over as the Lexus roared to life. He turned back to Alex. "Looks like your ride is back in service. It'll probably take a few minutes to cool off. Let's make sure it's not going to die again before you head out. Can Mario get you more water?"

She shook her head no. Stephanie walked over to Joe. "Here." She handed him her business card. "You can contact me if you want to. If there is *anything* you need just call me. You know, if your boss needs some kind of explanation what happened here. I'll be more than happy to explain—or in case you want to call me for any other reason." She gave him a wink that could only be interpreted one way.

"Well I don't think I'll have to worry about any explanation to the boss, but thanks for the offer." He pocketed the card.

Having finished cleaning her up, he turned to Alex and put his hands on her hips, bringing her down from the truck's lift. Then he took the shoes from her hands, crouched down and put them on her feet. They were some kind of black thong things with a little heel and leopard skin on top. If he thought barefoot was sexy, his groin tightened when he slid these hot little numbers onto her feet.

He straightened up. "Well ladies, what can I say? This has been an interesting start to the day, to say the least." Then he looked at Alex thoughtfully. "Look, I'm sorry I yelled at you. I know you didn't mean to do intentional harm. You just took me by surprise. That's all. And don't worry about paying for the damage. We'll get it fixed up."

Alex smiled, and then she walked over to Mike to thank him again for saving her shoes. He shot her a big sarcastic grin. "Any time."

Then she turned to Joe. "Again, I'm really sorry. Thanks for cleaning me up." Without any hesitation, Alex got on her tiptoes and kissed him gently on the cheek. "I know I made a mess of things, and well, your apologies are accepted, as I hope mine are."

Joe wanted to grab her and kiss the heck out of her silky, glossy lips. *Am I nuts?* Instead, he cautioned, "Take it easy, okay? And promise me you won't be so impulsive. The next time you might run across some guys who will do more than yell at you, and you might get yourself into some really nasty trouble."

They both just stared at each other a moment. She couldn't read anything from his eyes. Although he gave nothing away in his expression, she could tell he was thinking about something. What?

"So, thanks again. And I'm very sorry," she repeated.

Joe never took his eyes off Alex as the two women walked away and got into the Lexus. He continued to watch until the car was out of sight and he could no longer see Stephanie waving through the sunroof.

"Earth to Joe!" Mike said. "I'm surprised at you, bud. You looked pretty smitten with Miss Jimmy Choos. I'd have thought you'd go for the blonde.

That mean you're gonna give me *her* number? And by the way, her name is Stephanie."

Joe reached inside his pocket and slapped the card into Mike's hand. "You're welcome!" he said, with a knowing grin.

"You know I didn't see any rings on their left hands 'cause I checked it out," Mike said excitedly. "I'm gonna give her a call and see if she wants to go out to dinner or something. You want me to get the other one's number for you?"

He shook his head. "Thanks, but I think I'll save myself some trouble. I think she's probably more than even I could handle."

"Suit yourself," Mike shrugged.

Mike decided to go for it. He would call Stephanie soon. He was pretty sure that by giving Joe her card, Stephanie was letting him know that she was both available and interested. It had been a long time since he had found anyone he was so attracted to. She was dynamite in the looks department, and not bad with conversation, either. He wasn't going to waste any time and let this one get away.

Picking up the phone the next evening Mike was disappointed when Stephanie's machine picked up. "I can't take your call right now, so please leave me a message," her greeting oozed sensually in that breathy voice of hers. *Mmm.* He left his name and number asking her to give him a call. He was anxious for her to call back.

The next morning, Mike mentioned to Joe that he had left a message on Stephanie's machine. "Do you think it looks too interested if I try her again tonight?" he asked Joe anxiously.

Joe had a feeling she was more interested in him than in Mike, but he didn't say it. "Sure, why not? Maybe she was busy or didn't check her messages. Or just wait another day, if you don't want to seem pushy."

"Yeah, you're right. I should give her a little more time to call back," Mike agreed.

He waited a day to call again, but he found himself listening to Stephanie's machine again. A day went by. Three strikes and you're out, he figured. Mike had nothing to lose, so he called a third and final time a few days later. This time he changed his message. "It's Mike again. Somehow I'm getting the feeling the reason you're not calling back is you're not interested, so I'll let it drop." He was irritated, but he figured she obviously didn't feel any attraction. Clearly, she had the hots for Joe.

Steph actually had received all three of Mike's messages.

"Criminy," she groaned to Alex. "He left three messages, and on the last one he sounded kinda pissed that I didn't call him back. Well, sorry. I'm not really interested in him. Yes, he is good-looking and nice, but for God's sake his lashes are longer than mine. It's like he's almost too pretty, you know?"

Alex looked at her friend in disbelief. "Too pretty? The guy exudes masculinity, and you think he's too pretty? I just don't get you. Last week you were praying to see these two guys and drooling out the car window at them. Now, one of them calls, and you're not interested. You've been looking for a while now, and if this guy doesn't have a chance who does? Who are you waiting for, Brad Pitt?" She couldn't resist throwing that last bit in to make her point. "Well, honey, I'm sorry, but he's taken. I'd wait for Clooney, though, if it were me," Alex laughed, trying to lighten things up a bit.

"I was hoping Joe would call me. He could have gotten my number from Mike, but he obviously isn't interested or he probably would have called by now," Steph explained.

Alex had to admit that she was probably right. "Who knows about men," she sighed. "Why don't you just forget about both of them and focus on something else. It's not like we'll see them again other than when we're on the road." She decided to change the subject.

"Did you decide what you're taking to the convention? I've been checking the weather and can't make any decisions," Alex stated. The two of them were going to a women's law conference in Las Vegas. They would be in seminars for a couple of days, but they had worked in a full day of freedom. Alex and Steph's nights were free, and they had made a couple of dinner reservations and planned to see a show. They were both getting excited about their upcoming adventure.

CHAPTER 3

Arriving at O'Hare, the two legal ladies checked their bags curbside and headed inside to grab a Starbucks before flight time. The skycap told them the flight was on schedule and they would be departing at 10:10 a.m. from American's Gate D-12. It was going to be hot in Vegas, but it didn't really matter. This was all about a little fun in the sun.

Sitting at a small table at Starbucks, Alex could see Stephanie was in a funk. "Look, get over it, will ya? You should be happy such a cute guy is after you, even if it is not the cute guy you're pining over. A guy that hot has got to be attached, so don't take it personally."

"Well I can't help it. It's easy for you. You have Richard. I have no one."

*Geez,* Alex thought. *I love her to death, but sometimes she gets so needy and has such tunnel vision she can't see what is right in front of her.*

"Having a man in your life is not the be-all-and-end-all. Yes, I have Richard, but sometimes I still feel pretty alone. It's kinda hard to explain, but believe me, I understand where you're coming from," Alex explained.

Stephanie thought a minute. "Yes, you are right about that. What is it with men? You're with them but it's like a blank canvas sometimes. The frame is there, but it's empty." She sighed and looked at her watch, realizing they were getting close to boarding time. They needed to start making their way to the gate.

"Well, we aren't alone—we have each other," Alex said brightly, then added, "We should head over to the gate."

In the meantime, Joe and Mike were making their way to D-12 for their annual trip to the World of Concrete Conference. Although they had first class tickets, the two men preferred to board last. It was an irritation they could live without, having everyone else march past them, taking forever to get situated, messing with their overhead storage bins, looking for blankets, and God knows what other boarding chaos that made it impossible to relax. The approximately three hours they'd be airborne was long enough to deal with being on a plane.

Once aboard, the men took their seats. Immediately, the flight attendant buzzed over to offer her services. "Hello, gentlemen. Welcome aboard. What can I get you to drink?" she asked with a flirty smile. It was obvious their looks were not lost on the cabin attendant.

Mike thought a minute. "I'll have a Jack and Coke. Joe, Miller Lite?"

Joe nodded.

"I'll be right back with your drinks. And if there is *anything* else you need, you just let me know," the hostess bubbled, coyly.

As they buckled up, Joe chuckled, and said under his breath, "Well, yeah. She could give me something I need. You know, I never have joined the mile-high club."

Mike smiled back jovially. "There will be plenty of opportunity in sin city, if you choose to end your period of celibacy."

Joe shot back, "Riiiiight."

In the meantime, Alex and Stephanie were settled into seats 11A and 11B. Alex sat in the seat by the window. She was busy buckling her seat belt and retrieving the latest novel she had been reading. Stephanie was watching the boarding passengers and suddenly squealed, "Oh… my… God!"

"Now what?" Alex asked, slightly annoyed. Stephanie was speechless as she looked at Alex with huge eyes. "You absolutely will NOT believe who just sat down in first class!"

"Oh, I don't know… George Clooney?" she shot back sarcastically. "How the heck would I know? How about you give me a little hint."

Before Steph could utter another word, the pilot's voice rang over the loud speaker that they had to prepare for take off. Alex leaned over. "So, who has you so ruffled—is it Clooney, Dempsey?"

Stephanie's face revealed that little smile she always showed when she knew something Alex didn't. "Well, you'll just have to wait and see.

Alex buried her head in her book, as Stephanie continued to look up the aisle to catch a glimpse of what the guys were doing.

Joe had relaxed enough to take a little catnap. When he woke up, he needed a little walk. As Joe ambled down the aisle, Steph spotted him and leaned into the walkway, smiling. Joe stopped dead in his tracks. *Holy shit. What's she doing here?* Then he looked over at Alex. Alex sensed movement near her and looked up to discover Joe staring at her.

*Crap!* she thought. She tried to bury her head back in the book, hoping he would just go away.

"Well, hello, ladies! This is quite a surprise." He couldn't take his eyes off Alex, who refused to look up. Stephanie, however, put on her best *I'm your girl* face.

She tried to look enticing. "Well, fancy meeting you here! Yes, this is most certainly a surprise."

*Go away. Go away,* Alex chanted in her head. When she finally looked up again, she could see his eyes boring straight into hers. Against her will, she felt herself go weak. *This is so not what I want to do. I'm on a kind-of vacation, and he's on this plane looking all hot and staring at me. So he's not mad about the concrete anymore?*

"So, you girls heading to Vegas for a convention, or for some other kind of fun?" he asked. Alex cowered back again. *I'm so embarrassed about that day. And here he is right in front of me looking gorgeous... and looking at me like... well, like he likes me. He likes me?*

"Yes, we are," Steph explained. "Actually a little of both. You, too?"

When he nodded, Steph chirped, "Oh, how fun. We should get together. We're staying at the Bellagio. How about you?"

Joe took it all in to process—the convention, the fact they were staying at the same hotel. *Holy Cow! What are the odds?*

"What a coincidence. We're at the Bellagio, too. Maybe we'll see you around."

"Oh, you can count on it," Stephanie chirped.

Alex never uttered a word. She let out a sigh of relief as Joe finally moved on, on his mission to the rear of the aircraft.

He was amused by the way Alex seemed embarrassed and had tried to wish him away. Somehow, he found her behavior an inviting challenge.

When Joe returned to his seat, he shared the surprise with Mike. Naturally, this gave Mike all the excuse he needed to make his own trip to the rear of the plane. A moment later, he was delighted to find himself standing in front of Stephanie. But now it was Stephanie's turn to hide from male attention. Alex was sparing with her conversation as well, leaving Mike a little confused. He thought that the women would be warmer, given the men's hero status and the fact that Steph had given Joe her card.

*Hmm. What gives?* he thought. Yet, Mike remained undeterred. Hopefully, they would see the girls at the Bellagio, and then maybe it would be more comfortable for them all. Then he would have his chance to ask them out for drinks.

After landing, the couples made their way to the baggage claim separately. Once there, Joe could see Alex was trying to avoid the two men. In fact, she was actually standing on the other side of the turnstile behind a pole. As the luggage belt began to turn, finally, Alex came out of hiding, and Joe quietly moved over to stand next to her. For her part, Alex did her best not to acknowledge his presence. Somewhat amused, Joe leaned in, "Let me know what bags are yours, and I'll get them for you, okay?"

Her terse response quickly shot him down. "Really, that's not necessary. I can handle my own luggage. I'm a big girl."

Joe exchanged a "what the fuck" glance with Mike, who had just sidled over to the group. Joe's bag appeared, and he quickly grabbed it and set it down. He looked back over at Alex. Her taut face was anxious.

"That one coming up yours?" Joe offered hopefully.

"Uh, I think so. But I told you, I can get it myself," she chided, as she studied a black garment bag coming toward them. When it was in front of them, Alex hunched down to look at the ID tag and went to grab it. Joe shouldered his way in, lifted the bag, and set it down next to Alex. "Is this it, or is there another one?" he asked, undaunted.

"There's another small one. But I told you. I'm perfectly capable of handling my own luggage. I've done this dozens of times without your help."

"I know it's the millennium, but can't a guy help out a lady now and then, if he wants to?" Joe asked flirtatiously. "I hope chivalry isn't dead yet." Alex just glared. Joe was disappointed, but he got the message. So, he pulled up the roller handle on his own bag and stood to the side. Alexis was about to be relieved as her second piece of luggage came into view, until she realized it was stuck. She was considering how best to dive onto the carousel without attracting too much attention, when she saw Joe efficiently lift the bag and deposit it in front of her.

Alex was obviously annoyed, but he could tell she was thankful, too. A charming pink rose up through her cheeks. She looked perfectly adorable.

The soft look in his sea-blue eyes suddenly reminded her to be polite. After all, he had come to her aid. Again. "Thanks. I—well—it got hung up. Otherwise

I could have handled it," she stammered.

Joe grinned knowingly. *What was up with her attitude?* he thought.

Mike decided to take advantage of the situation. A second rescue had just taken place. Maybe the girls would be more receptive to the two men now. He had just thought of another way to be of service to these two fine women.

"Now it's time to play the 'let's wait in line half an hour and wade through a gazillion yards of people to get a taxi' game. Hey, why don't we save some time and get a taxi together? When we reach the numbered area I'll tell them there are four of us. That work for you guys?" Mike asked, impressed with his own genius.

*No that is not okay with me,* Alex thought. *I don't want to share their taxi, and I don't want to be staying at the same hotel.* She was afraid this trip was going to be too much temptation. Instead of being an educational networking experience and a bit of fun it was going to be a pain trying to avoid running into Joe. Fortunately, Vegas was big enough and busy enough that maybe the girls wouldn't run into them, she reasoned.

But Steph wasn't about to miss a chance to get Joe's attention. So, she pleaded with Alex. "He's right. The airport is especially crowded today. And the money we save on cab fare we can use to win in the casinos."

Alex fired back a skeptical glare, as Joe chimed in, "Right!"

"I'll take that as a yes," Mike responded, making for the taxi line.

In the cab, an uncomfortable silence permeated the air. Stephanie perked up and broke the spell. "God, I'm starving. What is it with these airlines not even feeding you anymore?" she said, for conversation's sake. "It's bad enough they hardly have time to serve you a cocktail, but a bag of peanuts? Ugh. I'm dropping my bags and heading for Carnage's Deli at the Mirage for a corned beef the minute we arrive."

Mike smiled at her knowingly. "My favorite bar's at the Mirage. I'm dumping my bag and heading over there, too, since our rooms probably won't be ready yet. You girls know the Mirage?" he continued. "They have great bands and strong drinks over there."

Stephanie replied excitedly, "I love The Mirage. I have to go there at least once and get my fix looking at the exotic fish tank and the walkway with the dome and tropical plants. It's kind of like paradise, don't you think? And the hotel isn't far from my favorite bar."

Mike wanted to know about her favorite bar. "Where is that?" he asked.

"Oh, I'm sure you guys have been there. It's the Carnaval Bar next to Harrah's. The music is terrific, its outside, and they have the best bartenders ever. I love it when they blow the whistle and the bartender gets on the bar and pours a shot down your throat." Mike's heart pounded. That was one of his favorites, too. "Hey, I love that place," he replied.

Alex cringed. She had no intention of spending time with them at the Carnaval Bar, or any other bar. The girls had taken the first bench seat of the mini van, with the guys climbing in behind them. Alex could almost feel Joe's breath on her neck, and it made her very nervous. *We've got some very long days ahead of us, and you're just gonna have to find a way to dump these guys. But how, with Steph encouraging them at every turn?*

Finally the taxi pulled up in front of their hotel. Bellmen loaded the men's and the women's bags onto separate carts. At check-in, things went as Mike had predicted. The women's rooms were not ready, nor were the men's. They couldn't help overhearing each other's conversations. The four looked at each other.

"Well," Steph chuckled, "I'm certainly up for a cocktail and then I've got to get my deli fix, so do you guys want to head over to Mirage together?"

Mike nodded, Alex looked uncomfortable, and Joe looked down. *What the hell,* he thought. Joe noted her discomfort, but he knew she could also do worse. She needed to get over whatever grudge she was holding against them. A drink sounded like a good way for them all to mend fences.

"Hey, whatever you guys want, I'm in. A cocktail sounds good to me," Joe conceded.

"Ready, ladies?" Mike said, stretching out his arm in an "after you" gesture. "Let's go get Stephanie her tropical fish fix and a few drinks." The main bar rocked at all hours, and Mike hoped they'd get lucky with finding seats. He figured if the guys had to shell out some cash to make it happen, these ladies were worth the effort.

Joe looked over at Alex, who looked none too happy when their eyes met. *What is up with her? Is she spoken for?* he thought.

At the bar, the foursome found luck in their favor. Another foursome was just vacating a table with a sofa for three and a comfy chair. Mike plunked down in the chair, so the other three scrunched in on the sofa. Joe found himself sandwiched between the girls, which was not at all unpleasant. Stephanie made sure she was next to Joe, and her intentions were obvious. Alex looked annoyed.

Noticing the look of distress on Alex's face, Stephanie asked, "Honey, what's wrong? You look like you don't feel well."

Alex shook her head. "I'm fine. Really. Just tired. And, well, you know how anxious I get about flying. I'm glad we're on land, that's all." *Geez, I could kick myself for admitting that in front of him.* "I'll have an Absolut. That should make me feel better."

Soon a scantily clad waitress approached the table, and the group gave her their order. Two Miller Lites, and two Absoluts on the rocks with blue cheese olives. Life was good, at least for three of them. Silence descended for a few seconds while they relaxed their way into Vegas mode. The guys found refuge in the large flat-screen TV in front of them, which was broadcasting a golf tournament. Alex put her head back on the sofa and closed her eyes, trying not to think about the hard, manly thigh pressing against hers. Why couldn't she just enjoy what life brought her? Live in the moment, so to speak, like everyone else seemed to do?

*My God, I haven't even thought about Richard since the moment I laid eyes on Joe during the flight. I suck as a fiancée. I should have called him already to say we're here. Instead, here I am enjoying the close encounter I'm having with Joe's thigh and wondering if the rest of him is equally toned. What the heck is wrong with me?*

As Alex was mentally flogging herself, the waitress reappeared with their drinks. Joe raised his glass and proposed a toast. "To Vegas, to some fun and sun, and to new friends." He hesitated a moment and then took a chance, adding, "And don't forget what happens in Vegas stays in Vegas." He winked at Alex. Then he thought about it again. "Or better yet," he jokingly ventured, "how about what happens in Vegas depends on who you meet in Vegas?"

His sentiments had been risky, but his instinct told him to go for it. Three of them clinked their glasses and laughed, but the fourth remained unconvinced.

By the time Joe ordered another round of drinks and the band started playing, even Alex's mood had begun to lighten. The band had just played the intro to "Highway to Hell," a popular AC/DC song. The girls looked at each other and smiled. Stephanie knew what they were both thinking: They would love to dance.

Alex stole a sideways glance at Joe who was clearly appreciating two young girls in tight short skirts and low-cut tanks. But Alex was more relaxed now, and she really wanted to get down to this song. Their eyes met as Joe reached for his beer. He looked down at her tapping foot and thought about the red toenails that might be hiding under her shoes. He grabbed the opportunity.

"Wanna dance?" he asked.

Without giving her a chance to say no, Joe pulled Alex to her feet. "Come on. This is a song that shouldn't be wasted."

Worried for half a second, Alex allowed herself to be led to the dance floor. She really wanted to dance, but she wasn't sure she should be dancing with him.

Mike wasn't about to miss his own chance and had pulled Stephanie out onto the dance floor.

Alex danced fervently, like she hadn't in a long time. Was it the Vegas influence, the vodka, or... him? All of the above? Joe was no slouch with the moves. And it was incredible how much sexier he was with his body in motion. Alex found herself getting hot and bothered, something she rarely did. Why was this happening with *him*? Dancing with Richard never made Alex feel this way.

The band continued playing classic rock, which suited this group perfectly. After a bit, Alex and Stephanie traded partners, but before long, they had given way to just dancing as a foursome. It felt good to enjoy a night out.

Joe was a bit difficult to read. But one thing Alex did notice was that even though he seemed to be enjoying himself, the man rarely smiled. What kept the grins from his handsome face?

When the band took a break, the foursome returned to their table. The discussion centered around how music today just wasn't the same as the old stuff. To their surprise, the four discovered that they all liked the same types of music. Half an hour later, the girls decided it was time for a visit to the restroom.

With the women out of earshot, Joe told Mike, "Look, I don't want them to know we used to play with the band, okay? And I don't want them to know who I am. You know, that my last name is Baker. I don't want them to know there is any connection with me owning the company. Things right now are better left unsaid," he urged. "I'd like to get to know Alex better, and I know for sure you want to get to know Stephanie. So, let's try to hold back and let things progress naturally."

"Sure—whatever. Can you believe they were on the same plane? And at the same hotel, no less? Are we lucky or what? It's gotta be fate," Mike replied. Then he added, "We've got four more days, so maybe we can talk them into having dinner with us. I did notice neither one of them is wearing a ring."

"Why not?" Joe agreed. "No ring on the finger doesn't mean a thing these days, but we can try to find out for sure whether the ladies are attached. At least Stephanie is giving all the signs that she's available."

When the girls returned, the band had started to play again. Alex was thinking they really should eat something. She was hungry, and she didn't think continuing to drink on an empty stomach was wise because she was already feeling a bit tipsy. Relaxed was a good thing, but she wasn't sure being buzzed was a good thing—especially around *him*. No sooner had the girls returned to the table when Alex looked up to see the son of one of her very good friends standing in front of her with a big grin on his face.

"Hey, beautiful! What are you doing here?" the young man asked. Alex jumped up and threw her arms around him, giving him a big kiss.

"Steph and I are here for a convention. What are *you* doing here?"

Brad was a strapping kid, built like a wrestler, with short blond hair and big green eyes. "We came in for the weekend. My buddy is getting married and this is the last hurrah. Too bad we're leaving tomorrow. Is Vegas fabulous or what!"

Joe was eyeing the interaction between the two of them and looked none too pleased. He was wondering how Alex knew the guy and instantly disliked him. *What am I, jealous? I hardly know the woman.* Still he didn't like another man potentially moving in on his turf.

Just then, the band started playing "Thank You" by Dido, and Alex grabbed Brad. "Come on, handsome!"

*Yes, I AM jealous*, Joe realized.

He watched as the two danced a little too intimately for his tastes. When they continued to dance to the next song, Joe started to do a slow burn.

A group of twenty-something females was at a table nearby, and Joe had noticed some of them eyeing him and Mike. Sure they were young, but he decided then and there that turnabout was fair play. He walked up to their table and asked the best looking one to dance. She gladly accepted. Joe danced his partner over toward Alex and Brad. Joe was giving her the once over, instead of focusing on his own dance partner, which Alex thought was a bit strange.

When she and Brad took a breather, Joe followed suit and escorted his partner back to her table.

"So, aren't you going to introduce us to your friend?" he asked.

Stephanie could feel the tension emitting from Joe and gave Alex a knowingly raised eyebrow.

"Oh, I'm sorry," Alex offered. "That was so rude of me. This is Brad, the son of a very good friend of mine," she explained proudly. "Isn't he a hunk?" She grinned. Then she hugged him and planted a kiss on the young man's cheek. "Honey, you know Steph, of course, and this is Mike and Joe." Brad looked a little uncomfortable after Alex's "hunk" comment, but extended his hand to both Mike and Joe. "Pleased to meet you both."

Joe looked from Brad to Alex and back to Brad and, believing what she said, slowly let out the breath he had been holding. "Hey, nice to meet you, too," he said, extending his hand as Mike did the same.

"Well, sorry I can't stay, but I've got to get going," Brad announced. And with him taking his leave, the foursome realized it was probably time to find some food. Next stop, Carnegie Deli.

An hour later, satisfied and tired, the group returned to the Bellagio. In the elevator enroute to the girls' twelfth-floor room, Mike asked them for their room numbers. "Let's keep in touch over the next few days," he suggested hopefully. Stephanie gladly complied, telling them her room number while specifically looking at Joe. Mike gave Stephanie his room number, too. Alex did all she could not to haul off and throttle Stephanie for giving out the information.

Alex had a hard time falling asleep that night, replaying all that had transpired on their travel day. Fortunately, the next day she and Steph did not have any work obligations, so she could sleep in. All the girls had planned for sure was to spend the day shopping for some fun Vegas clothing.

The phone rang much too early the next morning. Stephanie was ready and raring to spend her hard earned cash.

"Will you be ready by nine? I thought we could hit the coffee place first and fortify ourselves before we head out," came Steph's chipper, excited voice over the line.

"No I'm not really... um... up and um... at 'em yet. And certainly not very perky. But I'll drag my sorry self out of bed and get going. I slept like crap last night and had all kinds of weird dreams. I'll tell you about them later. I'll meet you at the elevators."

"Okay, sounds like a plan," Steph replied with curiosity in her voice. "I'm planning on finding something cool to wear to the show tonight. What do you think?" Alex remembered they had reservations with a group of their fellow colleagues that evening, so she agreed.

"Okay, great. See you in a bit." The conversation ended and Alex stepped into the shower. As she soaped herself down, her thoughts returned in blow-by-blow detail to the previous day's events and the shock of seeing Joe. She was embarrassed at first, but something inside her was glad to see him, too. Sure he was a fantastic-looking guy, but it was more than just that. She had to admit she was attracted to him. She tried her best to resist, but there was just something undeniable about him. He had a great body, for starters, and she liked the way he dressed. Then there was the way he carried himself. He exuded confidence, yet without any conceit. Or maybe she was attracted to the way that he always seemed wary—not smiling much. He seemed to always be thinking. She just couldn't put her finger on what made him tick. Yet Alex knew in her heart that she wouldn't mind finding out.

Shopping in Vegas was a dream come true. There, glitzy stores were packed with feminine delights. Alex bought a short, flirty, gauzy black skirt with a handkerchief hem and a Victorian blouse in ecru that would look great with her salvaged black Jimmy slides. She also bought a great short red dress that went over one shoulder. Stephanie purchased a simple turquoise sheath to wear that evening. Neither of them had been to Cirque de Soliel before but had heard fabulous things about all their shows. They were going to see "O."

A couple of times during the day, Alex found her thoughts drifting toward Joe and wondering what the guys were doing. They did say they would be at the convention, because it was opening day. Each time she thought about Joe, which was annoyingly often, she willed herself to stop. She was hoping they wouldn't run into the guys for the rest of the trip. But damn Stephanie, who *was* betting on seeing them again and was ensuring the odds in their favor, for giving them her room number! Steph still had the hots for Joe, and in all honesty, Alex couldn't blame her. That evening, the women and their legal group had show reservations for the 9:30 performance at the Bellagio. The two women were in the theater lobby swapping stories with their colleagues and discussing tomorrow's conference when Alex heard a familiar voice.

"Hey, Mike. Our friends are here."

Alex froze. Stephanie looked pleased.

"Did you tell them we were coming here?" she whispered to Stephanie in an accusing tone.

Suddenly, standing before them were their two "friends," along with four other gentlemen, who were apparently waiting for the show themselves.

Joe approached Alex with what she could only describe as this "dumb" smile on his face. *Well, he does know how to smile after all.*

"Wow, I'm so glad to see you," he remarked as he looked her over approvingly. "You look fantastic!" Alex was wearing the red dress she had purchased earlier that day. He stepped forward and, with that same goofy smile, planted one on her.

Alex was taken aback. For an instant she was shocked and embarrassed, especially in front of her colleagues. The kiss only lasted a few seconds, but it got her all flustered. They both pulled away about the same time, and when she looked up at Joe he still had the same grin on his face. He stood back and looked at her dress again.

"That's a nice little number. Love the color. Do you know that red exudes confidence?"

Mike quickly stepped up and whispered quietly in her ear. "Oh God, I'm sorry. I mean he's for sure a beer man, and he gets squirrelly when he drinks wine. Some of our vendors took us to Kokomo's tonight, and they have this thing about ordering a bunch of wine. They mean well, but Joe can't handle wine. It makes him act, well, different."

Stephanie was studying Joe. "And you know, you look like McDreamy, don't you mister?"

When he gave her a blank look, Mike intervened. "Figures. You know, Joe, the guy on that hospital show," he harrumphed.

After thinking a minute, Joe frowned. "Oh, you mean that Derek guy? Well I'm flattered, but I don't look like him. He's a hell of a lot better looking than me."

Alex disgustedly piped in, "Please, your eyes are blue and his are green, so how could you possibly look like him? She's overdue for her eye exam," she nodded toward her friend.

Joe looked back at Alex, figuring he must have annoyed her by kissing her.

"I'm sorry. I didn't mean to embarrass you in front of your friends, but I was just happy to see you."

*Good Lord. Is this how the trip is going to be? Running into him all the time? Maybe I should just pretend I'm sick and go home. Too bad probably no one would believe me.*

There was no more time for chitchat. The doors were now open, and people were beginning to take their seats. Ushers urged the patrons inside, so the girls pulled out their tickets and prepared to go in. Joe followed them and looked over Alex's shoulder. "Where are you guys sitting?" She could feel the front of his chest close to her back. When she replied with the section and row numbers, he responded with disappointment in his voice. "Hmm, bummer. We're in Section G. Too bad we're not sitting together."

As they continued to make their way into the theater, an attendant looked at their tickets and directed the ladies to the correct location. Joe continued to watch where Alex was headed as another attendant did likewise directing them to their seats after looking at their tickets. Once Joe was seated, he directed his attention back to where the girls were seated. He started to climb over Mike and excused himself.

"Hey, where are you going?"

Joe replied, "Just sit tight, I've got some wheeling and dealing to do."

*Oh, brother—way too much wine,* Mike thought as he watched Joe make his way over to the section where the girls were seated, climbing over several people in the row immediately behind them.

Joe began to whisper to the gentleman who sat directly behind Stephanie. He pled his case, offering the elderly gentlemen five-hundred dollars if he and his wife would relocate to Joe and Mike's seats. Noting those seats were far superior to the ones he and his wife were occupying, the man eagerly accepted. Joe pulled out his wallet and counted out five one-hundred dollar bills.

"Thank you sir. I appreciate your making the swap."

Alex could not help overhearing what Joe had just accomplished and had turned around to watch in horror as Joe paid the man five-hundred dollars to switch seats. Joe motioned Mike to come over, as the couple made their way to the other seats.

"What do you think you're doing? You bribed that man so that you could sit behind us?" she asked in a scandal-tinged voice.

His look was all innocence.

"No, I just offered him money for these better seats right behind you guys. It wasn't a bribe. I think it's a fair trade. Besides, the scenery in front will be much better than where we were sitting," he reasoned, coyly.

"Five-hundred dollars! Just like that you throw away five-hundred dollars?" She was thinking it was not a wise move even for someone who had a lot of money, but for a guy who worked construction? She knew they made good money but this seemed a stretch.

"How could you just throw away five-hundred dollars?!"

He got right in her face. "Because I can. And because it was necessary."

Alex just turned back toward the front, ignoring him, and shook her head.

"Wow, you guys are sitting behind us. How great is this?" Stephanie gushed.

By then Mike had made his way over and sat down giving his pal a quizzical look. He knew better than to say anything. Joe did what he wanted when he wanted, and by now Mike knew never to argue. Besides, he was happy to be sitting behind Stephanie. They turned their attention to the show as the lights dimmed.

The show was highly entertaining and the time passed quickly. When it ended and they began to make their way out of the theater, the four stopped to say their goodbyes. Mike had already decided he was going to invite the ladies to a party being hosted by one of their vendors.

"So, do you ladies have plans for tomorrow night? I'd love for you to join us for a function at Mandalay Bay. Their outdoor terrace has great views. The food is always awesome, and each year they have a surprise guest. Rumor has it that, since NASCAR is in town this week for next weekend's race, there may be an appearance by last year's Cup winner. Does that sound like fun?" Though he directed his question to both of them, he was looking directly at Stephanie.

When she gazed over at Joe, and then back at Mike, she opened her mouth to accept; but one look from her friend told her she had better say "no." Being none too pleased, she shot Alex a look that clearly said she really wanted to go. After several seconds of uncomfortable silence, Stephanie plowed ahead.

"That sounds wonderful. I'm actually a huge NASCAR fan and have been to several races. It would be so exciting to actually meet a driver in person! We really don't have any plans, and it sounds like a good time. Just call my room tomorrow and leave a message when and where you want us to meet you."

Alex was less than thrilled. She planned to fain a headache or a work obligation to get out of going. That was that.

The following day, the twosomes attended their respective conferences. Mike had left Steph a message on voicemail saying they would meet at the taxi area in front of the hotel around 6:45 to travel to the party together. He also stated that it would be a semi-casual affair. The men would be wearing jackets, but no ties.

Back in their rooms at day's end, Stephanie rang Alex's room to share Mike's voicemail information with her. Alex explained that she was tired and had a headache. She was going to skip the party and get to bed early.

"Oh sure. You felt fine all day," Steph argued. "This is just an excuse not to have to see them. We're in Vegas for God's sake. This party sounds like a lot of fun, and besides I've heard great things about the hotel. Frankly, I don't care if you ignore the guys. Just go with me, please?"

Alex closed her eyes and sighed. She opened them after thinking of a way to get out of this. "Look, you want Joe to pay attention to you so tonight you can have him all to yourself. You can have BOTH of them to yourself. Just don't totally snub Mike. He's a super nice guy."

Stephanie replied in a tone that made it clear she was not happy, "Fine. Do what you want, but don't go back home and talk about how bored you were in Vegas." She hung up.

Alex did not want to spend any more time with a man who turned her insides to jelly. It was bad enough she was thinking long and hard about whether marrying Richard was truly the right thing to do. And all being around Joe did was distract her.

A few minutes later, Alex's phone rang, and naturally it was Steph. "Okay, so I apologize that I got a little bitchy before," she said contritely. "If you go with me, I promise I'll owe you the rest of my life. At least go with me for a little bit, and then you can say you don't feel well and can take a taxi back. Please?"

She always did that—made Alex feel guilty. Accepting defeat, Alex agreed. "Fine, just fine. I'll go. But on one condition: when I decide to leave, and it will be early, I don't want any backlash from you. Agree?"

Her friend was a happy camper. "Oh, thank you, thank you! I promise if you want to leave early, I won't say anything. So what should we wear? I've looked at everything I have, and I think I'll wear one of the outfits I just bought. You?"

Alex just rubbed her forehead. Why would she even care? "Yeah, I'll wear one of the things I bought yesterday, I guess. I should be able to wear a pair of the shoes I brought with—maybe the Choo sandals. Look, I've gotta run. I need to check in with Richard, and then before you know it, it'll be time to leave."

At 6:45, all four met at the front of the hotel. Mike looked very happy to see them. Joe, on the other hand, looked a bit apprehensive. He sensed that Alex wasn't exactly keen on the idea of spending the evening with the two of them. Alex did have to admit both men looked exceptionally fine, just as they had the prior evening. Couldn't Joe just for once look something less than yummy?

"Ladies, good evening. You both look very lovely," Mike said, giving Stephanie the once-over. "Very nice." He nodded at her.

Joe glanced over and locked eyes with Alex who was giving him one of those annoyed looks that seemed to grace her face every time they were in each other's company. He spoke first. "Yes, ladies. You look great. I hope you're up for a fun night. We've done this party in the past and I must say it's a blast."

When the taxi pulled up, Joe figured he'd climb in the front seat and let Mike sit in back with the ladies. He didn't want miss prickly pear to get cranky before the evening even began. He wanted the night to be as much fun as it always was.

Once there, Alex had to admit it was indeed a great party. As the four seemed to enjoy their time together, the food, the drinks, and the view, Alex decided not to leave early. As hinted, the celebrity racecar driver walked in unannounced, and many clamored to get a word with him. Stephanie was able to flirt a little and get an autograph, much to her pleasure. Perhaps it was the two quick cocktails Alex had consumed at the beginning of the evening, or maybe it was just the festive atmosphere, but before she knew it, the clock's hands were showing nine, and the event was winding down.

The night was still young, so Joe made a suggestion. "Ladies, how about you let me do the honor of one nightcap when we get back to our hotel. One of the lounges has a live band until 2:00 a.m. Of course we won't keep you up that late. We've got an early day tomorrow ourselves. Anybody game?" Joe asked.

Of course Stephanie was up for anything involving these two, even though she was starting to get it through her head that Joe had no interest whatsoever in her.

But Joe was surprised to hear Alex saying "Okay." *Yes!*

The group managed to find two stools at the bar, where the guys helped the ladies settle in. Mike took everyone's drink orders. Alex was still on Cosmos, but Joe had switched to water in the interest of keeping a clear head. The band favored country and was playing a Little Big Town tune. All seemed to be going very well, as the four reminisced about the party. When their drinks arrived, Mike made a toast to the ladies and to what had ripened into a most enjoyable evening.

Suddenly the band segued into one of their hits, "Bring It on Home," which was one of Joe's favorite songs. He touched Alex's arm, and she looked up to find herself staring into the most handsome face she had ever seen.

"Could I have this dance, mademoiselle?" he asked, chivalrously. It took Alex only seconds to accept his offer.

Mike had excused himself to use the men's room, and Stephanie, sitting by herself, frowned as Joe reached for Alex's hand and led her to the dance floor. When he put his arm around her waist and she put hers around his neck they looked at each other a few brief seconds. His was a look of challenge with some seriousness mixed in. Hers was not of annoyance, as he had seen earlier, but of possibility.

Joe's strong, muscular arms pulled her closer. Somehow dancing tonight was totally different. Alex realized that something had changed. His body was warm and inviting, and he was having that same affect on her as the day they had first met. There was absolutely no way she could ignore it, nor at the moment did she want to.

Staring into each other's eyes, the windows to their souls seemed completely open. Almost afraid of the power in their gaze, Alex looked over at Stephanie to get some relief from the spell she seemed to be under. Stephanie, who was taking in the scene unfolding in front of her, gave her friend a thoughtful, appraising look, and then finally smiled. Even though Alex was unaware of it, Stephanie realized Richard was toast. He couldn't hold a candle to Joe, and Alex's life was about to meander down a much different path.

The smile seemed to reassure Alex, and she returned to the planet she and Joe seemed to inhabit there on the dance floor. They both knew the words to the song and were singing it in their heads. Joe knew the words pretty much conveyed how he felt, but he still didn't really have any idea if Alex had any attachments. He thought to himself how much he wanted to be the one waiting for her at home every night. He wanted to be her "safe harbor." As the song was ending, Joe whispered into Alex's ear and sang the last line. *"You've got someone here wants to make it alright, someone that loves you more than life right here."*

As the last strains of the music faded, Joe smiled at her. It was one of the rare times she had seen him with a real, genuine smile. Alex smiled back, but then looked down at the floor, not knowing what to do next. They were still standing on the dance floor when the band continued with another of the group's songs. He looked up and briefly closed his eyes to thank God for playing this song next.

Strains of "Lost" filled the room as the couples began to dance again. Joe took Alex in his arms as if it was the most natural thing for them to be doing. Alex closed her eyes and enjoyed every moment he was holding her and moving to the music. He did likewise marveling at how he could feel this way about a woman in such a short period of time. Physically, for sure, it seemed clear that they were meant to be together. Given his past history and track record, he couldn't believe this was happening. He knew that before the trip ended he had to have a definitive answer about her relationship status. She was a special lady, and he knew she was worth pursuing.

Mike had earlier brought up the "status" subject because he wanted to know just where he might stand with Stephanie. She had replied she was a free agent, as had the two guys. Alex was the only one who hesitated before declaring she was "basically" spoken for, whatever that meant. She offered no further explanation, and no one pushed her. Joe doubted she was married, because happily married women always wore a wedding ring. So he had yet been able to find out exactly what basically spoken for meant.

As the song ended, Alex felt reluctant to leave the haven of his arms and the miraculous feeling of his strong body pressed against hers. She would have to leave this fantasy with a hot and handsome guy in Vegas and return to Chicago and to her regular life. A life that included her becoming Richard's wife... Maybe.

They stood on the dance floor looking at each other awkwardly, trying to imagine what the other was thinking and feeling. Joe knew exactly how he felt—hot and bothered. His dance partner's feelings mirrored his own, although neither of them said anything.

Alex thanked him for the dances and remarked that it was getting late. Tomorrow they had an early start. Approaching the table, their friends were waiting for them.

Joe took care of the tab, and the group walked to the elevators.

"We've got another function tomorrow night if you ladies are interested." Mike was anxious to spend as much time with them as possible before they had to return home. "Mack Truck has this awesome thing planned at the Speedway. I know it may sound kind of hokey to you guys, but it's an outdoor basketball game between heavy-duty equipment. It's a cool way to show off their stuff," he marketed.

The elevator opened and they all stepped in. Alex, thinking that this game had finally played itself out, decided it was time for this charade to end.

"I think I'll take a pass, but maybe Steph wants to go. I've got some things I want to do after the conference winds up tomorrow." She and Joe locked eyes. He knew she was lying and gave her a look that said so. He still intended to pin her down about her relationship status before they returned home.

Earlier in the evening, when they were talking about their plans for returning home, Joe gleaned information from the women about their return flight. As soon as he got to his room, he was going to make a phone call that would ensure he and Mike would be on that same plane.

Alex, true to her word, did not accompany Steph and the guys to the Mack party. Even though Stephanie had finally figured out Joe was totally hung up on Alex, and she had concluded that Mike was a nice guy but not really her type, after all this was Vegas, and a party sounded like a lot more fun than hanging out at the hotel.

When the two women met for breakfast the next morning, Stephanie was very excited to talk about the previous evening's activities. She'd had a blast.

Alex, having spent a quiet night in her room, didn't care to hear about it, but listened anyway. Alex had spent the evening trying to relax and get involved in a novel, but she could barely finish a page before she started thinking about Joe. She spent a good deal of time talking herself out of the fact that maybe having a relationship with Joe might be a good thing. She finally concluded that her "hot shorts" would probably die off in due course, and then where would she be? Joe would be tired of her and on to his next conquest, and she would have given up a decent marriage prospect in Richard. No, he was not worth a quick fling. As tempting as the prospect of Joe might be, she decided that she would just thank him for all the Vegas fun and then let him know that she had someone waiting for her back home. Her mind was made up.

On their last day in Las Vegas, the ladies had quite a bit of time to kill before their four o'clock flight. So, Alex wanted to make a visit to the Ceasar's Forum Shops. Stephanie had mentioned the pre-flight shopping excursion to the guys the night before. Mike hadn't seen the venue before and expressed an interest in joining them. Steph was glad to invite the men to come along.

The Forum Shops at Ceasar's Palace was a destination itself. The multi-level extravaganza was quintessential Vegas. The over-the-top stores formed a kind of Disneyland for shopping adults. All four group members were excited to be there.

Alex, however, intended to follow her own plan and to follow her own agenda, as if the men were not even there.

Naturally, first stop was a visit to the Jimmy Choo store—her favorite. "Okay, I'm heading to Jimmy Choo first, just to make sure we don't run out of time," Alex announced as she began speeding off in that direction.

Joe quickly caught up with her. "You mean this Jimmy Choo dude has his own store?"

"Of course he does—several in fact." Men. They knew nothing about fashion.

"Hey, hold up. We're coming," Mike huffed as he and Stephanie caught up. "Don't want to miss this."

Stephanie stopped and turned to the guys. "This will be a good eye-opener for the two of you."

Inside the store, the guys absolutely could not believe the price tags on the merchandise.

"Hey, these cost more than a good pair of cowboy boots," Joe noted a little too loudly.

"Please keep your voice down and don't embarrass me. I may be someone who spends more money on a pair of shoes than you, but that's none of your affair," Alex hissed.

Glaring at him, she got back to business. Her labors paid off when she discovered a great pair of pumps that had been marked down. Although the shoes were a not-to-be-missed bargain, they were still a splurge. So, she promised herself that she would refrain from buying anything else for two months. Alex made a very good living, but these lovely leather beauties were still a stretch in her budget. Interestingly, she found Joe supportive of her purchase. He had told her not to pass up a good deal in case she regretted it when they got home. You really never could tell about men.

The group spent the remainder of their time window-shopping. The ladies had to give these guys credit for their patience. Stephanie was generally a store or two in front of the others anxious to see what they would encounter next. When she spotted David Yurman, she turned and waved anxiously.

"Hey, they've got a Yurman store!"

Joe looked at Alex with his eyebrows raised and a questioning look on his face. "Don't ask," she explained.

Steph had spotted a fabulous pendant necklace in the window, which coincidentally matched a pair of earrings she knew Alex had bought a while back. She grabbed Alex, dragging her into the store. She whispered, "Let's just ask. I'm just curious what they want for it."

The salesman was happy to comply by showing them the piece. The men seemed rather interested and leaned over to get a closer look. Joe was also looking in the various cases to check out why the girls found Yurman so fascinating.

The price tag on the necklace read $750. She and Steph exchanged glances. Alex told the salesman the piece was lovely, but she would have to think about it. After all, she had just made a vow of no more purchases for a couple of months.

"You can always order it on line or by phone later," Steph offered encouragingly, as Alex began to walk away.

Joe grabbed her arm. "I'll buy it for you."

She looked at him like he was crazy. "Absolutely not! *You* cannot buy *me* something like that. Why would you do that?"

"Because I want you to have it," he stated confidently, his deep blue eyes boring into hers. "Don't worry. I can afford it."

*You have to be kidding me. He wants to buy me a necklace? He barely knows me.*

"No." She shook her head. "No, but thank you for the offer. We should go now," she said, unsettled. Alex thanked the salesman and walked out of the store with the others trailing her.

Joe was mumbling, "Maybe sometimes a guy just wants to buy something for a beautiful lady. I don't see what the big deal would be. I know you think I'm some kind of poor sucker but I am in fact… um… I'm kind of a foreman."

She stopped in her tracks and faced him. "NO!"

Somehow, Joe was starting to be amused by the challenge. *Hmm. We'll just see about that.*

When the ladies were satisfied with their trip to the Forum Shops, the group decided to stop for lunch before heading out to the airport. After the group placed their orders, Joe excused himself to visit the rest room. Giving himself a pat on the back for cleverness, the man's real motive was to zip back to the Yurman store and buy the necklace for Alex. He deduced that if he waited until they reached Chicago to present it to her, she'd have to accept the gift because she couldn't return it. He smiled as he made his way back to the table, thinking about the scene.

Just then, his cell rang, and he was surprised to hear the voice of an old friend. Joe had talked to Ben, his partner during his Special Forces years, just last week. Ben was now with the Department of Homeland Security and thankful to have his old buddy and teammate. The government had just raised the terrorist threat level. Ben knew Joe would be on a plane back to Chicago and knew he could be counted on to assist in any type of intervention. As with 9/11, air transportation between two major cities had been targeted.

"Obviously I'm not armed, but I'll do what I can if anything goes down," Joe assured Ben. Then he remembered Alex and Stephanie.

"You should know I'm traveling with Mike plus two ladies. Yeah, you're probably surprised, but we can get into that later. It is absolutely imperative they sit with us. I want them right there if anything happens, so I can protect them. So you've gotta get me two more seats in First Class. I don't give a damn what strings you have to pull. Just do it. If the government can't afford to bribe a couple of passengers with a couple a thousand bucks, I'll pay for the seats myself."

Ben understood perfectly. "Okay, two seats adjacent to yours. When you get to the airport have the ladies go to the desk with you and exchange their boarding passes. They'll be held with your name on them, and all you need to do is pick them up. Let's just hope this is a false alarm. You be safe, okay? And call me when you land. Just be alert and cautious."

"Yeah, I will. You be safe, too."

When he clicked off his cell phone he ran back to the restaurant, trying to figure out how to put on, and keep, his best poker face.

"Sorry it took me so long. I got a business call I had to take," Joe apologized. He looked at Mike and the two ladies and addressed all three of them. "We need to get going right away so we make sure we don't miss that flight." He motioned for their waiter to bring the check as he handed him his plastic. "We're in a hurry, sir. Thanks."

Alex noticed that Joe's jaw was twitching. She wondered what that might mean.

At the airport, waiting in the check-in line and at security Alex noticed Joe's eyes were everywhere, checking out everybody and everything. His jaw continued to twitch. If she thought he looked serious before, that was nothing compared to the way he was now. *Well, I guess if I'm ever in danger he's my guy*, she thought.

At the check-in counter, the girls were in for a surprise. Not only were the men on the same flight, they had been bumped up to first class seats, adjacent to them. Steph was thrilled, but Alex thought it was another underhanded scheme of Joe's.

As the group waited to board, Alex recalled Joe saying something about having once been in the Special Services. Was that why he seemed nervous and on high-alert? Did he know something the rest of them didn't?

"Geez, first class! Whooeee! Free cocktails and all that," Steph gushed. "I've only traveled this way one other time in my life and I'm going to enjoy it."

*Good Lord,* Alex thought, wanting to slap her forehead for emphasis. The things she had to endure for friendship's sake. Only Steph would be thrilled that now they were stuck in a confined space with these men for a minimum of three more hours. Would this craziness never end?

During the flight Joe made a couple of trips up and down the aisle, supposedly to be stretching his legs, but in reality he was checking things out. Both times when he returned to his seat Alex didn't say anything but just gave him a questioning look. His face gave away nothing. Somehow, Alex got the impression that this was a man who could and who wanted to protect her.

As it turned out, to Joe's great relief, the flight was uneventful and without incident. As they made their way to retrieve their baggage, everything seemed normal at O'Hare. Even so, Joe continued to be on high-alert.

Joe had hired a limo, and he insisted that the driver drop off the ladies before continuing on to Mike and Joe's homes. Although the women protested, they were actually very glad to be taken home in style at the men's expense. It was a perfect ending to a perfect trip.

Goodbye came awkwardly to the couples. During the ride from the airport, Joe had finally asked Alex if she was seeing anyone seriously. She had had to inform him about Richard. In addition, it had become obvious that Stephanie wasn't into Mike. So, none of them said anything about seeing each other again. It looked as though what had happened in Vegas was going to stay in Vegas.

When the car arrived at the women's brownstones, Mike kissed both ladies on the cheek and thanked them for a great time. Joe said goodbye to Stephanie and then turned to Alex. After the days spent together, she still didn't know his last name or his real identity. He held her eyes for what seemed like an eternity trying to convey to her that he cared for her without putting his feelings into words.

"Take care of yourself, okay?" was all he could muster. Alex just nodded, hating to walk away from him.

Distracted by the potential security threat, Joe had forgotten all about the necklace, still secure in his pocket.

CHAPTER 4

It was August and another hot day with atrocious humidity. Joe's guys had been working nonstop trying to catch up because of recent rains. It was impossible to conduct a decent-sized concrete pour in the rain, and it certainly was not recommended when the heat index was over 120. Today, the favorable forecast meant the crew was going to get overdue tasks accomplished.

Joe had been thinking about Alex since their return. He could not get her out of his head. She was a woman he could see himself spending a lot of time with, a sentiment he hadn't felt for some time. It had been years since he had experienced a connection like the one he shared with her in Vegas.

With a sigh, his thoughts drifted back to the fact that the woman who made his heart come alive had finally showed up, and she had plans to marry someone else. It figured. The good ones were always taken. He had to get her out of his thoughts and get on with his life.

His reverie was broken by the sound of crashing metal. His head followed the sound. He looked behind and to his left saw what appeared to be a large panel truck that had rear-ended an SUV, and it looked like a hard hit. The SUV had run into the back of another vehicle and was sandwiched between. He yelled for Ramos to call 911 and began running toward the crash. Mike and a bunch of others followed to see if they could provide aid to anyone injured.

As Joe got closer to the crash, his stomach clenched as he realized the SUV was a silver Lexus. He began to run faster. When he got to the vehicle, he noticed the air bag on the driver's side had deployed. When he made his way to that side and peered inside the open window, his worst fear was realized. Alex was sitting behind the wheel. His gut started to knot up, and he felt like he couldn't catch his breath.

Stephanie had managed to open the passenger door and was climbing out, screaming for someone to help her friend.

Joe yelled over to Mike. "Take care of her. See if she's hurt. I'll see what I can do on this side. Ramos called 911. Hopefully they'll be here soon."

The driver-side door was jammed, so Joe rounded the front of the vehicle to get to the passenger door. Once inside, he grabbed his service knife and cut the air bag away from her. He assessed her overall condition. She was unconscious but breathing. Although there was no blood, that didn't mean there weren't any internal injuries. His years of training in the military gave him the ability to assess these things quickly. He leaned out. "Someone get me a goddamned blanket or something. She may be in shock."

One of the road crew workers quickly grabbed a light canvas cover and brought it to Joe. He covered Alex as best he could while making sure not to move her body more than necessary.

Facing her and taking her hand into his he began to talk to her quietly. She needed to know someone was with her and she was alive when she came to.

"Where the hell is the damn ambulance!" he yelled out at Mike, who had finally managed to calm Stephanie by assuring her that Alex was breathing and there were no apparent signs of blood.

"They'll be here soon, man. Ramos called again, and the dispatcher told him they are on their way."

As Joe was whispering to Alex that help was on its way she stirred slightly, and her lashes flitted as she tried to open her eyes. When she finally managed to do so, she looked at Joe, confused. He could barely hear her.

"What happened?" She squeezed his hand with desperation.

Joe's heart was pounding. Whatever the truth might be, he knew he had to make her believe she was going to be okay.

"Alex, there was an accident, but you're going to be fine. Help is on its way and should be here any minute. In the meantime, I'm here with you, and I won't let anything happen to you," he reassured her, still holding her hand.

Alex closed her eyes and whispered, "Don't leave me," and then she was out of it again.

When the ambulance did finally arrive, Joe moved out of the vehicle so the paramedics could take over. He watched nervously as Alex was carefully lifted onto a gurney, covered with a blanket, and then loaded into the ambulance.

"I'm going with," he shouted. "And don't give me any crap," he growled.

Acquiescing, they allowed him to climb into the back as he yelled at Mike to follow them to the hospital. In the meantime, they had loaded Stephanie into another ambulance to transport her to the hospital for evaluation.

When they arrived, he had to wait in Emergency while they ushered her behind closed doors. In the meantime, the second ambulance had arrived with Stephanie. Mike ran in after that. The two men did all they could to keep calm given the circumstances.

Joe sat down with his elbows on his knees running his hands through his hair. "What the hell… Why did this have to happen? I hope to Christ they're going to be okay. I mean Stephanie is totally conscious, so I have a feeling she'll check out—Alex, I'm not so sure."

His friend tried to console him and put his hand on his shoulder. "You know more about this kind of stuff than I do, but it didn't look as bad as it did at first. She'll probably come to soon. They'll run her through some tests and then probably release her."

Joe wasn't so sure.

Knowing that there would be only one way to get into the intensive care unit to be with Alex, Stephanie—who had been checked out and pronounced fine—devised a plan to get herself and Joe into their friend's room. Stephanie lied, claiming to be Alex's sister. Then she added, "And this is Joe, her fiancé."

Joe looked at Stephanie like she was from another planet, but she gave him a look that told him to just go along with it. "Yes, that's right. She's my fiancée," he confirmed, secretly relishing the thought.

That was all it took for them to be able to be enter her room. Mike patiently sat in the waiting room outside ICU waiting for Alex's parents to arrive. Stephanie had called Richard, who was traveling, but agreed to catch the first available flight. She figured in the meantime she would explain to Alex's parents the reason Joe had hung around. She would tell them that he was the first one at the scene of the accident and wanted to make sure she was going to be okay.

By afternoon, Alex had still not fully regained consciousness. Stephanie left again to get some coffee and check in with Mike. Alex's parents had arrived and the three of them took turns going in and out of the room. Joe didn't want to leave until she regained consciousness, even though he figured he should not be around when Richard arrived. It would be too awkward.

Joe was exhausted from worry and napped on and off in the recliner next to her bed. He had taken off his work boots and deposited them next to the chair, and his white-socked feet were comfortable on the footrest. He had scooted the recliner as close to her bed as he could so he could hold her hand. When she woke up, which he figured had to be soon, he wanted to be there so she wouldn't be frightened.

Mid-afternoon Joe had been snoozing when he felt her begin to stir as her hand began to move. He was on his feet in an instant and leaned over to assess her condition. When she opened her eyes it took her several seconds to comprehend her surroundings and recognize Joe. When she smiled, he felt immediate relief. As he grinned at her he spoke softly, "Didn't I tell you I wouldn't leave you?" She nodded as he pushed the button for the nurse.

Alex took in his disheveled appearance. His five o' clock shadow was beginning to surface and, as she looked down, she saw he had taken his boots off.

"You've never left me?"

He continued to hold her hand, now with both of his, as one of his thumbs stroked her palm.

"No. They tried to kick me out, but I told them they'd have to drag me. I wanted to make sure you were okay before I left. I know I shouldn't be hanging around. Richard should be here soon."

"What about Stephanie? She's alright?" she anxiously asked.

"She's just fine. They checked her out. She was a little in shock at first once she realized your airbag had deployed, but I put Mike in charge of calming her down. Do you want me to get your Mom first?"

When she responded "Yes please," he left the room to get Mrs. Parker as the nurse entered to take Alex's vitals. Shortly thereafter, the doctor came in to check on her and told Joe he wanted to keep her overnight for observation, and then, if all was well, he would release her in the morning. Joe was relieved and decided it was time for him to get going before Richard arrived.

There was a sudden commotion in the hallway.

"What the hell do you mean I can't see her?! She's my damned fiancée!" Richard's voice rang through the hall.

The three attending nurses looked at each other, none of them knowing just how to respond. Wasn't her fiancé already here? The senior nurse took it upon herself to respond.

"Sir, I am sorry but you'll have to wait in the lounge while I check with Miss Parker. She is conscious now and doing well. There seems to be a little, uh, misunderstanding. Her fiancé is already in there with her."

Richard was incensed. He pushed the woman aside and entered the room yelling, "What the hell do you mean her fiancé is with her? I'm her damned fiancé!"

Joe and Stephanie were in the room at the time, and he, Stephanie, and Alex looked up as he barged into the room. In the same vociferous voice he boomed, "Alex, what the fuck is going on? Who the hell is this guy?" pointing his finger at Joe. No one spoke. Alex looked over at Joe with panic in her eyes. It was unfair to put her through this situation when she was lying there injured. Yet, here they were.

Alex was obviously upset, and Joe was angry that this guy was being such a jerk.

Joe, being the gentleman he was, held his tongue and extended his right hand. "Joe. My name's Joe." He hesitated and turned to Alex. "I'm—my name is Joe. Joe Baker." He continued to gaze at Alex.

She gasped. "As in…"

He finished the statement for her, "Baker Concrete." He didn't say anything further, just looked at her.

Alex could barely believe her ears. Stephanie looked as shocked as Alex felt. "You own Baker Concrete?"

"Yeah." He grabbed his boots and started to pull them on.

"I guess my job's done here and I'm no longer needed."

It suddenly came together for her. Joe *owned* Baker Concrete. She had heard that his father had sold the company. What she didn't know was that he had sold it to his son. *No wonder he could afford to throw money around in Vegas.* She grabbed his arm, pulled him close and whispered, "Why didn't you tell me?"

He shrugged. "Would it have mattered?"

"You take care of yourself, okay? I'll get in touch somehow and check on you." He turned to Stephanie, nodded, and started to walk out of the room when he hesitated for several seconds before turning around. Addressing Richard directly, and with a look of fury in his eyes, he said in a tone that made Alex cringe.

"You know, the *least* you could have done is ask her how she is and tell her how relieved you are that she's going to be okay. That's what I would have done if she were my fiancée."

He looked back at Alex as her gaze rose to his. She scowled, unhappy, confused, and looking as uncertain as he felt.

*I must be getting old*, he thought. His emotions had been getting the best of him since they had met. Holding her gaze one moment longer, he calmly walked out of the room, and, at that moment, out of Alex's life.

The nurses entered and asked Richard and Stephanie both to leave immediately to give their patient a break from the circus atmosphere to which she had just been subjected.

Mrs. Parker was appalled at Richard's behavior. They could hear everything that was going on from outside the room and never had she witnessed any type of outburst or vulgar language from him. She was very distressed at the way he had acted. When she entered the room she held her daughter as tears spilled down Alex's cheeks. There was so much Alex needed to tell her mother, but at the moment she didn't quite know how to put everything into words. Her feelings about Richard and about Joe were so confusing. Alex hated that Joe had left, and with him, the feeling of being in a safe little cocoon. And what of her fiancé? Alex had never seen Richard display any type of rage. Was there a message in this behavior?

When Richard returned to the hospital room, he apologized profusely, explaining that it was the shock of Alex's accident and of then being told another claiming to be her fiancé was by her side. Alex wasn't about to tell him about having met Joe at a prior time, let alone that she had spent time with him in Las Vegas. Richard accepted the fact that Joe had only accompanied her to the hospital because he was at the scene of the accident, and he felt compelled to make sure she was going to be properly taken care of.

CHAPTER 5

The month following the accident had passed quickly for Joe, as Baker Concrete was having an unusually busy year. After the accident, Joe had called Steph several times for an update on Alex's progress. She had seemed hesitant to give him any contact information for Alex, which he assumed was at Alex's request. Hell, he wasn't stupid. She was engaged to another man, and he had no business talking to her let alone spending time with her.

Joe was also thinking he had endured just about enough of Mike's whining and pining over Stephanie, who wanted nothing to do with him. Ever since the accident, he had shown a renewed interest in pursuing Steph, but she just wasn't interested. Joe felt sorry for Mike, and he could relate to his friend's dilemma—he felt the same way about Alex.

Joe felt his buddy was a good catch and that Steph really should give the man a chance. So, he decided to put Mike—and himself by default—out of misery by finding out why the woman refused to date him. Perhaps it was just a case of no chemistry, but whatever it was, he owed it to Mike to find out why Stephanie refused to date him. Maybe then the man would finally move on, leaving everyone in peace.

There were many ways to get Alex's number. He was a resourceful and well-connected man. But he also realized Alex probably would not appreciate a phone call from him. He reasoned that a face-to-face talk would be best. Joe had no guarantee that she would tell him, if she knew, but he had to make the attempt. His best friend was miserable, and Joe felt it was his duty to help, if possible. The thought of seeing Alex again sent tingles through his body. He recalled her beautiful face and warm brown eyes. The memory of her smile got to him every time he thought of her. He knew he probably had no chance with her—after all, she was marrying Richard. But on the other hand, how could she deny the electricity generated between them since the moment they had met?

Fate emboldened him, and Joe chose Wednesday to pay Alex a visit at her office. What was the worst that could happen? Either she wasn't in or she was too busy to see him. He had Googled her and found the name and location of her firm. As he browsed through the firm's website, he noted that Alex and Richard Churchfield were both partners in the senior Mr. Churchfield's firm. A law firm partner, he had reflected, delighted. She was as smart as she was gorgeous.

He arrived late afternoon—thinking that she might be less busy at that time of day. He looked up at the imposing twenty-story building that was home to Churchfield and Bryant. It was an older building on LaSalle, and he had read that the building was in the historic Landmark Preservation Group. He had researched the firm, which had been in existence over one-hundred years with many generations of Churchfields at the helm. He also knew that Dickhead, as he had begun to think of Richard, was the next in line to inherit the throne of the family's legal empire. As such, Joe imagined that Richard probably felt pressured to marry and have children, not only to keep up appearances in the legal world, but also to carry on the family business. Joe easily pictured Alex as a mom. Then he realized he had no idea how old she actually was. Probably still within childbearing range, if Richard planned to marry her.

Joe entered the building and took in his surroundings, noting that the reception area had marble floors, rich cherry paneling and an imposing reception desk. The entire place reeked of old money. Generations of it.

"Hello," he said, giving his best smile to the crusty guardian stationed at the lobby desk.

"I'm here to see Alexis Parker."

"Your name sir?" he asked.

"Joseph Baker."

"One moment Mr. Baker." He picked up the receiver and dialed. "Hi, Heather. I have a Mr. Joseph Baker here to see Ms. Parker."

Heather didn't remember seeing him on the schedule so she checked her computer.

"Well, he doesn't have an appointment. Hold on. I'll ask Alex." Heather buzzed her.

"Alex, I don't see it on the schedule, but they just called from downstairs and said there is a Joseph Baker here to see you."

"Who?"

"Joseph Baker."

*Holy crap. Joseph Baker, Sr.? Or Joseph Baker, Jr.?* A few years back she had assisted the senior Baker with drawing up paperwork for a joint venture. Corporate law, specifically mergers and acquisitions, was her specialty. Baker senior did seem the type to make an appointment in advance. She'd have to take her chances.

"Tell them it's okay to send him up, and buzz me when he gets here."

Joe was directed to the elevator that would take him to the twentieth floor of this architectural masterpiece. As he stepped into the elevator, he noted that even this small space had been decorated with intricate brass work, which had been meticulously maintained.

Heather, Alex's assistant, walked down the hall into the twentieth floor reception area. Since there was only one visitor, she had to assume it was Mr. Baker. *Wow, what a hunk of man,* Heather thought. He looked like something out of one of those Chippendale dancer or firefighter calendars. Regaining her composure, she remembered her manners. "Good afternoon," the young lady said, extending her hand. "I'm Heather. Ms. Parker's assistant. I'll show you to her office."

At the end of the hall they came upon a large glass door that read "Alexis Parker, Vice President," and he followed Heather through the door.

"Please make yourself comfortable. I'll let her know you're here." Heather picked up the receiver and dialed Alex.

"Ms. Parker, Mr. Baker is here."

"Heather, don't say much. Just answer me "yes" or "no." Is the Joe Baker sitting there young? AND is he the most gorgeous guy you have ever laid eyes on?"

Joe observed that Alex was obviously saying something to her assistant because Heather was nodding her head up and down and muttering "Uh huh. Uh huh. Yes." And then she addressed him as she hung up the receiver.

"She will be with you in a few moments. Can I get you something to drink, like coffee, tea, bottled water?"

"No thanks. I'm fine."

Alex took a moment to get her head straight, took in a deep breath, walked to the door, and opened it. "Hello, Joe. Nice to see you." She smiled as she extended her hand. "Come in."

"Well, this certainly is a surprise." She opened her hand toward a chair facing her desk. "What brings you here?" she asked, standing in front of him. She was doing her best to act and sound professional, but inside she was a nervous wreck. *God he looks good.* She took a quick glance down at his Italian loafers that matched his belt. He could look outrageous, even in khakis and a button down.

Joe didn't sit down right away. First, he just looked her over from head to toe. *What is it about her that makes me want her so much?* He forcibly redirected his thoughts to the task at hand.

"It's nice to see you. You look great. No after-effects from the accident?" He had a serious look on his face. Alex found that she couldn't tear her eyes from his. Before she could respond, he whispered, "I've missed you."

*Oh, God—I've missed you, too*, she thought.

"I've been fine," she replied. She bit her lower lip and he knew then that she had missed him, too.

Joe's gaze wandered down to her feet. Her toenails were once again done in red, set off in a delicious way by her heeled sandals. He couldn't resist: "Nice. Is that your friend Jimmy Choo?" He grinned, pointing to her feet.

"I'm sure you didn't come here to talk about my sandals," Alex replied, skeptically.

"Um, no. Actually, Alex, I need your help with something. It's an issue that's probably best dealt with in person, so I hope you don't mind that I just popped in unannounced."

"Of course not." She settled into the chair behind her desk. Alex willed herself to remain calm and professional, as her heart was beating intensely and her stomach was doing flip-flops. It was best to keep the office thinking that Joe was here on official business.

"I'm happy to help if I can, especially with what you have done for me. I mean, with the accident and everything," she said, sweeping her hand toward him. "Do you need legal advice of some kind?

"No," he said, shaking his head. "It's about Mike. Well, actually it's about Mike and Stephanie. You probably already know that Mike has been calling her and she keeps turning him down." He looked down, sadly. "Mike's got it bad for her, and frankly he's driving me nuts. Every day he talks about her and how she won't give him the time of day. You know yourself that he's a great guy and a great catch." He paused to gauge her reaction. She seemed receptive, so he continued.

"He really doesn't understand why she won't date him. Does it have anything to do with the fact that he's a construction guy and not some high-buck lawyer? Because if that's it, I can tell you for sure that he makes a *very* nice salary," he said, smiling weakly, unsure that what he was saying was making any impact.

Of course Alex knew Mike had been calling, and of course she knew Steph kept turning him down. But Alex actually didn't know the reason why. She thought maybe it was because Steph still hoped that Joe would break down and call her. She *had* given her card to Joe and not Mike, after all. And Alex had made it clear to Joe that she was not available. There was no reason for Joe not to call Steph. But was that still what was on Steph's mind? Alex couldn't be sure.

"I'm pretty sure what he does for a living has nothing to do with it," Alex concluded. He gave her a sympathetic look of understanding and then smiled slightly. Seeing the rare turn of Joe's lips upward, suddenly her insides turned to mush. *My Lord, get a grip, Alex. How can you let him affect you like this?* She was powerless against this man's smile. For a split second, she pictured herself with Joe Baker.

"But possibly it has something to do with the fact that she thinks his lashes are longer than hers," She blurted out with a laugh.

Joe nodded and chuckled back. "Yeah, she's probably right on that one."

*Oh, God. Just let him keep smiling...* she thought.

Alex decided to take a risk. "But let's be honest here," she said, looking down, and then again into his eyes. *Just tell him.* She took a deep breath.

"Stephanie has the hots for you. That's it in a nutshell. She is so wrapped up in hoping that you'll call her that she can't see what she might be passing up."

Joe looked surprised. "Ooohhhh," he acknowledged. He was sure he had done nothing to lead Stephanie on regarding his intentions. "She certainly is a beautiful and nice lady, but... I'm interested in someone else. Someone who's... not available at the moment." He gave Alex a raised eyebrow and a knowing grin.

Alex threw him a look. "Married?" she asked him, both of her own eyebrows now raised. She hadn't grasped his little joke.

"No, not yet. Technically you could consider her as still being somewhat free."

He studied Alex's face. She still wasn't getting it. For a lawyer, she had no common sense, it seemed. He would have to spell out the situation for her.

"Look, it can't be a surprise that I care for you. I know you are spoken for, and I have to accept that, but I'm hoping we can be friends. But anyway, I have a proposition on how to get Mike and Stephanie together and am asking that you'll help me put the plan into action. Want to hear it?" he asked.

She couldn't imagine what kind of plan he was talking about.

"Okay. We need to get them together somehow, without either of them knowing what we're doing. I was thinking we could meet up somewhere. You bring Stephanie, and I'll bring Mike. We'll act like it was this big coincidence, and then we'll leave them alone so they can hopefully discover why they should be."

The thought tickled her. He was adorable, trying to play matchmaker and being such a good sport about giving her up to Richard. "I like the way you think. It's going to be like a conspiracy or something?"

"Or something. I have a few ideas. But first I want to find out from you a few things about what Steph likes. What does she like to do? Is she into tennis or some other sport? Does she like boating? Where does she like to hang out? Which bars or restaurants? And, most importantly, what kind of music does she like?" he rambled, breathlessly.

"Oh, she definitely would like something involving drinks and a live band. She likes all kinds of music." Alex smiled a conspirator smile. His eyes smiled back at hers.

"Hmm. That's good! Mike plays the guitar, actually," Joe informed her.

She was surprised. "I can't tell you how many guys she dated in high school and college that played," Alex revealed. "That's probably why her marriage failed. Steph fantasized about those types of guys but married someone who couldn't have cared less about music. Can you believe it? I often times wondered what she was thinking. He didn't even like to dance."

Joe was just looking at her with a boyish grin. *Damn, I think she's getting into this whole idea*, he thought.

"Well, I think we should meet somewhere for some live music, then," Joe said, pleased. "I'll check the schedule again, but I'm sure my friends are playing at Navy Pier two weeks from this Saturday. We'll meet 'by accident,' and while we're listening to the music, I can mention Mike plays guitar. Hopefully that will open the door to some conversation for them. Do you think that would work, or do you have other plans for that day and evening?"

She hesitated before replying. "I don't know… I usually see Richard on Saturdays. Maybe I can just change plans and tell him Stephanie and I are having a girls' night out. I mean that wouldn't exactly be a lie. Lying isn't my thing."

"Check with her and make sure she can make it, and I'll get the game plan set up. Why don't we plan to meet at five sharp? Of course we'll be in touch before then to firm up all the details. Can we make it work?"

She cocked her head to one side and looked at him. "It should be fun, but we have to go into it with the attitude that the setup could turn out marvelously or end up a complete disaster. But I'm game if you are," Alex giggled conspiratorially. "I *do* love setups."

Before Joe could reply her phone rang. She hesitated. "Uh, excuse me," she said, grabbing the phone impatiently. "Yes, Heather. What is it? Do you know what he wants?" She sighed. "Okay put him on." She looked at Joe. "Hi…yes… well, I'm just finishing up. NO, don't come down. How about if I just meet you in the lobby at 5:15. Sure, yeah, okay. Um—me, too," she said, and hung up.

"Betcha I know who that was," Joe smirked. His mischievous eyes had changed from that cute expression to, for a split second, a look of jealousy.

She let out a sigh. "It's been a busy day, and we haven't connected, so he…"

"Wanted to connect?" he said with wide questioning eyes.

What was it about him that always challenged her? It was as if he was intentionally trying to irritate her, but then again she let him have that affect on her. God knew he didn't like Richard. That was obvious from the hospital incident.

"I'm sorry, but I only have a little time to finish something, and I told him I'd meet him in the lobby soon. You really need to get going unless you want to cross paths with Richard. He'd wonder what you're doing here, and this is our little secret, right?"

"Okay, call me as soon as you can about the date." And with that, Joe took out his business card and handed it to her. "If that doesn't work we'll have to go to Plan B."

Alex looked at him quizzically. "You have a Plan B?"

"Always… Just as soon as I think one up," he taunted. They both stood and

Alex came around to the front of her desk. Joe stepped closer to her, invading her space, as he seemed to enjoy doing. He was looking at her again with that serious look.

"What?" she asked innocently. Her heart beat faster than normal.

His heartbeat suddenly kicked up a notch, too. He reached out and softly stroked her cheek as he continued to look at her.

*He isn't going to kiss me again is he? You know you want him to, and you are so bad.* As if sensing her thoughts he did just that—softly at first, but then he hitched it up a notch, pressing his mouth into hers like he wanted to devour her. The heat between them was unmistakable.

Joe pulled her entire body into his and she could feel his hardness through his khakis. When she grabbed his triceps with her hands she was pretty sure she could feel him trembling. Then he pulled away just as quickly as he had leaned into her.

"See what you do to me? You make me lose my head and just give into the moment," he said. Then he brought her hand up to kiss her palm. Alex closed her eyes, allowing herself to "feel," if only for a moment.

Just then her engagement ring caught his eye. He dropped her hand like it was a piece of hot charcoal.

"Nice ring. He must have paid a lot of dough for that one. Did he pick it out?"

The moment was lost just as quickly as it had begun. "Oh Joe, you're not here to discuss my ring," she said in an exasperated tone.

"Why not? You kiss me like you want to crawl inside me but you won't answer a question about a ring?"

He had a point. She *had* kissed him back like she wanted inside him. Or rather, she wanted him inside of her. She sighed and answered him.

"Yes. It really is lovely but a bit over the top. I couldn't hurt him by telling him it's a bit much."

"If you ask me, if he knew you as well as he should he would know exactly what you would want. But that's just my opinion." He gave Alex a sharp, knowing glare. "Call me this week and let me know if that date works."

With that, Joe started for the door. Then suddenly hesitated. "Alex?"

"Yes?"

"Make that date... And be on time."

"And Joe?" She gave him a mocking look. "You know you look rather cute wearing pink lip gloss and a hard on," she said, winking.

He thought a moment and then wiped his lips with the back of his hand. He opened the door and closed it behind him.

Alex walked back to her desk on somewhat unsteady legs. The kiss had shaken her. *What was I thinking kissing him back like that? God, that was like an open invitation.* She was helpless in his presence. She had to admit, she had *wanted* to kiss him back. And more. *Oh, God!*

She sat down and put her head back in her chair and thought about seeing him again in a couple of weeks. She found herself actually looking forward to spending more time with him. *This is not a good thing*, she thought. She knew she was forcing herself to honor her commitment to Richard, but knew she had to work through her uncertainties.

She nearly forgot she had to meet up with Richard, she was so engrossed in her thoughts. She had replayed everything Joe had said, how he looked at her, the smiles, and the kiss, analyzing it all. Thoughts of her attraction to him were agonizing.

After tidying up her desk, Alex sighed, retrieved her purse, and walked to her door. She turned back to gaze at the spot in front of her desk where she had felt Joe's desire. Closing her eyes for a second, she allowed herself to remember the kiss. She felt that kissing Joe was very unfair to Richard. Yet, on the other hand, maybe she should give some serious thought to calling off her engagement. An engaged woman shouldn't be acting the way she was.

The following day, Alex phoned Stephanie while they were both still at the office.

"Hey, it's me. You busy two weeks from Saturday? I've been thinking we should do something fun for a change. Just the two of us. Whatcha think?"

Steph thought a minute.

"Am I busy?" She chuckled. "I guess you could say I'm not busy. I mean I don't have a date planned yet. So what did you have in mind?"

"Why don't we take the train in and go to Navy Pier. We haven't done that in ages. I read they have some awesome band playing there. We can check that out and then grab dinner or something." Stretching the truth was not her style, but Alex had given Joe her word she would do her best to set this up.

"That sounds great to me. But what about Richard? You guys usually see each other on Saturdays," Steph responded.

What the heck *would* she tell Richard? Well, she would just tell him she needed some girl time. Time to not talk about work for once and just get caught up on other non-work related stuff. That was actually true.

"Well, he'll understand that sometimes women need some girl time. I mean it's not like missing a Saturday together will kill either of us. We are going to be spending a lifetime together. At the moment, I think it would be good for us to be apart a little. We've been arguing so much about this wedding thing that I think I need a break."

Steph couldn't agree more.

"You're right. I'm up for some fun. Just the two of us—it sounds great. Do you know what time the band starts?"

"I'll check to be sure, but I think they start kind of early. I'm pretty sure they end by nine, and then a different band comes out when the heavy metal younger crowd arrives. We can grab some dinner after, if we feel like it."

"Sounds good to me. What's the crowd like, do you know? I mean, what should we wear. Jeans?"

Criminy; Alex had no idea. She'd have to look on the Internet. She'd never heard of this band.

"I'll find out and let you know," Alex assured her.

"It sounds like fun. Thanks for asking me on a *date*."

Alex laughed. "Sure, honey. Just put it on your calendar, so you don't forget, okay?"

*Whew!* With that settled, Alex made a mental note to call Joe the next day and tell him they were set. As if she would have to make a note. Every time the man showed up in her life, he stayed in her brain like a slow flame on the back burner. Alex wondered what kind of "mysterious" coincidence Joe had planned. Now all she had to do was convince herself they were only entering into this co-conspiracy as two friends doing something for the betterment of their mutual friends.

The next day Alex's stomach was doing flip-flops as she prepared to call Joe. When she dialed his cell, he answered immediately.

"Baker."

She took a deep breath, exhaled, and closed her eyes. "Joe. Hi. It's Alex. I talked to Stephanie and she's okay with that Saturday. Is the plan in place?"

She sounded kind of breathless and nervous, but it was good to hear her voice. "Yeah, it's still a go," Joe answered. "Just make sure you guys are there at five, okay? You said you'll take the train in, right?"

"Yes, I told her Navy Pier at five. I just told her we would go to listen to the band and then we would catch dinner or something—you know, just play it by ear. She wasn't suspicious at all." She hesitated a moment, feeling rather silly asking him what to wear.

"Uh, what's the dress code? We haven't been there in ages, and I have no idea. The Pier is pretty casual right?"

*She was asking him what to wear? Mmmm. How about you show up in something slinky and revealing. Or better yet, just show up wearing nothing but a smile,* he thought. But instead of saying this, he replied, "Nothing fancy. Jeans. You two always look nice." He thought a moment, and then added, "No Jimmy Choos necessary. But bring something warm in case we decide to do something outside, okay?"

"Ha, ha," Alex replied sarcastically, though she couldn't resist smiling at the inside joke. "Something warm? Want to clue me in, or is this part a surprise, too?"

"Darlin', you *will* be surprised, that's for sure. Don't want to give away my plan. You'll just have to trust me. Just remember we are doing this for Mike and Stephanie's benefit."

"Sure, *darlin',*" she mocked him, "Whatever you say. We'll be there at five sharp."

"Yeah, I'll do the same. I'm really looking forward to it. Besides, I know you can't wait to see me."

She snickered. "You wish."

"Can't blame a guy for trying." He smiled to himself.

"Cut the crap, Baker. Do your job and we'll get along just fine. Remember, we're on a mission. If anything changes let me know. Otherwise I'll see you there."

Joe would have loved to talk with Alex for hours, but he knew she was probably at work and had to get back to her billable hours. He couldn't wait until Saturday, when he could spend a whole evening in her presence.

CHAPTER 6

Joe was excitedly pulling together his master plan. He had made a visit to the venue to talk to the manager about reserving a special table for the ladies. The band would join them, when the time came.

What the women didn't know was that Mike and Joe had originally been part of the band, Taylor Street, that Alex and Stephanie were going to be listening to. While most of the other guys continued to play full-time, Mike and Joe had moved on to other careers; however, they still jammed with them just to keep up with the music scene.

Joe had confirmed, even before he talked to Alex, that Taylor Street would be at Navy Pier on the evening in question. He had explained to the leader what was on his mind and had convinced his old buddy to let him put together the music in the sets.

The big surprise was that at some point Joe and Mike would join the band on stage for a few songs. It was guaranteed to be a memorable event, and Joe had not been so excited about anything in a long time.

After her conversation with Joe, not a day went by that Alex wasn't thinking about their setup and what she should wear. Even though Joe had said jeans, she wanted to look her best. She had changed her mind a dozen times, and finally decided to go with classic black slacks, a lightweight red sweater, and her funky, new short black leather jacket with the cute hardware. And of course her Jimmy Choo short boots with the little heel. She'd decided to wear her hair down and to finish the look by donning the silver hoop earrings that matched the hardware on her jacket.

When Steph called to confer on the wardrobe for the night, Alex remembered to tell her to bring a jacket, in case they wanted to walk around a bit outside. It was difficult but delicious keeping such a cool secret from her friend.

When date night finally arrived, the girls took the train in as planned.

"Do you think there will be any decent, age-appropriate guys there?" Steph asked on the ride in. "I heard there is a huge age range that frequents the place.

Maybe I'll finally meet Mr. Right," she said, with lots of enthusiasm.

Alex nearly burst out laughing, thinking about her plans for the evening, which actually included Steph meeting Mr. Right. Steph's problem was that she didn't recognize what was right under her nose the whole time.

From the train station, the ladies caught a cab right away, so they actually arrived at the designated bar exactly on time. The place was packed and noisy.

*Yikes. How am I supposed to find him in this crowd?* Alex thought.

The band was playing Boston's "Don't Look Back".

"Ooh, one of my favorite songs," Stephanie shouted excitedly.

"Where the heck are we going to find a place to sit?" Alex groused. Most of the tables were already taken. The bar area looked packed, too. A number of people were standing. As Alex tried to locate Joe, an official-looking guy walked up to them.

"Hello, ladies. Would you like me to find you a table? Some folks just vacated a nice spot close to the dance floor."

They made their way through the crowd, and finally a table for four. Alex was about to sit down, when she glanced toward the bandstand.

*What the heck? Was that Joe playing drums?*

Joe had noticed the girls had arrived and managed to catch Alex's eye.

Alex's jaw dropped. She could hardly believe what she was seeing. And there was Mike… playing bass?

Alex shot Joe an "I can't believe you" look. He countered with an "I'm innocent" pose. He had one-upped her and was very pleased with himself.

While Alex was staring at Joe in disbelief, Stephanie grabbed her arm and squealed, "Oh my God! Joe and Mike are in the band? Did you have any idea? What a hoot!"

Alex pulled her down.

"Alex, why are you looking mad?"

"Because I thought that they were out of our lives, and now, here they are interrupting our girls' night out. And no. I did *not* know they even played music, let alone were part of this group." She'd had to think quickly to mollify Steph with a plausible excuse.

"This is great!" Steph gushed. "I've been wanting to see Joe again, and you know it."

*Oh brother, this is not the direction we're supposed to be headed*, Alex thought.

It was all coming back to her now—the conversation she and Joe had had about musicians and Steph having a thing for guys in a band. Clearly Joe had dreamed up this whole thing. They must have been playing for years, because they looked pretty at home with the band members and being on stage.

When she looked up again and caught Joe's eye, he flashed his biggest melt-a-woman's-heart smile. She took in his white shirt, partly rolled up his forearms, jeans, and gray cowboy boots. As usual, he was completely hot. Then she glanced at Mike, who apparently had not yet spotted them. He was concentrating on playing his guitar.

"Well, how cool is this to see two totally hot guys that we actually know up there?" Steph remarked, as she gave Joe her little wave. He nodded back.

*Okay, you're here for a reason. So just get it going here*, Alex thought.

"Yes. A little shocking, but cool. Look at Mike playing guitar. He looks pretty darned good," Alex commented.

"Yeah, he looks pretty good. Well, actually they both look good!" Steph agreed.

The band launched into another Boston song. "This is great music! I'm so glad we came, aren't you?" Stephanie was definitely excited.

Alex lied for her best friend's sake. "Yes I'm glad we came. You're right, the music is really good. Do you suppose they'll come over and say hi when they're done with the set?" Alex was playing her.

Steph gushed. "I certainly hope so. If not, I'll just get up and go talk to them. It's not like we're strangers or groupies."

They continued watching Mike and Joe. Mike finally sensed someone checking him out and realized it was Stephanie. He looked extremely pleased to see her.

Alex had to admit she *was* enjoying the music. And it was actually cool to know a couple of the band members. Alex noticed that Joe just happened to be a fantastic drummer. He made it look so easy.

She had to give it to him. Planning this event was a stroke of genius.

The women ordered a couple of Blue Moons when the waitress stopped by their table and enjoyed the classic rock play list the band was working through. Toward the end of their set a tall attractive woman stepped up to the stage. She looked like a model—slender, beautiful shiny blonde hair, and an enviably endowed chest. Alex concluded that the woman's short, trendy hair cut enhanced her beauty.

Alex watched as Joe gave up his drums, walked up to the blonde, and grabbed the microphone. She and Joe started singing the Bon Jovi/Jennifer Nettles hit "Who Says You Can't Go Home." Would this man ever cease to amaze her? Not only was he a drummer but he had a great voice as well. As the duo belted out the song, Alex began to have the sense that these two knew each other intimately. Joe had his arm around her hip, and they sang together as though they had performed together hundreds of times before. When the song ended Joe gave his song partner a hug and a kiss that suggested they knew each other well.

Alex was surprised to discover that she felt jealous and a little angry. Why? Was it because of the kiss they had shared in her office recently? It was silly of her to assume that a man as hot as Joe remained unattached. And after all, she was engaged to Richard.

This song ended the set, and Joe made his way over to Alex and Stephanie's table.

"Ladies, what a most pleasant surprise!" He motioned to a huge corner table where the band members had seated themselves for the break. "Would you like to join us and meet the others?" Joe looked at Alex and winked. She closed her eyes and just shook her head. *Very funny Baker.*

"Oh gosh that would be great—we'd love to," Stephanie replied. "Joe, I'm so excited to see you," she said, giving him a quick hug. "Come on Alex, let's go meet Joe's friends."

Reluctantly, shaking her head, she looked at Joe and frowned. Stephanie was not supposed to be excited to see Joe. That wasn't the plan. They would have to redirect Stephanie's attention soon.

Joe walked the girls over to his table and introduced them to the band, while Mike just stared at Stephanie, still shocked to see her. "Everyone, I'd like you to meet Alex and Stephanie. They're new friends of Mike and mine, so I thought I'd invite them to share our table."

He then proceeded to introduce the group and delved into an explanation of how he and Mike occasionally jammed with the group. He disclosed how they had grown up together, practicing in Joe's parents' garage on Taylor Street and playing at clubs when they could. It turned out that gorgeous Carolyn, the female vocalist, had, like Mike and Joe, moved on from the group toward another type of career. She now owned a trendy boutique on Michigan Avenue. Though the girls regularly frequented Mag Mile boutiques, somehow they had missed hers. Like Joe and Mike, Carolyn still enjoyed occasionally sitting in for a song or two to keep in touch. So, apparently Joe had known this beauty most of his life. Alex found herself wondering whether the two of them had previously had a relationship. That was a fairly common thing in bands.

When the break ended, the regular band members took over, while the part-timers sat out. They began to play Little Big Town's "Bring it on Home." Stephanie looked on in dismay while Joe grabbed Alex and started pulling her toward the dance floor.

"What are you doing?" she asked, in a low voice.

"I like this song. I wanna dance, okay? Remember, we danced to this in Vegas." As if she could have forgotten.

"If we dance, it will encourage Mike and Steph to get out here," he added.

Alex shot him a frown. But not wanting to make a scene, she moved into Joe's arms. He pulled her so close she could barely breath. He was clearly enjoying their "mission." A little too much for Alex's tastes.

"I have to hand it to you, Baker. Setting this one up must have taken quite a bit of imagination and work to pull together."

"Hey, I told you to trust me and it would be great. Neither one of them seems suspicious. Relax and try to enjoy yourself, okay? We're doing a good deed, here," he coaxed.

She nodded. At the final lyrics Joe pulled back and their eyes locked and he sang to her as he had in Vegas, "You've got someone here wants to make it alright, someone that loves you more than life right here." She flushed at the way he was looking at her. *Why did he have to have such power over her? Stay in control, Alex. Don't fall for him.*

The band moved right into the next song, which was the same Little Big Town hit she and Joe had also danced to in Vegas. Two such memorable Little Big Town hits in a row? Had Joe planned it that way? Was he scheming on her in addition to trying to get Mike and Stephanie together? What if he was?

When Taylor Street played the last notes, Joe squeezed her. "Thanks for the dances, darlin'. I know you won't admit it, but I think you're very glad to see me and are already having fun."

When they returned to their table, they were glad to discover Mike had ordered another round, and he and Stephanie were engrossed in a light-hearted conversation. Alex was delighted by the look of rapture on her friend's face. Maybe this had been a good idea after all. Mike looked especially hot tonight, and Alex was glad for Stephanie. Carolyn had remained as well. She chatted with the group and seemed genuinely nice.

Joe kept insisting Alex dance with him. She couldn't fight it—she was having a great time despite the warning bells going off in her head.

Joe was hoping, but not necessarily expecting, Alex would let down her guard. The truth was that Alex found both Joe and the situation irresistible. She was enjoying herself immensely, even to the extent of doing a little dirty dancing. Mike and Steph seemed to be having a great time as well, and Joe could not have been more pleased with the situation.

After the next break, Joe and Mike rejoined the band. Stephanie couldn't stop gushing about what a great guitar player Mike was. For the moment, Steph seemed to be over any doubts she'd harbored about the man.

Carolyn then took center stage and began to belt out Bonnie Raitt hits. Was it Alex's imagination, or were all these songs suggestive of love and getting together? "Something to Talk About," "Thing Called Love," and then "I Can't Make You Love Me." Alex could just imagine who had selected these songs.

Alex found herself itching to know more about the Joe/Carolyn relationship. Had they ever been more than friends? Yet, Alex noticed that Joe's attention seemed to be focused on her. And she could still feel the sparks that he emitted when he was around her.

During the last song, during the words "I can't make you love me," she could have sworn a look of sadness filled Joe's eyes as he gazed at her across the room.

The set included a couple more love songs, interspersed with some up-tempo tunes to keep the crowd out on the dance floor. Finally, Carolyn came back to sing "Insensitive." Joe's eyes never left Alex's face during the entire song.

Suddenly she got it. Warning signals went off. No doubt about it. This song was clearly intended to send a message to Alex without him ever actually having to utter a word. "I need to get some air," she told Steph, then shot Joe a dirty look and walked out.

Watching her walk away he figured he had pushed it too far. As soon as the song finished he left his drum set to the regular drummer and went out to look for Alex.

Joe tracked her down, standing at the boardwalk railing with her back to him, arms to her sides, gazing out at the lake. When Joe approached and put his arms around her waist, Alex tried to pull free.

"Don't!" she instructed.

He turned her around to face him and saw she was crying.

"What's wrong?" he asked her gently.

"You've been playing me this entire time haven't you? I mean with all those songs. Are you trying to make me feel bad or something? I'll bet you planned this evening as much for yourself as you did for Mike and Steph. I'm right, aren't I?"

He was busted. At a loss for words, he didn't know how to respond to her. He reached for her cheek and wiped the tears from one of them with his thumb. He stood back from her to give her some space. They stood facing each other, neither of them saying anything for a moment.

He looked at the ground and then back up again. "Okay, I confess. I picked the songs. The guys and I practiced a lot these last couple of weeks. I confessed to them, well Carolyn, too, that I wanted this day and evening to be something very special. And yes, this night was not just meant for Mike and Stephanie."

He shoved his hands into the back pocket of his jeans. Not looking at her, he went on.

"Look, I'm not exactly good at conveying my feelings. Hell, the fact is I *suck* at it. I'm not your typical guy about this kind of stuff. I'm worse than your typical guy. I have feelings for you and don't know how to handle it. So, since I couldn't put these feelings into words I tried to convey them with music. Can you ever give *us* a chance?" He looked back up at her with a heart-wrenching look of expectancy.

She forced herself to keep her distance and sighed.

"Joe, I can't give *us* a chance. There can't be an "us." I've made a promise to another man. A promise of marriage. I didn't enter into that promise lightly, just as I'm not taking our friendship lightly. It is just something we're going to have to work through. Richard is expecting that I will honor my promise to be his wife. If I had given you that promise, I'm sure you wouldn't want me to break that promise and start spending time with Richard or any another man."

He responded with bitterness in his voice. "You're right about me not wanting you to spend time with Richard. Hell, anybody *but* Richard." Now it was Joe's turn to be angry.

Alex reached out and took both of his hands in hers.

"So far, I think we have succeeded in our plan to get our friends together. *Finally.* Let's not spoil it for them. This night isn't about us. It's about them. We need to concentrate on that and try to enjoy the rest of whatever it is you have planned."

He knew she was right, but that didn't mean he had to like it. He stood there looking at her, thinking about what she had just said.

"Come on, let's go back inside. They'll be wondering where we are. Besides it's getting cold out here and you don't have your jacket," he said.

When they walked back in, the band was taking a break before their final set. No one mentioned anything about Joe and Alex having gone missing. Joe and Mike planned to join the band for the last set, and then Joe had made plans for the four of them to have dinner.

Joe was not happy about what Alex had just told him—that he had no chance with her. How could she prefer a man like Richard, so dry and boring, to someone like himself, so alive and passionate? He would have to get through the rest of this evening somehow. And Alex was right. Part of the reason why he was here was to see that his best friend got together with hers.

Before going back on stage, Joe made sure the girls had another round of drinks. During the last set, Mike and Joe played their hearts out, and Joe hoped it was a performance the girls were not likely to forget. Richard, indeed! He'd never hold a candle to Joe's lively drumming.

The song Joe had chosen as the last for their guest appearance was none other than the classic rock anthem "Free Bird." The song started out slowly, but culminated in a frenzied drum set at the end. Mike had taken over lead guitar for this number, and hopefully Steph would be impressed. Joe still hoped Alex would see what he had to offer. So much more than the dull, socially impotent attorney she had clearly mistakenly bound herself to. He was going to win her heart, or die trying.

As they entered into the last part of the song, the two of them did the classic drummer/lead guitarist thing of playing to each other. Mike had turned his back to the audience, and the two of them were seemingly each trying to outdo the other. Joe was amazing on drums, as was Mike on guitar. When the song ended, Alex and Stephanie both jumped from her seats, clapping and whooping in appreciation. It was truly a fantastic performance. Other members of the audience began to move to their feet as well. The band basked in their celebrity moment.

Both a little out of breath from their hard work, Mike and Joe left their instruments and walked toward the ladies. Alex threw her arms around Joe. "God, you were fantastic! I can't believe you guys can play like that. Everyone loved you!" she said, enthused.

Taken aback, he enjoyed the moment of adulation and hugged her back. As he glanced over, he noticed Stephanie had given Mike a hug and a quick peck on the cheek.

"Ladies, if it wouldn't be too much of an inconvenience for you to be seen with two such outstanding musicians, would you care to join the drummer and the guitarist for dinner?" Joe queried mischievously. Though his heart was heavy with the thought that Alex wasn't going to give in to his charms, he went along with his well-made plans for Mike and Stephanie's sakes.

Both women were clearly delighted and accepted without hesitation.

"I just happen to know a great spot," Joe said.

As they made their way out of the establishment, Joe explained he had his own boat waiting for them at the pier, just a few short steps away. He had hired a chef to prepare their dinner, which he hoped would be romantic, as well as memorable.

Their dinner cruise along the shore of Lake Michigan was both relaxing and romantic. It seemed a fitting ending to an exciting, slightly-over-the-top evening. Afterwards, Joe insisted on driving everyone home. He refused to let the ladies ride the Metra at this hour, but his ulterior motive was simply to prevent the evening from being over quite yet.

As Joe pulled his Tahoe up to the women's brownstones, suddenly they were all silent a moment. It was hard to have an evening like this one end.

Mike was the first to break the silence. "We'll walk you ladies to your doors."

Joe sat there a moment contemplating what he should do. It wouldn't look right if he didn't walk Alex to her door. He cut the engine, and they all got out. As Mike walked Steph toward her front door, he called out, "Fifteen minutes." Joe nodded from the steps leading up to Alex's door. But then Joe shook his head and mouthed to Mike, "No. Thirty." Mike shot him a questioning glance, but nodded in agreement.

Joe suddenly had a plan. He might have to give up on Alex, but the Yurman necklace he'd bought for her in Vegas wasn't doing him any good gathering dust in a drawer at his house. He needed to give it to her and wondered how she would react, given all that had transpired during the evening. Knowing her, she would probably try to refuse it. But he had made sure she couldn't. Since learning that there was a Yurman store in Chicago, and thinking she might just return it without telling him, he decided to have it engraved. He was a little nervous about how the gift-giving might go.

Alex unlocked the door and went inside, with Joe following.

"Make yourself comfortable. Can I get you anything?" she said, wondering how she was going to entertain him while Mike said good night to Steph next door for fifteen minutes.

"Depends on what you're offering."

"Oh, ha ha. You are so pathetic Baker. What I'm offering you is something like a beer, coffee, water—something along those lines."

All he really wanted was her.

Joe took in his surroundings, noting a very well decorated home that suited Alex perfectly. It was classy, but comfortable, warm and inviting. Possibly a little too inviting, given his state of mind.

"Nice place," he said as he followed her into the kitchen.

"Thanks." She opened the fridge and got herself a bottle of water. "I think all that alcohol made me dehydrated."

"Come on, you didn't drink that much," he said.

"Well, more than my normal consumption, anyway. Want one?" She took out another bottle and offered it to him.

Joe took the bottle from her, screwed off the cap, and took a long drink as Alex began to talk about their success.

"You know, I think we succeeded big time tonight. Don't you think they both are in deep right now? I think Steph finally gets it," she remarked, for the sake of conversation. Obviously Alex was attempting to cover up her nervousness.

"That was the most fun I've had in years," she continued. "Thank you so much for all the hard work and planning. And I know you guys must have spent hours practicing those songs." She chuckled. "You are such a schemer, Baker."

She had just given him the perfect opening, thanking *him* for the evening. Now it was his turn to thank her.

"Yeah, it was a great time wasn't it?" He said.

Alex just smiled at him and then there was a moment of long silence—too long, while their eyes met. She was a nervous wreck being there alone with him, even though it was her own house. Joe cleared his throat, then stepped closer. He steeled himself, and then said, "I want you to know that tonight you stole my heart. Again. Even more than you did the first time. I know you don't want to hear this, but I need to try to tell you how I'm feeling right now. In real words, not music."

Alex's smile faded and, as their eyes held, what he had just said began to sink in. This was not supposed to be happening.

"Say something," he pleaded.

But Alex didn't know what to say. So, Joe watched her for a moment and then went on. "Look, I'm sorry I said that, okay? But I had to." He sighed and hesitated. Then he left the kitchen to retrieve the Yurman box from his jacket pocket. When he returned to the kitchen, Joe extended his hand with the box in it.

"Here. I bought you something to thank you for going along with my plan and for not thinking I was crazy. Actually, I've had it a while."

She looked hesitant and confused. This was crazy.

"You didn't have to do that Joe. I went along with the plan because I wanted to. I certainly don't expect you to give me a gift as payment. A simple thank you suffices. Along with our friends' happiness."

Joe remained undaunted. He put the little box into her hand. "Go ahead, open it."

"Well, alright." She removed the ribbon from the box and opened it. Inside was the Yurman necklace she had seen when they were in Vegas. The one that matched her earrings. It was beautiful and she really wanted to keep it. But Alex knew she shouldn't accept it.

"Joe, it's beautiful! But I can't accept such a generous gift. Besides, I told you I don't need payment for tonight. We did this together with their best interests at heart. When did you get this anyway?" She tried to hand it back to him.

He shook his head. "Sorry, no can do. If you look at the back you'll see I had it engraved." He gave her a look that said he was satisfied with himself for doing something that would require her to keep it.

Alex read the inscription: YSMH, and under it the letter J. She looked at him nervously. "Is this a puzzle I need to solve? What is YSMH? Am I to assume the J would stand for Joe?" She looked at him quizzically.

Joe stepped closer and whispered in her ear, "YSMH stands for you stole my heart. I bought it for you because I don't want you to ever forget that." Then he backed her up against the refrigerator.

"What are you doing?" she asked, her eyes wide as she looked up at him. He took the box and necklace from her hands and put them on the counter.

Then he placed both hands against her refrigerator above her head pinning her there.

"I'm going to do what I've been dying to do all night."

She was afraid to really look at him, because she knew she would just get lost in his eyes and probably do something she'd later regret. Alex was sure he was going to kiss her, but to her surprise, he didn't. She looked up at him again and held his gaze. What was he waiting for? He just kept staring at her, willing her not to take her eyes from his. She allowed her gaze to travel to his mouth until she couldn't stand it any longer. This might be her only chance to explore what she might have had with this gorgeous man. Throwing caution to the wind, she leaned in and kissed him very tenderly. When he kissed her back, sparks of intensity flew.

He removed his mouth from hers and started nuzzling her neck and making small sucking movements up and down her throat, not enough to mark her but enough to get her breath to quicken. Then he ran his tongue up and down the curve of her neck and then started sucking again. He was lost in the feel and taste of her. He realized it was going to be difficult to maintain any semblance of control. Joe caressed her cheek as he continued to suckle her throat. He dropped his hand caressingly down her arm and interlaced their fingers.

Alex felt like exploding. She was getting swept up in what he was doing to her, and she liked it way more than she should have. She wondered what it would be like to have him make love to her.

Somehow he sensed she wanted more. He cupped both her cheeks and kissed her with all the meaning his lips could convey. His raging passion was obvious, as his lips caressed hers and his throbbing manhood pressed against her. Joe plunged his tongue into her mouth and intertwined with hers. Joe hoped she wanted more. She hadn't given him any sign that she wanted him to stop, yet he couldn't be sure that he was making the right move. He decided he would continue on, until she gave him a signal.

He let his hands travel very slowly down her body, briefly pausing to explore her breasts before progression lower.

Alex moaned with delight and an "Oh, my God," escaped as he clasped her tightly. He continued caressing her. Finally, Joe pulled down the zipper to her slacks. The sight of her sexy red lace drove him mad with desire. It was now or never. He'd better check to make sure this was something she really wanted to do.

"Do you want me, Alex? Tell me what you want. I think you know that all I want is you," he whispered seductively in her ear. "Do you want me?"

Alex was completely helpless against his lovemaking. "Yes," she replied in the barest of whispers. She was dropping into a deep vortex as he continued to massage her and suck on her neck. She was so close to giving herself to him, and she wanted to so badly she was shaking.

Joe kept whispering encouragements to her. She was surprised by his erotic vocabulary. His words were so sensual. Alex felt sure that Richard would never, ever, talk to her like this or make her feel this kind of intense passion.

Suddenly, through the fuzzy haze of desire, they heard the doorbell. At first neither of them acknowledged it, hoping it was imaginary. But it rang again. After the third ring, Joe accepted reality and pulled away.

It had to be Mike. "Shit! It's probably Mike. I'll be right back." Joe left the kitchen, took a few seconds to straighten himself out and opened the door.

Indeed, there stood Mike with a quizzical look on his face.

"What are you guys doing? I rang the doorbell three times. Didn't you hear it?" Mike said, although he could guess that something more was going on than just a friendly goodbye chat.

"I'm sorry, we didn't hear it. We were, uh, in the kitchen. I guess we lost track of time." He turned to the sofa and grabbed the keys out of his jacket and put them in Mike's palm.

"Here, go ahead. I'll say goodbye, and I'll be right out okay?"

Mike just nodded knowingly. "It sure takes you a long time to say goodbye." And then he mumbled, "Take your time."

When Joe walked back into the kitchen, he found Alex sitting at the table with her head in her hands. The moment was gone, and they both knew it. He crouched down in front of her and lifted her chin.

"Hey, what can I say? I'm sorry. I got way carried away. I guess I just wanted this so badly." She gazed into those undeniable sea-blue eyes.

"Well, yeah. It's my fault, too. But you know this is probably for the best. I'd probably have hated myself after. You made me feel so good—so wanted—and I just wanted to let myself go. You know, do something unexpected and totally wild," she confessed.

"You should probably go now. It's late, and Mike is waiting." She looked at him and smiled slightly.

"You know you look a mess, don't you? I mean your hair is all out of whack and you look like you've just been kissing somebody silly," she giggled.

"Yeah, I'm sure I do, and I'm sure I'll get the third degree. But I won't say anything that would compromise your reputation. Thanks again for an incredible day and evening." It was going to be so hard to walk through her door and even harder to try to forget her. "I had a wonderful time, too. Thank you for the necklace. I love it, but that doesn't make it right my accepting it and all. I wish you would just take it back." He just shook his head "no" and said nothing further.

They both looked at each other seriously for as long as they dared. Finally, Joe broke the silence. "I guess I'll be seeing you around. You know you can call me anytime. For anything. I've told you how I feel, and I meant every word. And if nothing else, I am still your friend," he said sincerely.

Alex just nodded. She didn't want him to go as much as he didn't want to leave her. The moments they had just shared would remain a bittersweet memory for them both.

CHAPTER 7

Time was flying, and thoughts of her romantic, electric evening with Joe kept creeping up. As hard as she tried to explain to Richard that she had doubts about becoming his wife, he shot her down. The man came from generations of stock who were accustomed to getting their way, so he was well versed in arguments such as these.

She decided that Richard was probably right. After all, hadn't she wanted a man like him for most of her life? She would be a fool to give him up to gamble on a sex symbol like Joe, she argued to herself.

Most of her energy was now channeled into her commitment to Richard and their future together. She really needed to choose a wedding date and get on with the event plans.

In the meantime, Stephanie and Mike had started seeing each other exclusively. After their evening at Navy Pier, Stephanie had agreed to give dating Mike a chance. They found they had so much in common and their relationship flourished. How could she have not gotten it at the very beginning?

Although Steph was now investing time she normally would have spent with Alex in Mike, Alex couldn't fault her for this. She was glad for her best friend's joy. It was disturbing, however, to realize that she didn't feel the same kind of gut-wrenching fire for Richard that Steph did for Mike. And she worried that if the Mike and Steph were to get married, Joe would become a permanent part of her life. She didn't know if she would be able to handle it.

Alex decided it was time to see a professional who could help her sort through her inner turmoil. It helped to vocalize her feelings and fears to an objective outsider who could give her direction. Therapy steered Alex's thoughts and feelings toward Richard. Once again she began to see him as the man she desired and with whom she wanted to spend her life. She believed that she was beginning to heal and was finally on the road that would lead her away from Joe.

After a whirlwind courtship, by Christmas Mike had proposed to Stephanie. Alex found their romance ironic: how many times had she pointed out to her best friend that this man was obviously perfect for her?

Joe insisted on throwing an engagement party for the happy couple. He had made all the party arrangements himself, from the invitations to the catering. The event was scheduled for just after his return from his annual ski trip to Colorado.

Alex could deal with the whole engagement party thing. What she couldn't deal with was seeing Joe again. The week prior to the party, she made another visit to her therapist and finally felt prepared to face Joe. It wasn't going to be easy spending a night in his presence, but she felt sure the party wouldn't be as hard as she might have previously expected.

The night of the engagement party, Alex felt upbeat. In fact, she was in such a good mood that she made an unusual choice of attire for the event. She slipped on her sexiest dress and a pair of killer heels.

When Richard picked her up, he could scarcely believe his eyes. "Hi, honey. Wow! You look fantastic," he commented. He couldn't resist giving her an approving kiss.

When Alex and Richard arrived at the clubhouse, the guests of honor were busy greeting everyone—Stephanie bestowing kisses and looking like she couldn't have been happier. Although Joe was the evening's host, he was nowhere to be seen.

Carolyn had offered to pick up Joe, who was on her way. But she also had another reason for playing chauffer: she had a feeling that it might be difficult for her old friend to see Alex and to be forced to spend a whole evening watching her with Richard. She knew Joe still loved Alex and wasn't over her. Just as Joe had helped Mike and Stephanie get together, Carolyn thought she would prove her friendship to Joe by trying to get him together with Alex.

When Joe and Carolyn walked in, Stephanie was on hand to greet them.

"Hey, Mr. Host. You're late. Hey, Carolyn."

Joe feigned annoyance. "I'm not late. I'm *fashionable*."

Steph chuckled.

Joe scanned the room. He zeroed in on Alex about the same time she noticed him walk in. He took in her face, her figure-hugging dress, and the three-inch heels. Alex blushed a little as his stunning blue eyes took inventory. She turned up her glossy red lips in a slight smile as she nodded at him. Richard was several feet away talking to some redhead Joe didn't recognize.

Carolyn saw she was right. The chemistry between them was undeniable. *Good,* she thought; *she's looking. Implement game plan, now.*

The tall blonde beauty grabbed Joe's hand and kissed him on the cheek. She pressed her body close to his in a possessive manner, hoping to annoy the woman who had been the object of his attention.

Joe turned to her and murmured, "What the hell are you doing?"

"I'm going to ensure an exciting evening," she whispered. Looking over toward Alex, she noticed that Alex seemed irritated.

"I can tell you still care for Alex, and I'm going to make sure you get her. Let's just see whether a little competition brings out her true feelings. She can't possibly want to spend the rest of her life with someone else when she could be with you!"

"I really do appreciate how much you care about me, Carolyn," Joe explained, "But this is Mike and Stephanie's engagement party. It's not right to be scheming during their big occasion. Alex has made it clear that she's committed to Richard. She doesn't want me. I gave her an open invitation the last time we were together and I haven't heard from her, so she's made her decision."

Suddenly, all Alex's therapy and coping methods seemed to fly out the window. Just looking at Joe stepped up her heart rate. Her original suspicions about Carolyn also seemed confirmed. She and Joe certainly looked like they were a couple the way she was cuddling up to him. Darn her! Carolyn was perfect in every way. Who could blame Joe for wanting to be with her? Despite her killer outfit, which she definitely looked great in, Alex was beginning to feel very inadequate.

Alex concluded that for Mike and Steph's sake, she needed to acknowledge Joe as the party host, if nothing else. After all, they would have to exchange polite pleasantries for the foreseeable future, now that their best friends were getting married. Might as well get used to it.

Richard was still deep in conversation with the redhead, so Alex took a deep breath and walked over. She extended her hand.

"Carolyn. Hi. Nice to see you again." She smiled as cheerfully as she could. Then she willed herself to be brave and turned to Joe. "Hi, Joe," she ventured, gently kissing his cheek. "It's nice to see you again, too. You're so thoughtful to give this party for Mike and Steph."

If he thought she had looked hot in Vegas at the "coincidental" concert, it was nothing compared to her look tonight. She looked positively scrumptious. "Hey, lady. How've you been? You look fantastic."

Richard, seeing that Alex was in conversation with Joe and a mystery woman, broke away from his conversation partner. He had no idea who Carolyn was and his curiosity was piqued. Judging by the iron grip she had locked on Joe's arm, she must have been someone he was dating. She looked like someone who could handle him. And keep him where he belonged: away from *his* fiancée.

"Hello. Joe? The construction guy from the hospital, right?" He made sure to make the word construction sound unsavory, like the man belonged on the bottom of his shoe.

Joe shot Alex a look that asked "and you're with *him* because...?" Yet, ever the gentleman, he responded tactfully. "Yeah. Glad you could make it. This is my good friend Carolyn."

Joe was not about to spend one more second making small talk—or any conversation for that matter—with that pompous ass Alex insisted on marrying. Not wanting to be rude, he continued. "Well, I haven't finished up my official welcoming duties quite yet. So, I hope you'll excuse me. I'll look forward to catching up with you later."

As they walked off, Alex noticed the way that Carolyn had glued herself to Joe's side and was draped off his arm.

Joe noticed that she noticed.

He whispered to Carolyn, "I don't think this is a very good idea. Give me some breathing room, will ya? You're going to give people the wrong impression about us."

She gave him a sweet as sugar smile. "Honey, that's exactly what I'm trying to do." Joe shook his head. *Oh, no.* He knew that there was no stopping Carolyn when she'd made up her mind.

Indeed, Carolyn's strategy was succeeding. Seeing Joe and then watching Carolyn plaster herself all over him was becoming increasingly tough for Alex to take. Although the party was in high gear, she knew she had to get out of there. She waited until the big toast to Mike and Steph had been made, then feigned a headache and asked Richard to take her home. Therapy had been useful for something: it gave her the courage to walk away when she needed to.

# Chapter 8

The next few months, Alex did her best to avoid Joe. It was not the easiest task, but she felt she was doing well.

Sunday, Alex's phone rang. It was Steph on the line. "I've got cool news. Mike got four tickets to next Saturday's game at the Cell, and on top of that, they're those scouts' tickets like we got last year. Gosh, we were waited on hand and foot and treated like royalty. Remember? And the food and drinks were fabulous."

"I take it you're telling me this because… What, you're inviting me, or just rubbing it in that you're going?" Alex mock scolded her friend.

"Of course I'm inviting you. A vendor gave them to Joe, but he gave them to Mike because he knew we'd want to go and so would you and Jason. Joe remembered that you're a big Sox fan. I thought that was really nice of him to give us the tickets and want us to include you, don't you think?"

Alex countered in a sarcastic voice, "Oh, of course, that was *really* nice of him, being the *really* nice guy he is. You know. I'd love to go. But on one condition. I'm only going if *he's* not going."

Stephanie thought a moment.

"Well, I don't think he's going. There are only four tickets that I know of. So, what you're saying is just because he might be there, you'd pass this up? You've been doing great these last couple of months. You know you've gotta get over this. You'll be seeing him more often now that Mike and I are getting married. Anyway, I'm pretty sure he won't be there. Do you want me to check with Mike, just to be sure?"

"No, don't ask him. I don't want him to think that I spend my time trying to avoid Joe," she replied. "Thank Mike for me and just let me know all the particulars. Let's hope for great weather and a win."

Mike and his son Jason picked up the girls at 11:00 a.m. the following Saturday. It was a perfect spring day, with moderate temperatures and plenty of sun. When they arrived at the ballpark, the foursome entered through the special scouts' entrance. They were escorted to their private table, where a waitress took their drink order and invited to help themselves to the buffet.

Alex noted with relief that Joe wasn't there. Two cocktails later, and after enjoying the wonderful buffet, there was still no sign of Joe. With her anxiety subsiding, Alex started to look forward to the game. The four fans made their way through the walkway to their seats in the third row, right behind home plate, to watch some of the warm-up action and then the national anthem and player introductions.

In the middle of player introductions, Alex was looking around, taking it all in and smiling. Suddenly, she froze. There *he* was. Joe was sitting in a seat adjacent to hers across the aisle. He noticed that he'd been discovered. He tipped his ball cap and nodded hello. Alex saw the smug look on his face. He looked quite pleased with himself. Steaming, she turned her attention back to the field. But she could scarcely concentrate on the player introductions.

The next thing she knew, out of the corner of her eye she could see him making his way toward her group. "Hey, guys. Fancy meeting you here!"

*Surprise my ass!* Alex thought.

Joe looked at Jason. "Hey, Bud, you wouldn't mind switching seats with me would you? There's a couple of nice-looking young ladies sitting in front of my seat," he nodded his head in that direction. Jason got his drift. Let the old folks sit together, while he checked out the scenery on the other side of the aisle. No problem. He gave Joe a knowing smirk as he slid out of the row.

Joe climbed over Alex and plunked himself down in the seat next to her, which had just been so conveniently vacated. Alex took in his Sox hat, cargo pants, topsiders and a long-sleeved Sox tee that looked like it had seen better days. Joe turned to Stephanie and gave her a hug and winked at Mike. Mike shook his head. Finally, Joe turned toward Alex. "Hey," he offered, trying to act like an old buddy, as he leaned in and softly kissed her cheek.

"Hey," she said back, in a tone that let him know she wasn't pleased. She shot him a look of disgust as she turned back to watch the beginning of the game.

In his heart Joe refused to believe that she would actually go through with marrying Richard in the end. How could she have such a physical connection with him and yet be set on marrying another?

Mike had recently told him Alex and Richard had finally set a wedding date. Joe vowed to not waste any time. He would be in her face as much as possible. Maybe that was a bit unscrupulous, but he didn't care. They were two people who were meant to be together. And in that case, the end justified the means, right? In addition, Stephanie had pretty much given Joe her blessing by confiding in him she believed Alex's marriage to Richard would be a disaster once the shine had worn off and she realized what she had signed up for.

So, here he was. Making an opportunity to win her over. The weather was perfect and the food and drink plentiful, so Alex finally relaxed, not letting it bother her that she was in Joe's company. He didn't crowd her or force conversation so the day turned out better than she would have expected.

Following a Sox win, the group high-fived each other and agreed what a great game it had been. They collected Jason and began to walk to their respective cars.

This gave Joe a moment to formulate how he was going to get Alex alone for a few minutes so he could talk to her in private, that is *if* she would agree.

Nearing their cars, Joe slowed down and stated his intentions.

"Hey, guys. Do you mind giving us about five minutes?" he asked as he grabbed her hand.

Turning to him, and giving him a somewhat annoyed look, her response was pretty much as he had expected.

"For God's sake, what now? What more could you possibly need to talk to me about? We've been together for how many hours?"

He shrugged. "Well, Alex I only want five minutes of your time. Can that be so tough?"

Casting a glance skyward, then at Stephanie and back to Joe, she responded, "Okay, but make it quick. I'm sure these guys don't want to wait around here any more than they have to."

He nodded and addressed the group.

"We won't be long." Continuing to hold her hand he headed in the direction of his car, which was several rows away and out of sight of their companions. She was silent, as predicted, while he dragged her along. He remained undaunted. She was a tough nut, but he believed that eventually she'd crack.

At his car, Joe stopped and pulled Alex over to the driver's side. Positioning her between the car door and himself, he made his intentions quite clear.

"Upon inquiry, the general consensus is that you're still intending to marry him. Heard you set the date," he began.

She sighed and shook her head in the affirmative. "Yes, I *still* plan to marry Richard. Can't we just once get off of the subject?" She flashed her left hand in front of his face. "What else would you like to talk about? And make it fast, because you're on the clock, and your five minutes are almost up." She pointed to her watch.

He closed in, reducing the space between them.

"OK. Then let's talk about you and me. You know what I think? I think you've got feelings for me and you won't admit it. Come on, Parker. You're hot for me and you know it."

She shoved him, trying to gain some breathing space.

"Your over-inflated ego never ceases to amaze me. Sorry to burst your bubble, but you're dead wrong." She tried to get around him but he blocked her. While she struggled against him, he caught her, pulling her tightly to his chest. She looked up and saw the fire in his eyes. Before she could protest, he leaned in and kissed her.

He was a man in love, on a conquest. His lips revealed the intensity of the flames in his heart. She could feel the hard steel of his chest as his well-honed biceps sealing their grip around her. There was no mistaking the message his body was sending.

As hard as she tried to resist, she just melted. What was it about this man? Alex was horrified by her own body's response to his. She was overcome with guilt.

When he finally broke away, having made his intentions clear, he interrogated her. "So, now do you still want to lie and tell me I'm dead wrong? Look at me and tell me you're sure you want Richard."

Alex was still trying to catch her breath. She looked down for a moment. When she finally looked back up at him she looked confused and sad. He hated her looking like that, but damn, he just couldn't let her marry another man. Deep in his heart he knew there could be something truly wonderful between the two of them. She was just cheating herself, denying herself the right to true and lasting happiness.

Joe had been discouraged numerous times in his life but had never given up without a fight. Besides, nothing really worthwhile in life ever came easy and without some form of endurance and energy to go the distance. He would always keep going after what he wanted and little by little, and finally by the grace of God, he would somehow achieve it. It had always taken great determination and not knowing when to quit, and he wasn't about to quit now. He was sure she had feelings for him. She had made that quite obvious to him many times, even though she always tried to hide it.

He took her chin in his hand to hold her eyes steady with his so she wouldn't look away.

"This was to prove a point, and I think I just did," he whispered softly. "You need to think about this before you make a mistake." Letting go of her chin, he gently kissed her on the forehead.

After they took a few steps, she stopped. He turned toward her.

"Okay, you proved your point," she said. "Yes, there is some chemistry between us. Attraction and arousal are uncontrollable. But that's just physical. It's not *love*. Love goes beyond that. Love is a choice, and I've made that choice in Richard."

He was getting upset. Now she heard an angry tinge in his voice. "You know that's bullshit, Alex." He continued to walk back toward their friends with Alex tagging behind him. Approaching them, he made his apologies. "Sorry to hold you up, but I appreciate it. We just needed to clarify something which, uh, I think we did."

Stephanie looked at Alex for some kind of non-verbal answer, but all she saw was her friend's flushed face and what looked to her like somewhat puffy lips. Steph approached Joe and gave him a hug.

"Well, I'm happy that you two have come to terms with *whatever* it was that needed clarification. Honey, it was a fun day. I'm glad you were able to join us. And thank you, Joe, for the great tickets."

Before he walked away, Joe held Alex's eyes, making clear, one last time, how he felt about her.

CHAPTER 9

"Look," Stephanie patiently explained, "it's no big deal. It's just a scramble. I know you don't think you golf well enough, but this is a piece of cake. It's for a good cause, and you've always been a charity-supporting kinda girl. Besides, this will be a lot of fun."

Alex considered the proposal. A scramble format would probably keep her from embarrassing herself too much, and Steph was right, she did like to support non-profit causes. Then something occurred to her. "And I suppose *he* will be there. Right?"

"Well, yes," Steph guiltily acknowledged. "He will, but you might not even see him. I told Mike not to put him in our foursome. And you don't have to stay past the awards ceremony. You should make nice with him though, because you'll have to see him in a month at the wedding. After all, you'll be walking down the aisle together."

Oh, this was miserable. How could anyone expect her to ignore her feelings for Joe when he was constantly in her face? She'd done everything she could to avoid him, but it was difficult with all the get-togethers supporting Mike and Steph's engagement. Alex thought she had done well, thus far, throwing herself into Richard's life and social agenda. She had managed to quit thinking so much about Joe. Except when her best friend would bring up his name about some thing or other, and then she'd have to force herself to stop thinking about him all over again.

What was it about him? Clearly the sexual attraction was obvious. But Alex was well aware that "hot pants" was not a solid foundation for a lasting relationship. Once the fire died down, there was nothing left. Substance, mutual respect, and friendship. Now those were things one could build a relationship on. Richard offered all of those qualities. That's why she knew she and Richard were a sure thing.

She thought about how much they had in common. Enjoying activities together made it easy for friendship to flourish. Alex also had a lot of respect for Richard. He was a successful attorney from a well-established and well-respected family. She found that aspect of her fiancé very appealing. But their sex life... it was mundane, that was for sure. His travel schedule didn't leave much time or energy for fooling around. But even when they were in the mood, there wasn't much flame to the fire. She was hoping that once they were married and settled into a routine, their romantic life would pick up. Yes, she concluded, what Richard offered her in life was solid, enduring. A relationship with Joe seemed like it would be a frenzied frolic. He didn't seem to have the kind of long-term possibilities that Richard did.

The charity golf outing rolled around on a gorgeous, warm, sunny late spring day, when everyone is thankful to be outside in the sun, enjoying the fresh air. Alex donned some basic golf wear and had invested in a pair of golf shoes, which everyone assured her would improve her footing. Goodness knows her game could use any help she could give it. She dragged out her old Lady Cobras and dusted them off. Maybe if she played on a regular basis she would begin to like the game, or at least get better. But who had half a day to spend on the golf course on a regular basis? Alex was convinced this event would be a disaster, between worrying about hitting the darned ball and wondering whether Joe was going to witness her playing badly. She had made a trip to the driving range the weekend prior in hopes of warming up her game before the big day. Ugh. She still couldn't hit the ball to save herself. Well, it was all too late now. There she was at the course for her twelve o'clock tee-off time.

She met up with Mike and Stephanie, who were towing their clubs over toward the carts.

"Honey, you need to go over to that table to register and get your package of freebies. Then we'll grab our carts and head for the third tee. That's where we're gonna start," Steph informed her, cheerfully.

"So, did we get Jason as our fourth, like you thought?" Alex asked, hoping her anxiety wasn't coming through in her voice.

Mike and Stephanie looked at each other. Joe was on the planning committee and had placed himself with their foursome. Mike had learned the news from Joe the night before. He knew that Joe hoped he could convince Alex not to marry Richard and to see that he was perfect for her. Mike knew that having to golf with Joe might cause fireworks, but on the other hand, he had to support his best friend, the way Joe had supported his attempts to win over Stephanie.

"We'll argue that being together for this outing will help she and I and get us primed for your wedding," Joe said confidently, hoping Alex wouldn't stay mad for long, once his charms won her over for the day.

Stephanie came to the rescue by causing a distraction. "Hey, you should check your bag-holder strap again. It looks a little loose."

Alex got out of the cart and took a look at her bag. No. It was secure. Now she was back to wondering where the devil their fourth was. It was nearly tee time.

As she was getting back into her cart, she spotted Jason and the remainder of his foursome heading down the first fairway to their tee box. What? So, he wasn't their fourth? She was really suspicious now. *Don't let it be him, don't let it be him*, she chanted to herself, as if she could prevent what was probably inevitable.

"There goes Jason with another group," she announced, looking at her friends suspiciously.

As Mike and Steph struggled to come up with an excuse, the predicament became obvious.

"Hey, guys. Sorry I'm late," they heard Joe's voice ring out as he jogged up to them, clubs in tow.

*It figures. Great. Just great. Not only did she have to spend the better part of a day with him, she had to suffer through the embarrassment of him witnessing how crappily she played. Oh, just perfect.*

Alex studied him as he approached. Eye candy. Did he always have to be so freakin' attractive?

Joe planted a kiss on Steph's cheek, and then slapped his pal on the shoulder. Then he looked over at Alex, trying to read the message in her eyes.

"Hi," she said, in an "oh, brother—here we go again" way.

He stepped closer and softly kissed her cheek.

"It's nice to see you, too," he chuckled. As predicted, this was going to be a challenging day. But he was up for it. She was worth it.

Joe strapped his clubs to the back of Alex's cart, while she sat staring straight ahead. What was there to say?

Joe quickly jumped into the driver's seat and took off, nearly giving her whiplash.

"Hey, if you're gonna drive like that, I'll be taking over as soon as we get to the first tee," she yelled over the drone of the cart's engine.

He just looked over at her and grinned. The man was infuriating, the way he just thought he could do whatever he wanted.

They stopped at the blue markers on the third hole so the guys could tee off. The two men flipped a coin. Mike won, so he chose to be second. Joe pulled out his driver and hopped up to the tee box, did a few stretches, and took a few practice swings. He was thinking about his shot.

*Show off,* Alex thought. *Who does he think he is, some professional?*

She had to admit, he was dressed like one. Joe had on a black Greg Norman shirt paired with khaki shorts. His feet were covered by classic black-and-white saddle-style golf shoes, with… no socks? Of all things. She wondered whether he regularly golfed without socks, or whether he'd have eighteen blisters by the time they were done today.

Joe finished setting up, he took another practice spring, stepped up closer to the ball, and finally, after so much ado, hit a drive so far she lost track of it.

Mike gave him the high five. "Right down the fairway," Joe confirmed. "Good thing I didn't take that bet you wanted." Smugly, he stood to the side while Mike set up, took a quick practice swing, and guided his own shot straight down the fairway. This drive the girls could see, because it didn't go quite as far as Joe's. They high fived again.

When Joe jumped back into the cart, Alex chuckled.

"What? What's so funny?" he asked.

She pointed to his shoes. "Did you forget something? Or do you usually go commando on the golf course?" She laughed.

He looked down. "Yeah, I forgot my socks. That's a first," he grimaced.

When they moved up to the red markers Alex started getting little stomach flutters. The first hole was always the worst for her. But then again, it really didn't matter because this was best ball, and obviously the best ball was not going to be hers.

The girls decided Stephanie would go first. Alex determined that she'd tell them she planned to wait and hit on everyone's second shot, which clearly would be from Joe's drive.

Steph launched a pretty decent drive. The ball didn't travel very far, but it was largely straight.

Alex was getting more apprehensive by the minute. She would eventually be required to hit the ball. "Honey, that was a great shot," she complimented Steph. "Well why should I even hit? It's obvious I won't be hitting it as far as you guys." Her voice was a little too high-pitched with an anxiety they all recognized. Joe patted her on the knee.

"Come on, everyone has to have a turn. Don't worry about it. You need to just have fun. Go on. Get up there and hit the snot out of it," Joe said.

*Is he kidding*? Alex thought. All three looked at her, waiting, and she knew they wouldn't take no for an answer.

Reluctantly she exited the cart and grabbed her driver. She put her little pink tee between the red markers and deposited one of her new balls. Taking a deep breath she let it out slowly and swung. She wanted to die of embarrassment when she realized that her club had not connected with the ball. She had missed it, of course. She looked over at the others.

"Geez, I hit it so far I don't see where it went," she joked. *Nice recovery, Alex!*

"Darlin', now that you've had your practice swing, you can relax. Take another practice swing, relax, and let 'er fly," Joe encouraged.

She just glared at him. She was going to die listening to him coach her terrible game all day. But she did as he said, took a practice swing and then missed it again. She picked up her ball and tee.

"That's it. I'm not making the third strike because I'd be out, so I'll just quit right now and stop wasting everyone's time."

Joe jumped out of the cart.

"No. It's easy to fix. You're just out of whack—pun intended. Come on, it's been how long since you've played? Here, I'll help you." He pulled her back up to the markers, took her tee and ball, and placed it where she was positioned to make it down the center of the fairway.

"First, let's check your grip, and then we'll check your set up," he coached. When Alex's set up was corrected, Joe stood behind her with his hands on hers adjusting her grip and had her facing in the right direction. He took his knee and knocked it gently into the back of hers.

"You need to bend both of those knees a bit, and don't grab the club like you're gonna strangle it. No death grip. Just relax. Put your weight forward a bit and play the ball off your right heel. Yup, that's right. Okay when you swing, keep your arms straight, your body down and *don't* take your eye off the ball. Swing easily and let the club do the work. Don't try to kill it. You can do it."

His body was behind hers, with both of his hands on top of hers holding the club as he took her through the back swing and follow through.

Alex was way too conscious of the front of his body pressed to the back of hers. *And I'm supposed to concentrate?* she thought. She caught a whiff of his aftershave and the laundry detergent from his shirt. Glancing down at his large hands on top of hers, she had a mental flashback of just what those hands had done to her that evening after Navy Pier. She was supposed to hit a golf ball when she was getting all hot and bothered?

"Hey, you with me?" he whispered in her ear. "Let's try one more swing just to make sure you've got it."

Two bodies swinging back and forth again. Joe suddenly stepped back. He had to pull away before he embarrassed himself and the world could see she was turning him on, too. "Okay darlin', you can do it. Just run it through your head real fast and relax. I guarantee you won't miss it this time. And remember to follow through."

With determination and gritted teeth, she quickly went through the drill in her head, swung back with arms straight, and followed through.

"I hit it. I hit it!" Her ball didn't make it as far as the others, but she got it into the air and it went straight. Joe picked her up and spun her around.

"Told ya! That was great!"

Her partners were clapping and she smiled. When he put her down she gave him a quick hug. "Thanks, coach," she whispered in his ear.

They jumped back into the cart and made their way down the fairway as Joe picked up both of the girls' balls. Then they continued down the fairway to see which of the guy's balls would make a better second shot. Joe's hit was a bit further, but the next shot from there would require them all to clear a bunker. Mike's drive would allow everyone to shoot straight down the fairway, so they decided on his ball.

"Okay, Palmer. We'll take yours. You get honors, since it's your ball," he grinned at Mike. Mike's shot landed just short of the green. Joe's was on the dance floor, but would require a pretty hefty putt.

Alex started to get nervous again. "You go first, Stephanie. I'd prefer to go last, okay?"

Stephanie nodded and got her seven wood.

"I used to be good at these, but it's been awhile. I'll do my best. Thank goodness at least Big Gun here is already on the green," she fretted.

Steph's shot wasn't bad. She didn't quite get under it like she wanted and landed short of the green. Alex was a little jealous of her friend's abilities as well as how great Steph looked while proving them.

"Okay, Mr. Big Gun," she said, shooting Joe a nervous smile, "I mean, Coach. What would you suggest I use? My seven wood? Which I can't hit worth a darn. Or maybe my longest iron?" When she looked up at him for direction, their eyes caught and held. Because he didn't answer she waved her hand in front of his eyes.

"Hello, anyone in there?"

Her hand brought him back to reality. She was asking him a question, but he had been distracted looking at her back side when she got out of the cart and stood in front of her bag deciding on her club selection. He couldn't remember the question.

"What?" was all he could muster.

She looked at him strangely. "I asked if I should use my seven, which I suck at, or should I try my longest iron?"

He finally replied after shaking his head free of the cobwebs.

"Try the seven. You'll never learn how to use it unless you practice. You need some direction?" He looked back to make sure they weren't holding anyone up.

"Come on, there's no one behind us. I'll help you." They both approached the designated spot, and she placed her ball next to the marker. Joe picked up the marker, pocketed it and started giving her direction.

"Same drill as the first; but you play fairway shots a little left of center, not off your back heel like at the tee," he explained patiently. "Straight arms, follow through, and DON'T take your eye off the ball. Oh, and let the club do the work. Go for it, ace."

She nodded, approached the ball, and ran the drill in her head again. She pulled in a deep breath and let it out long and slow. She swung and hoped for the best. The club had connected, but the shot wasn't quite what Alex had hoped for.

"Not bad," Joe conceded. "We'll keep practicing with that one. There should be plenty of opportunities today to use that club."

She smiled at him. "Thanks, but I think you have a lot more faith in me than I have in myself." When they got back in the cart he patted her on the back. "Stick with me babe and I'll teach you everything you need to know," he said and smiled back.

*I'll just bet you can teach a girl everything she needs to know*, she thought.

After they picked up their balls and moved to the green, everyone putted out. The group ended up with a par. Not bad for their first hole. Today's game was supposed to be all in fun, and the score wasn't supposed to matter, but both guys were acting competitive. Despite the party atmosphere, clearly they were playing to win.

Their next hole was a par three. *Piece of cake*, Alex thought. Mike encouraged the girls, as par threes were known to be easier for women. Finally, the girls would have a chance to be heroes.

"Alright ladies, this is your hole," Mike announced. "Oh. And look," he said, pointing to a sign posted in the ground near the tee box. "This is one of the ladies' prize holes. Closest to the pin wins the 'big one,' whatever the heck that is. The rules say that we do have to use one of each of your tee shots today, so this is your chance, ladies. Who's first to bring our team to glory?"

Alex shook her head no. If Steph hit a nice shot, she'd be off the hook.

Joe looked at her and frowned. "Chicken. I can see it in your eyes. You know, sometimes going first is empowering. C'mon. Try it," he coaxed.

It was too much pressure. Yet the pressure from Joe was worse. "Alright, I'll go first. But since you're the *expert,* what would you suggest I do?"

*I love this girl*, Joe thought. *She's got spunk. And even though she sucks at this sport, she tries. I give her that. And her back side looks amazing when she bends over to put her ball on the tee.*

"Alright, Trouble. Let's use that seven again. If you connect you'll hit the green. If not, well, we'll be practicing for when you make the Women's Open as the oldest chick on record. So let's try it," Joe encouraged her.

She glared at him and shot back, "Shut up! I don't need you, Baker. You know, you annoy me."

He was hoping for that. It seemed like when he annoyed her she would do anything just to prove him wrong. He would keep trying to provoke her, if it would improve her game.

"You know, sometimes you annoy me, too." He looked over at his friends for support, but neither said anything.

"Do you want help or not? You want to figure the setup yourself, or do you want expert advice?" he continued, trying to get a sassy reaction.

She didn't like the game unless she was doing well. *Cripes I've got sixteen more holes to complete after this one and I'm already tired,* she thought. She stepped up, put in her tee and topped it with her pink ball. Her man gave her the thumbs up. "Don't forget the practice swing."

Despite all the advice and her good intentions, Alex's shot came out a worm burner. *Oh, crap!*

Joe walked over, put his arm around her, and told her it was okay. She didn't need the prize anyway. He said not to worry; he'd buy her whatever the prize was.

When it was time for Stephanie's shot, fortunately she landed on the green and put their team in the running for the prize. There were hurrahs all around and Alex gave her a high five.

The game progressed and the day wore on. Alex had to admit that if she had to spend a day with Joe, this really wasn't too bad. She had learned a lot about golf and her game had started to improve. All day Joe had served as her biggest cheerleader, fan, and coach. He kept encouraging her and telling her she had come a long way and was doing a great job. It made her feel good that he was so supportive.

As they moved into the final holes of the game, light rain started falling. At first it was just a few sprinkles, but then it became steadier.

"I'm getting tired. I've had enough for one day. I don't need to play in the rain. I'm just going to just sit this one out," Alex announced.

"Baby. A little rain won't kill you. It's not like you're gonna melt or anything. Come on Alex, you can't quit now when you've been doing so well," Joe cajoled.

"No, I am really NOT going to play in the rain," she said as she continued toward the cart. Joe was not going to let her get away with it. He wanted the last say.

"Hey, we guys play in the rain all the time. It builds character. Come on," he pleaded. She sat in the cart, staring ahead.

*God, she is so stubborn*, he thought.

After Joe and Mike teed off, Stephanie got up to the ladies' markers, and despite the rain, hit her drive well down the fairway. "Miss Parker, it's your turn. Come on, show us that spunk. I told you a little rain won't hurt you," Joe insisted.

After giving him a look of disgust she exited the cart, grabbed her driver, climbed up to the tee box, and whacked the ball. It wasn't a great shot, but it wasn't bad either. She cast him a "so there!" look.

Everyone's second shots landed them on the green. But putting was another story. They were all three-putts. At least the hole was over.

"Darlin', I'm proud of you for playing that hole in the rain. We need everyone's shots to finish up and do well in this tournament. We're nearly done, and then you can go get cleaned up. What do you think, will you help us work toward our victory?"

She looked over at him and nodded. Ok. He had won. This time.

At the next tee box, the men were quick to drive and return to the carts. Alex noted that Joe's hair was soaking. He looked hot. Like something out of a Calvin Klein cologne ad. He didn't seem phased at all, playing golf drenched.

He glanced over at her forlorn look. "Only two more holes. You can do it."

As if to test Alex, the clouds unleashed a more urgent round of water.

Joe looked up and then over at Mike. "Well, as long as there's no lightening," he remarked matter-of-factly.

Clearly, the guys were used to playing in less-than-ideal conditions, but the irritated women were not. Alex's mood was not lost on Joe. When he pulled up to the ladies' tee, Joe jumped off the cart to grab his rain jacket. He draped the garment around Alex. "Here, hon," he said tenderly, rolling the sleeves up and zipping it tightly over her throat. "Wanna put the hood up?" She stood there looking like a little girl in her daddy's big clothing, sleeves rolled three or four times and the jacket practically down to her knees. Joe reached back again for his huge golf umbrella. "Here. I'll hold this over you while you choose a club and get up to the tee box."

As they stood in the rain those few seconds she looked at him with uncertainty and confusion. Her emotions were starting to surface again. Joe was taking care of her. Protecting her. She thought about the fact that Richard never really felt the need to take care of her or protect her. He felt she was independent—which she was—and he told her so. But sometimes, just once even, she would like for him to think that she needed a big strong man to take care of her if the situation arose. It occurred to her that maybe she had misjudged Joe. Was there actually the heart of a nice guy beating inside this hot guy? Just who was the real Joe Baker?

The foursome rallied their courage and finished their game despite the downpour. After returning the carts, the group dried off and cleaned up as best they could in the locker rooms. Alex had tried to beg out of the dinner banquet and awards ceremony that followed, but the others told her she had to stay. They had actually come in third—thanks to Joe's brilliant drives—and needed to claim their prizes. In addition, all female participants would receive a dozen roses and a bottle of wine at the end of the dinner. Alex sighed and said she guessed all of that honor and glory would be worth staying for, especially if it meant that much to her friends.

After dinner, the men had walked the ladies to their cars. Alex had to hand it to him, Joe didn't approach her in any inappropriate fashion, only kissed her on the cheek and thanked her for being his partner. He told her how proud he was of her golf game and that she had done a great job. She was quite surprised he was being such a gentleman, because past experience had proven otherwise. Had he learned to control himself and be her friend?

In truth, Joe had recently decided to approach her softer side and make her really question her feelings for him. *Take baby steps*, Carolyn had advised. Chip away a little at a time. Break down the exterior, and soon you'll get to the interior where you want to be. Take your time. Don't give up. Eventually she'll come around. So far, his old friend's advice was effective.

CHAPTER 10

Two weeks later Alex was getting ready to attend the Printer's Row Lit Fest downtown, which was an annual pilgrimage for her. This year she was making the trek alone because Stephanie would be away at her cousin's wedding. Alex was fine with going alone. In fact, it was probably better to shop this sale without distractions. Book fair day started off with sun, though it was a bit cool near the lake. Alex dressed casually and comfortably. She was sporting a pair of comfortable Old Navy flip-flops, jean Capris, and a long-sleeved tee.

After strapping on her fanny pack, she grabbed the big shoulder tote she would use to carry home her purchases. Several other festivals were going on that day as well, so traffic was a guaranteed nightmare. She would take the train into the city, and then get some exercise by walking to and from the sale.

When Alex arrived, hundreds of shoppers had already assembled and were scrutinizing the loot, snapping up treasures. Her book fair shopping tended to follow a certain format: a bestseller, a couple of pieces of romantic fiction, and a self-help volume of some sort. Romantic fiction was the kind of reading that made her relax, feel all warm and fuzzy, and gave hope that there was a true hero out there for every woman. Not that she really needed one. Richard was her hero, or at least she kept trying to convince herself he was. Besides, she liked reading the sizzling sex scenes. She decided it could give you a few ideas of your own. Certainly, she and Richard could use a little help in that department.

Since she had met Joe, and he had awakened her sensuality, she was finding it increasingly more difficult to think of Richard as her hero. She wondered whose hero Joe would be.

After an hour or so of browsing, Alex was satisfied with her standard reading choices. Having covered her favorites, the best seller, and the romances, she could take her time going over the assortment of self-help books. A cookbook or something about health or exercise would be good. She discovered there was an entire section devoted to fitness. She was milling through a selection of dozens and picked up one she thought might be of interest. It had to do with eating your way to good health. She was already a pretty healthy eater, but decided a few tips wouldn't hurt.

As she flipped the pages, she felt a disturbance in the atmosphere. After quickly looking to her right and left, she decided nothing was going on and returned her attention to the book. Her senses crackled again. Was someone looking at her? She raised her head to scan the crowd in front of her.

Suddenly, her eyes locked with another's a short distance away. The other's eyes were a pair she knew well, set in a face she knew equally well. There was Big Bad Joe Baker, cruising the Printer's Row Lit Fest and standing there checking her out.

He'd been caught, but he didn't care. He made a beeline over to her.

Alex wondered how he happened to be at the same place at the same time as she was. Was this another of the "coincidences" he was so adept at dreaming up? She thought back to the golf outing and the Sox game. It would be a real trick to pull off an accidentally-on-purpose meeting in a crowd this large. Could this really have been the hand of fate?

He stood before her. "Hey, nice to see you. Glad to know I'm not the only closet bargain hunter when it comes to reading material," he said with a little crooked smile. He took both of her hands in his and drew her closer to him. His eyes went from her eyes to her mouth. Though he would have loved to devour her right then and there, he recalled that he was taking a softer approach and played the gentleman.

"I can't tell you what a pleasant surprise this is," he remarked, placing a polite peck on Alex's cheek.

*Well I'm happy to see you, too,* she thought. *You could be my fiction hero anytime.* In fact, Joe looked as though he had stepped from the pages of a romance novel and come to life. Looking as buff as always, he had on a Black Eagles Tour tee topping off a pair of greenish cargo shorts, and a pair of topsiders. His socks were missing. Again. His sunglasses were hooked into the top of his shirt. Casual attire, secure in his looks, Joe was who he was and put on neither airs nor pretenses.

She grinned at him. "You know I thought I felt someone staring at me, and then I looked up and saw it was you. How funny is this? Actually I was a bit relieved that it was you and not some pervert. For us to run into each other in such a big crowd is unbelievable. Do you come here every year like I do?"

He shook his head. "Nope, not always. But I figured it would make a great way to spend a sunny Saturday." He was stretching the truth just a little. Actually, Mike had mentioned Alex would be at the event. Alone. He thought fate was on his side, since in all the throngs of people he actually had managed to find her. He was encouraged.

She pushed a stray hair off of her face and tried to sound casual. Her heart continued to beat wildly, not slowing down since the moment their eyes connected. "Oh, yeah. I come pretty much every year." She laughed. "I can't tell you how many cookbooks I've bought over the years. I look at them once or twice and then they end up gathering dust on the shelf."

He studied her a moment. "I pegged you as more of a romantic novel type," he teased.

When she screwed up her mouth and frowned, but still looked guilty, he pointed a finger at her. "Ha, I figured as much! My sisters read that stuff, too. They tell me I should read a few myself and find out how a woman really wants to be treated by a man." He shrugged. "I do the best I can and I think I do alright. I don't think I need to read a bunch of books to figure it out. In my thinking, when you know it's right you just know it. Ya know what I mean?"

Then he looked at her tote. "Anyway, are you nearly done? I haven't bought a thing yet. I think my stomach is getting the better of me. Have you worked up an appetite carrying that bag around?"

"Why Mr. Baker, are you offering to buy me lunch?" she answered with mock surprise.

"Maybe," he countered. "An image of a Portillo's dog with everything on it keeps popping into my head and distracting me from the books."

"And a hot dog at that? Big spender, aren't you?" she laughed back.

He grinned. "So, you're in?"

"I'm in. But I'm a purest kind of chick. Just mustard on the dog, for me."

*Oh yeah,* he thought. *She would be truly delicious all by herself, just pure, with nothing on.* It was such a tempting image. Yet he dared not linger.

"Okay, then. Let's do it," he said, grabbing Alex's bag off her shoulder and slinging it over his own.

"Hey, I can handle that myself. I'm not an invalid you know." Here he was trying to take over again, and it annoyed her slightly.

She grabbed for the bag but he held on tight. "Parker, don't be a pain in the ass. Let's go."

They walked hand in hand toward the hot dog stand. Neither one spoke, as they were both lost in thought. Holding her hand, Joe couldn't help but be aware of the large ring on Alex's hand. She was going to be a married woman one day soon. Even so, his mind wandered into thoughts of what kind of underwear she might have on beneath her outfit. He couldn't help it. He figured until she was married it was okay to think about her underwear. He found her so appealing. His heart broke to think that once she was Mrs. Churchfield, he would have to forget her and get on with his life. He adored her and he wanted her for himself. He hoped that she would eventually decide not to say "I do" to Richard. Never would he have ever imagined he would meet someone who would turn his world upside down like she had.

As they waited in line for their lunches, Joe glanced down at Alex's flip-flop clad feet, checking out her toes. *Yup, red today. Oh boy.*

He decided to provoke her. She was so darn cute when she got fiery on him. "You do know," he blurted out, "that flip-flops are the worst thing for your feet. They're a podiatrist's nightmare. They cause all kinds of injury, offer no support, and can ruin those pretty little feet of yours."

It worked. Alex looked at him horrified. "What? Says who?"

"Well, I read an article in the *Tribune* a few weeks ago about how people are getting them caught in escalators and ripping off their toes and stuff. And it's bad for the arches, too."

"You know, you are one sick puppy. Is that all you have time to think about? Flip-flop hazards? I've worn these shoes for years, and my feet are just fine."

"Well, good to know," he countered, enjoying getting her heated up. "Ruin your cute little tootsies if you like, that's your decision. Just promise me you won't throw out your friend Jimmy's leopard things. They're hot."

"Oh, you are so funny," she returned, humoring him. "Don't worry about my Jimmys. They'll be around for a while. But, thank you. I'm glad you like them so much. I think they're still available if you want to buy yourself a pair." They were both thinking about that day when he rescued her from the concrete and about how the salvaged shoes looked on her in Vegas.

Hot dogs in hand, Joe and Alex made their way to a vacant picnic table.

He waited for her to sit down first and then sat down next to her as close as possible, making sure their thighs touched. She looked sideways and frowned. "Hey, give a girl some space, will ya? What are you, cold?"

"Just being friendly. Actually, I'm heating up quite a bit. You do that to me," he asserted.

Alex raised her eyebrows. "There you go being bad again," she chided. She saw the seriousness in his eyes. Their gaze locked, and Alex could feel the heat rising in her face. She couldn't let him discover that she was getting turned on herself. Her appetite for the hot dog dissipated, but increased for *him*. For them both, it seemed like the most natural thing in the world to be sharing lunch at a picnic table on a beautiful day, thighs pressed intimately together.

His lazy, sexy smile lit up his face. All was right in the universe. He couldn't help himself. He was overcome with emotion at the perfection of the moment. Joe turned to her, taking her left hand in his right, and squeezing it. Looking into her sweet face, dangerous things started flowing from his lips. "I want you, Alex. I want you so badly. I know I'm not supposed to say stuff like that, but please just hear me out. I care about you; I dream about you; I want to be with you all the time. And God, I so want to show you…to make love to you."

Alex's nerves buzzed raucously on high alert. She was so excited by what she had just heard, that she wasn't in control of what was coming out her mouth, either.

Her response was exactly what he wanted to hear. "I care about you, too, and I love being with you, too," she admitted. The next was harder and more dangerous. "I want you to touch me all over, and make love to me, but you know that would be very unwise."

His grip on her hand tightened. They had incredible chemistry, but he was reluctant to say exactly what he was thinking: *Then why the hell are you marrying someone else?* Instead he said, "You don't know how long I've waited for you to say that to me."

Alex looked sad as she started to get tears in her eyes.

He hated the fact that she was upset, so he decided it was not the time to have further discussion on the subject, so he let go of her hand. "Well, now that we've gotten that out of the way, I guess we should eat. I'm hungry for you but I guess for now a hot dog will have to suffice."

Alex was feeling very unsettled at the moment and no more wanted to eat her lunch than to jump off a bridge. What she really wanted was to eat him. She wanted to taste every inch of him. *Can't do that*, she thought. *I've got to control my thinking and start thinking with my head and not my stupid heart and body.*

They ate in silence, each lost in their own private thoughts.

*Oh, God. Here he is making me question my feelings for Richard again*, she thought. As always, the sparks flew the minute Joe's body was anywhere near hers. With Richard, there was barely a fizzle. She realized that the heat of passion did make for a long-term relationship. Growing old with someone required substance. At this stage in life, Alex wasn't looking for a fun summer fling or a quick romp in the hay. Although Joe probably believed everything he was saying to her, she also knew that men would say anything just to get into your pants. He'd probably walk away after he made his conquest and return to his usual gig—tall, blonde, and popping the buttons on her blouse. If she decided to give in to her physical attraction to him and a real relationship didn't develop, it could make being together at events very uncomfortable. Not to mention the fact that she'd have a big, unsavory secret to keep from Richard for the rest of her life. She wasn't sure she wanted to spend the rest of her life trying to forget about those kinds of indiscretions.

Simultaneously, Joe was hoping Alex was taking him seriously. He thought she was rather childish about her upcoming marriage—it was more about fantasy than reality. Why couldn't she see the real thing, when it was right here in front of her? Joe knew making love with her only one time would never be enough, not by a long shot. And he knew, too, that it would be a lot more than sex. They had fallen hard for each other, from the very beginning. He could easily picture himself spending the rest of his life with her. That was a scary thought for him, after the pain of his divorce. He had been relationship-shy ever since. Yet, he believed that being with Alex was the real deal. He wanted her to grab the ball and run with it—to score the touchdown and be on his team forever.

After an awkwardly silent meal, Alex finally spoke. "Well, I suppose I should think about going. If I leave now I can catch the 3:30 train."

He just looked at her, not saying anything. She rose from the picnic table and gathered her things.

"You took the train in? I'll walk you to the station," he said as he got up.

She shook her head "no." "That's not necessary. Really, I'll be fine. I ride the train nearly every day. It's not like I'm gonna get lost or anything."

He would have none of it. "Yeah, I know you're a big girl, but I don't have anything else to do today. Besides, the walk there and back will be good exercise. I'd enjoy it." *And we can spend more time together,* he thought.

"Well, sure, suit yourself. You're sure you want to?"

"Yup, come on. Besides you need a big strapping guy like me to carry your bag of treasures," he teased as he grabbed her tote.

They made their way out of the area and headed toward the Metra station, not saying much, just enjoying the walk and the weather. Chicago could be a bugger in the winter, but on a day like that you had to love it. The breeze off the lake was pleasant and lifted a few strands of Alex's hair.

Alex was thinking how she so did not want to have dinner with Richard that night. The question was how to get out of it. She'd been playing the headache card too often lately. She needed time to really sit down and search her soul. Was she doing the right thing for herself by marrying Richard? Trying to sort out her feelings about both Richard and Joe was overwhelming.

"So, what do you have planned for the rest of this weekend?" Joe asked.

"Uh, well, actually Richard and I are supposed to have dinner tonight, but I—uh—I'm kind of getting a headache all of a sudden, so I don't know. And tomorrow? Sundays are usually my day to get caught up on laundry, mail, my reading—personal stuff. Work's been busy, and I've been helping Steph with her wedding plans, so I'm really behind. You?"

Alex was so busy talking she didn't pay attention to the "DO NOT WALK" yellow flashing hand lit up at the corner. She began to cross the street under the busy "L" tracks at Wells. Joe grabbed her shirt and pulled her back.

"How long have you lived here? Don't you know Chicago cab drivers would just as soon run you over than stop? They're notorious for skirting through the lights. You're supposed to look both ways before you cross!" He was scolding her but she just shrugged.

When the hand turned white, and he looked both ways, they crossed the street. He looked at her a few seconds before saying anything. It occurred to Alex that this man had once again tried to protect her. Ten points Joe, Richard zero. The thought made her even more confused.

"Nothing planned really," Joe replied. "The guys are meeting at a sports bar to watch the Sox game. I may do that. Haven't made up my mind yet. Yeah, I suppose I should go. Who knows, I just might meet the *second* woman of my dreams." *Okay Joe, that was said with a little too much sarcasm,* he thought.

Alex gave him an assessing gaze. "Really, the *second* woman of your dreams? And the first one would be whom, if I may ask; Carolyn?"

His eyes narrowed. "Get real. There's nothing between us like that. She's like another sister to me."

"So she's not a previous romance?" Alex said, her curiosity piqued.

*Shoot,* Joe scolded himself. *Why did I have to open this can of worms? I just wanted to make her a little jealous, not rehash my past.*

"Okay, you seem to want to know all about it, so I'll tell you. Like I said before, we have known each other for as long as I can remember. Our friends thought it would be a good idea for us to get together as a couple. So we tried. It was a disaster. When we kissed, she said she didn't hear bells. And I didn't see stars. So we laughed. We agreed that we had tried, but we were better off as friends." Then he got serious. "When I'm in a relationship, I *want* bells. I want fireworks. I want it all."

Alex realized he was probably referring to her. Did he really believe that she was the real deal? Or was this just another part of his plan to get her into bed?

She didn't have to wait long to find out.

"I do have something to confess, though. You know, I once told you I'd never lie to you. Well, I didn't actually lie today, I just didn't tell you everything. I knew you'd be at the sale today. I'm being completely honest. I just wanted to see you."

She was taken aback. "Wow, and here I thought it was some huge cosmic force that brought us together." Then they both laughed. It was remarkable how being together came so naturally for them.

When they finally reached the station, he opened the door for her and they entered. He kept walking toward the train platform, intending to see her to her car and wait until she boarded. She grabbed his arm gently. "Hey, you don't have to walk me to the platform you know."

He stopped and his eyes searched hers momentarily. "Humor me. I can't help it if I want to spend as much time as I can with the *first* woman of my dreams."

She held his eyes. "Oh."

He gave her a boyish grin. "I was thinking, maybe I'll ride back with you and we could make it an adventure."

"Isn't riding Metra always an adventure?" she laughed.

"Yeah, but I was thinking about a different type. You've heard of the mile-high club haven't you? Maybe we could be one of the first to join the rail club or something like that."

She grabbed his hand and pulled him toward the platform leading to her line. "You are so bad, Baker. We'd die from the stench in those foul bathrooms before we got past the first kiss. Come on, you can walk me to the train, but when I get to my car, you'll have to be a good boy and go home, okay?" she chuckled.

"Alexis Parker, you are a very hard woman, you know that?"

She answered, "Of course I am. How do you think I've made it to where I am? Certainly not by being a marshmallow. Now hurry up, or I'll miss the train. I promised Stephanie I'd get her a bag of Garrett's caramel corn. She loves that stuff and forgot to pick some up yesterday. So I've got to stop here and get some for her." She started to walk faster as he trotted after her.

After her popcorn purchase, when they reached the open doors at her car she turned to him. Before she could stop herself, she threw her arms around his neck and kissed him. He returned the kiss with as much fervor as she had put into the kiss initially. When she quickly pulled away from him her cheeks had reddened. "Thanks for keeping me company and for lunch." With that she grabbed her bag from his shoulder, hopped up the steps, and turned around to smile at him before she opened the inner door to her car.

She took the first seat by the window on the side that looked out onto the platform. He had walked to the window where she was sitting and continued to stand there looking at her through the glass. She placed her open palm flat against the glass and continued to smile as he watched her intently. He reached up, placing his hand on the outside of the glass adjacent to hers. When they announced the doors were about to close and the train lurched and began to roll, she kept her hand on the glass and watched him until he was out of sight.

Her head went back on the seat, she took a deep breath and closed her eyes as a lone tear slid down her cheek. In a rare moment of clarity, she realized she had to call off her wedding. Joe stood there until the train had completely pulled out of the station, trying to control his emotions. He was happy to have spent time with her, but it took so much out of him to let her go.

CHAPTER 11

Where did the time go? Over a year had passed since that memorable day when Alex's destruction of a perfectly good section of roadway had brought the four friends together and sealed their fate. Alex was ruminating on this as she drove to the church Friday night for Mike and Steph's rehearsal. She recalled that spring day when she first laid eyes on Joe and the way he gently rinsed the concrete off her favorite shoes. Back then, Stephanie had insisted she had absolutely no interest whatsoever in Mike. How funny that Steph would be professing her love and pledging to spend the rest of her life with the man she had insisted wasn't her type.

Alex had not felt well the entire day, which she attributed to a case of nerves. It had only been a short time since she had seen Joe, yet it seemed like an eternity. She was supposed to be focused on planning her own wedding, which was only a few months away, yet she still found her thoughts wandering toward him constantly. Every time she tried pushing those thoughts away, they popped up again and at the strangest moments. She had gone back to the psychologist who assured her what she was feeling was quite normal. Knowing she would soon be committing herself to one man for a lifetime made it natural to doubt whether she was doing the right thing. Her thoughts and feelings, the therapist assured her, were normal— nothing to feel guilty about. But in her heart she knew her apprehension about her marriage to Richard was not normal at all. She had changed her mind about going forward, but Richard had successfully argued his case. As usual.

When Alex pulled into the parking lot in front of the church and turned off the engine, she took several moments to compose herself after checking her appearance in the mirror. Yet, as she approached the walkway to the church, her heart began to beat rapidly. She stopped momentarily to take in and release deep, calming breaths.

As she opened the large double doors she heard voices and laughter. Glancing around the vestibule, she quickly took inventory and saw that most of the wedding party had arrived. She didn't see Joe. They still had about fifteen minutes before the event began.

Approaching the chatting group, she gave Stephanie a quick hug. "Hi, Honey. You okay? I'm so nervous myself, I can't imagine how nervous you're feeling."

Stephanie just grinned at her. "I'm nervous, but more excited and happy. Gosh, can you believe this day has finally come? Sometimes it seems like it took forever to get here, but then it seems like Michael and I just met yesterday."

Steph assessed her best friend. "You look great, honey." Alex had dressed simply, but elegantly, as usual, in a short black skirt, white cap sleeve blouse that showed just a bit of cleavage, and her favorite Jimmy Choo leopard thong sandals. Had she had worn them for Joe?

"Hey, everyone! Hope I'm not late!" Joe's tenor tone rang out. As Alex turned to look at him, her heart started thumping again, and she began to feel lightheaded.

Joe seemed to have followed the Alex dress code: he was sporting black slacks, a white oxford shirt, and black loafers. She noticed that he'd even had his hair trimmed for the occasion. He looked gorgeous, as always.

He had barely said hello to everyone when he caught sight of Alex. When their eyes met, she swallowed hard, expecting him to give her the look she knew so well. Instead he stared at her with what momentarily looked like regret in his eyes and then he recovered, smiled gently, and walked up to her and Stephanie. Alex knew that the last few times she had been with him he had not been entirely happy with her, thus his famous look—the one that everyone knew was his way of silently expressing his displeasure about something. But Alex knew that this was just his way of masking his true feelings. It was like his protective shield.

Approaching them he said, "Hello, my two most favorite beautiful ladies." Bending over to first kiss the bride-to-be on the cheek, he then turned to Alex and held her eyes. He gently placed his hand on her right cheek. "Hey," he murmured, as he very gently brushed his lips against hers.

"Hey, yourself," she whispered. Then she put on her good face. "Good to see you. You're looking handsome as usual," she said, trying to sound casual while at the same time covering up her nervousness.

Mike came up behind him and the two of them embraced, slapping each other on the back and giving each other votes of confidence that they could pull off the groom and best man thing.

As Alex stood watching the two men banter back and forth, she suddenly felt dizzy and grabbed Stephanie's arm. Her friend became concerned. "Honey, what's wrong? You don't look well."

When Alex continued to hold on, and as her face began to become white, Stephanie grew concerned. "Joe," she said with alarm, "something's wrong. I think Alex is ill."

One quick assessment told him she was about to go down. He quickly made his way to her, scooped her up in his arms before she fainted, and walked in to set her down in one of the pews. As he sat beside her, he pushed her head down between her knees.

"Just breathe and keep your head down. Breath slowly. That's it, in and out," he encouraged. As she struggled to bring her head up he gently kept his hand on her neck. "No. Alex, keep your head down. You need to get some blood back to your brain so you don't pass out."

When she began to feel less faint she responded, "Okay, okay. I got it. Quit crabbing at me."

He began to massage her neck. "You scared me. I thought you would take a header and hurt yourself. Try to keep your head down a bit more, and then we'll let it up slowly, okay?"

She was now painfully aware of his thigh pressed tightly against hers and his warm breath on her neck. His hand held her neck down while his other shoulder was cuddling her to him.

*God this feels good,* she thought. *He always feels so good and here he is taking care of me. Again. He's always taking care of me. Richard never takes care of me like this.*

Slowly removing his hand from her neck he slid his hand gently to the back of her head and whispered in her ear, "Okay, let your head up slowly." He kept his hand there to make sure she did as she was told as he regulated the quickness of her assent back to a normal position.

"When is the last time you ate? I'm thinking this may have something to do with your blood sugar. Have you eaten today?" Joe asked.

Alex looked guilty. "No. My stomach has been upset most of the day, so I had no appetite. Excitement does that to me, I guess."

He just shook his head as Stephanie peeked her head into the church. "Is she okay?"

"Yeah, but she needs to eat something right away. Find out if anyone has anything stashed in her purse. You know, a granola bar, candy, or something."

Stephanie nodded, "Okay, I'll check. Alex, just sit there and try to relax, okay?"

While they waited for the bride-to-be to return, Joe and Alex sat in silence, both staring at the floor. Finally, Joe said, "Tell me the real reason you haven't eaten. Is it excitement or is it just a plain case of nerves? Does it have something to do with me being here?"

When she looked up at him she knew she couldn't lie—and that he'd know. Chuckling she just shook her head. "Baker, did anyone ever tell you what an inflated ego you have? Don't be so full of yourself."

He laughed then. "Well you must be feeling better, because you're your usual charming self. So, speaking of charming, where is Barrister Churchfield? I didn't see him anywhere. Does he just run away when you do your fainting act?"

"His plane was delayed, but he'll be here."

Joe gently took her chin in his hand and turned her toward him so she would look him squarely in the eye. Holding her head so there was no way she could look away, he asked her, "Still in love?"

"Why do you ask?" she replied. *Oh, crap*, she thought. Did he have to put her on the spot like this when she was vulnerable? "Of course I'm still going ahead with the wedding."

His eyes bored into hers. "You didn't answer my question Alex. I asked you if you're still in love."

She averted his eyes. Part of her wanted to believe she loved Richard with all her heart, but she knew it wasn't the case. She was at the point in their relationship when one doesn't turn back because of uncertainty. Those were Richard's exact words. She had always admitted to herself that she was physically attracted to Joe. But she was hoping some day, after she was married, that would wane and Richard would be the focus of her physical desires.

"Can't say it can you?" he pushed.

After taking a deep breath, she lied through her teeth. "Of course I'm in love. There, I said it. Now are you happy?"

He pulled her face closer to his. "Oh, I know you're in love. That's for sure, darlin'. You're just not certain with whom."

After what seemed like an eternity, Alex looked away, trying to come up with a good response. But for the life of her, she couldn't.

With his eyes not boring into hers she was able to look off in the distance. Fibbing again, she just shrugged and tried to make light of it. "I love many people, Joe, as do you. I'll make a deal with you. You quit asking me about my marriage to Richard, and I'll quit ribbing you about your inflated ego. Deal?"

He didn't want to let it go but figured he had no choice. One day he'd hear her admit how she felt—how she really felt, but this was neither the place nor the time to force it. This weekend wasn't about them. It was about Stephanie and Mike and their upcoming union. Reigning in his feelings, he nodded and stood up. "Sit tight. I'll see if anyone came up with a snack for you. Stay put, okay? Be right back."

She nodded and smiled up at him. "Thank you, my hero and protector," she said mockingly.

When Joe returned with a granola bar and a bottle of water, Alex gratefully took them. After consuming both, she was ready to proceed with the rehearsal. She noted that Richard still had not arrived and began to become a little more than annoyed. Why was it whenever she truly needed him, he seemed to be absent? Her thoughts briefly brought her back to her car accident. How long had it taken him to arrive at the hospital? Joe had been by her side the entire time. And when she nearly walked out into traffic after the book sale? Mr. Baker was on hand. In fact, Joe always seemed to be nearby, ready to shield her from anything and everything.

Just as the rehearsal began, Alex's cell rang and she grabbed it from her purse.

"Hello, sweetheart! It's me. I'm sorry but we just landed, and I know I'm a little late. By the time we deplane, I get my luggage, get to my car, and get back there, it will be late. Do you still want me to try to make it?" came Richard's voice through the line.

Why did she always seem to be on his schedule? Waiting around for him to show up? She rubbed her left temple. "No, don't worry about it. The actual rehearsal will only take about an hour, and then we're going to grab a quick bite."

"Should I just meet you guys at the restaurant, then? If I'm too late for dinner, I can at least buy an after-dinner drink," he offered.

Well, she supposed that at least was a compromise. "Alright. I'll convey your apologies and tell the others you'll meet us later. Be careful and just take your time, okay? I don't want you to get into an accident rushing to get there."

"Will do. I'll see you soon."

She walked back to the front where the others were waiting. "Sorry for the interruption. That was Richard, and he just landed. He won't be able to join us until later. He sends his apologies."

Looking over at Joe, she saw he just stood there with that smirk of his. *Oh he loves this for sure. Score: Joe ten, Richard zero. Again*, she thought.

The bridesmaids took their places in line for the procession down the aisle, each holding a single long-stemmed red rose. Each groomsman stood with his partner in the order the wedding coordinator had directed. Instructions were given as to the pace that should be kept, who would go first, and who would follow. Of course, Alex and Joe would be the last couple, immediately preceding Stephanie and her father.

Waiting for their turn, Joe kept glancing at Alex to make sure she was doing okay and not feeling faint again. "You okay?" he whispered. He had a death grip on her arm, which was entwined with his.

She nodded, although she really didn't feel all that well and wondered what the heck was the matter. She just kept telling herself it was just nerves because she had to walk down the aisle the next day in front of a bunch of people. Yet part of her couldn't deny that just being with Joe, and especially feeling the warmth of his body next to hers, made her calm.

Richard had, on more than one occasion, mentioned his not being happy that she and Joe had been chosen best man and maid of honor. She couldn't exactly say he was jealous, but he didn't like Joe because he felt he had ulterior motives as far as she was concerned. She knew his assumptions about Joe's interest in her were absolutely correct, but she would never admit it. He had a way of always thinking he was right anyway, and she just didn't want to give him the satisfaction.

When they reached the altar, they turned around to watch Stephanie. Her smile lit up the room, and the love that shone in her eyes for Mike was obvious to all. When Steph passed by Joe and Alex, she said a silent prayer, asking God to bless her by bringing her two friends together.

Following the rehearsal, Joe suggested that Alex ride with him, so she wouldn't have to go to the dinner alone. She reminded him that Richard was meeting up with the group at the restaurant.

At dinner, Joe managed to snag a seat next to Alex. He noticed that she was unusually quiet and kept glancing at the door, expecting her fiancé to arrive. But there was no sign of Richard, until just as Mike settled the bill and everyone was getting ready to leave.

"Hi, everyone! I am so sorry I'm late. It couldn't be avoided. You know how airline travel can be. Unfortunately it's just one of the many drawbacks of being a successful attorney who travels the world," he chuckled.

*I can't believe he just said that,* Joe thought. *And Alex told me I had a big ego? Wow, this guy takes the cake. Doesn't she see that about him? She doesn't see anything, even though it's right in front of her.*

CHAPTER 12

The following day was perfect for a wedding. The bride and bridesmaids arrived in a limo that had picked them up at Stephanie's place after their salon appointments. Likewise, the groom and groomsmen had been driven to the church. Later, the entire wedding party would depart for the reception in an oversized limousine. The reception was being held at the Hyatt, and they had all planned to spend the night, including the happy couple.

The girls were giddy on the ride to the church, but Alex didn't know who was more nervous, herself or Stephanie. When they had left the restaurant the prior night, Richard had walked her to her car, so she and Joe didn't have a chance for further discussion. In fact, she and Richard had ended up in an argument about his never being around when she needed him.

Assembling in the bride's room, the women were laughing and joking about the wedding night. "So, anyone want to give me some tips for my big night?" She was looking at Alex, specifically addressing her.

Alex's mind was completely elsewhere, and when she didn't respond Stephanie waved her hand in front of her face. "Hey, you with us? You look like you're on some other planet. Are you feeling okay?"

Coming out of it she apologized. "Gheesh, I'm sorry. Yeah, I'm fine. Just thinking about stuff. You know having all this attention has never been my thing, and I'm just a little nervous about walking down the aisle. I know it's stupid."

One of the other bridesmaids laughed and countered, "Well, I'd be a lot more nervous walking down the aisle with someone as hot as Joe than I would about people looking at me." She teased, "I begged Steph to let me be her maid of honor just so I could be on the arm of someone so sexy, but no matter how much money I offered she still chose you." She grinned. "You need to thank your lucky stars that you get to hang on to him walking to the altar. Plus, you get to have the first few slow dances with him!"

*Great, that's all I need—to be reminded just how desirable he really is. As if I'm not stressed enough about the entire day and evening ahead. And I'm sure he will take every opportunity to try to get under my skin. And that won't be all that hard to do either. Besides, Richard will pout and expect my attention, which is going to be hard since I'm in the wedding party.*

Stephanie wagged her finger at her other friend. "You should be ashamed of yourself lusting after a single guy when you have a wonderful husband and two children at home," she said, and then laughed.

"Well that may be true, but I'm not blind. I can look, just can't touch. Besides, everyone knows he has eyes for Alex."

Alex was not happy with the comment. Shoot—did the entire world have to know?

"Look, I agree with you that Joe is a fine male specimen; but let's remember that I'll be marrying a wonderful guy soon, too," Alex countered.

There was a knock at the door. It was the wedding coordinator advising the girls that it was time to line up. "Alrighty, then. Let's get this show on the road." Steph hesitated a few seconds and then looked at Alex. "Thank you, my friend, for bringing this day to all of us. If it hadn't been for you and Joe, none of us would be here right now."

The groomsmen were waiting at the back of the church, and Mike had taken his position at the front. When Joe saw Alex, his eyes lit up. He took in every inch of her from head to foot and then smiled appreciatively. The peach strapless gown and brown sash complimented her lightly tanned skin. Her peach toenails were peeking out from beneath her dress, displayed prettily in the heeled sandals dyed to match. She looked stunning as Joe moved to kiss her cheek. She smelled delicious, too.

While the coordinator was busy lining up each couple, Alex noticed Joe had never looked more attractive. Maybe it was the tux, or maybe it was just the whole wedding thing. Her heart started pounding, and it had nothing to do with being nervous about walking down the aisle. It had everything to do with the warmth of his body next to hers and the intertwining of their arms, anticipating their stroll down the aisle. Once they were lined up and waiting for the music to begin, he brushed his lips over her ear and whispered, "Alex, I've never seen you look more beautiful." Her eyes smiled "thank you" back at him.

As the music started and the others began to walk down the aisle, Alex noticed her parents and Richard sitting together on the bride's side. She caught

Carolyn's eye who, oddly, winked at her with a huge smile on her face. What was that all about? She knew now that there was nothing between Carolyn and Joe.

When Alex and Joe's turn came to walk down the aisle, Alex couldn't help thinking how ironic the situation was. It seemed strange that the next time she walked down a church aisle, it would be with Richard. Not with Joe.

As the couple reached the front, Alex turned to stand in her spot and Joe to his. They disengaged arms, and he reached for her hand, held it a moment, and smiled warmly at her. She smiled back through her wistful reverie.

As Stephanie began her walk toward Mike, the tender yet proud look of adoration on his face nearly caused Alex to lose it. They looked so in love, and it seemed so right for them to be together. She had a tough time holding her emotions in check. She realized she would probably never feel this way about Richard, nor he for her. And yet, she still dreamed that her big moment would be filled with heartfelt emotions on their own special day.

Mike and Stephanie's ceremony was beautiful. It took every bit of concentration for Alex to keep from glancing at Joe during the nuptials. Once, when she peeked, he seemed serious. Alex found herself imagining what it would be like if it were the two of them standing together exchanging vows.

After the requisite church pictures, the wedding party climbed into the limo. They headed to the lakefront to take more individual and group shots. It seemed surreal to her when she and Joe posed for individual couple shots, especially the one at the church where they stood at an angle to the photographer with her back to his chest. Her emotions ran wild as they posed by the water, each of them barefoot, his pant legs rolled up and she holding up her dress. He stood behind her with his hands on her hips smiling and laughing. It all just seemed so natural, and that really bothered her.

Before they piled back into the limo, Stephanie discretely pulled her friend aside. "So, is everything okay? Joe looks so darned serious—kind of like he just lost his best friend. He didn't lose him. We'll just be sharing Mike. Can you maybe talk to him?"

"You're asking *me* to talk to *him* about what he's feeling?" she laughed. "He's not exactly the open-up-your-heart kind of guy. But I'll try."

"Hey, you two beauties! The carriage awaits. We've got to get to the reception and greet our adoring public," Mike teased.

Stephanie threw her arms around him. "Yes, my prince! Alex babe, it's time to party down." Alex wasn't paying attention. She had caught Joe's eye, and he was staring at her deep in thought. She couldn't tear her eyes from his.

When they arrived at the hotel, the coordinator had set up the receiving line. As the two honor attendants, Alex and Joe were side by side. She was standing next to Joe greeting guests. It was actually the first time Alex had had a moment to speak with Richard all day. His demeanor toward Joe was not friendly, but that didn't seem to bother Joe in the least.

At one point, Alex was introduced to Joe's parents. Kathryn Baker was a striking woman, perhaps seventyish, yet she didn't look a day over sixty. She and Joe Senior made a handsome couple, and she could see why Joe had been one of God's more beautiful creations. The man had great genes. When Joe introduced her to his mother, Alex was a bit nervous.

"My dear," his mother said taking her hand, "it is such a pleasure to meet you. I've heard so much about you. Joe told me what a lovely woman you are, and now I can see for myself." Glancing at Joe, she could see a tinge of pink dot his cheeks.

"It is nice to meet you, too Mrs. Baker, and to see you again, sir," she said as she turned to Mr. Baker.

"Oh, please call me Kate. That's what my friends call me. Well, we had best not hold up the line. We'll look forward to getting to know you better and chatting later."

When the Parkers arrived, Joe chatted with Alex's father. Alex could see her mother was apprising the best man with a bit more scrutiny than she would have liked. While Mr. Parker was occupied with Joe, her mother whispered to her, "I can see why he's giving you second thoughts. No doubting the way he feels about you just by the way he looks at you. Richard never looks at you like that."

The evening was off to a good start, and the cocktail hour passed quickly. During dinner, Joe's toast to the groom was quite humorous and entertaining. Alex wished hers was more clever and less emotional. During her own speech, it was all she could do to keep from wiping away the tears as she talked about her best friend and about Steph's journey to becoming Mike's wife.

The bride and groom began their first dance as a married couple to Mariah Carey's "I Had a Vision of Love." Mike had actually chosen the song.

After Stephanie and her father completed the father/daughter dance, it was time for the wedding party to join the bride and groom. The next song was Little Big Town's "Bring it on Home." *Of all things! Wasn't this day challenging enough without my having to dance with Joe to this song?*

Taking her into his arms, Joe whispered to Alex, "Here we are again, dancing to one of our favorite songs. Why does this always feel so right?" He smiled at her, waiting for an answer. She couldn't really think of a reply. She knew what she felt but couldn't verbalize it, so she just smiled and shrugged. Joe pulled her closer and just chuckled.

After the requisite dances, Alex knew it was time to search for Richard.

Alex found him talking to Carolyn.

"Richard, I see you've met Carolyn. I just wanted to let you know I'm finished with my obligations for the moment, so I'm all yours," she said, kissing him on the cheek. "Carolyn, good to see you. Your dress is gorgeous." Carolyn's figure was set off by the form-fitting, ankle-length, simple black gown she had chosen. Surely it was by some famous designer, and her shoes were probably Choo or Blahnik. What else could one expect from the stylish store maven, Alex concluded.

Carolyn returned the compliment, then excused herself, saying that she knew the two of them probably wanted to catch a dance.

Carolyn approached Joe, who was at the bar enjoying a glass of red wine. "Hey, handsome. What's with the wine?"

He gave her a "what a stupid question" look. "My best friend—well my best *male* friend, just got hitched, is madly in love with a wonderful, beautiful woman, and she with him. My envy is getting the better of me. So, unless I can find a cooperating partner to join me in a lifetime of bliss, immediately, I'm planning to get stinking drunk and wallow in self-pity. So does that answer your question?"

She had to smile at his honesty. "Yeah, I guess that about explains it. I met Richard." She gave Joe a knowing smile and then continued. "He seemed to be enjoying his cocktails as much as you, so there you have it. Both of you have two things in common; trying to get shit-faced and loving the same woman. Two men—one woman—the basic triangle."

"Well, I might be getting shit-faced, but I owe it to Mike and Stephanie to be on my best behavior. So, I won't be doing anything about that situation tonight."

For most of the evening, Joe managed to steer clear of Alex, though at most times he basically knew her location in the room. He successfully ignored Richard until it came time to throw the bouquet and garter.

"Okay, I'll try to throw it to you. Just have a heads up and be aggressive," Stephanie said to Alex.

"No, I really don't want to participate. Don't you think it looks a little juvenile at my age? Let one of the younger girls have a chance."

Stephanie argued, "Oh come on, people will expect you to be out there. You're my maid of honor and you *are* getting married next!"

Alex finally relented, but figured she would just hang back and let someone else catch it. Besides, she didn't want it to look like a setup. But it was. And when the time came, Stephanie threw the flowers practically into Alex's face. There was no other option but to catch them. Joe enjoyed the scene immensely because the intended recipient was quite obvious. He knew he had to catch the garter, no matter what.

He looked at Mike, pointed to himself, and assumed the position. Since he was taller than a lot of the other guys, he figured it was a cakewalk. The stripper song began, and Mike pulled the garter down Steph's leg with his teeth. When it was off her foot, he held it up and pumped it in the air victoriously. Looking at Joe he mouthed, "It's yours man," turned around, and threw it. Joe jumped up and had his hand on it at the same time Richard—who was about the same height—grabbed the garter with his hand. The two struggled a few moments. Suddenly they stopped and looked at each other. At that moment, Joe, having honed his quick instincts from his past life experiences, decided to take advantage of Richard's hesitation and yanked it away, shooting him the smug "I told you so" look of a conqueror.

"Fuck you, man! I had it first!" Richard roared. Alex's ears burned. She was appalled and so were her parents. No one had ever heard him say that word or anything remotely like it. Not wanting to cause any further disturbance that would tarnish his best friend's wedding day, Joe turned on his heels and walked away with his prize.

The party went on peacefully after that. Joe took turns dancing with Carolyn and his mom. Baker senior was busy chatting up industry colleagues. As Joe two-stepped with his mother, she relayed, "You know, I only got to speak with your Alex briefly, but that was enough time to know she would be perfect for you and would make a lovely addition to our family."

Joe groaned. "Mother, I told you she's engaged. I've tried to get through to her, but she's told me repeatedly she has no plans to break that engagement. Trust me, I'm as disappointed as you are. I've done everything I could since I've known her to change her mind. I respect her for wanting to honor her promise, but it's really unfortunate. The fiancé's a jerk, as you could tell by the garter incident."

Mrs. Baker pondered a moment. "Honey, it is very apparent the two of you have some kind of feelings for each other. You should try to get through to her again, before she makes the biggest mistake of her life."

"Yeah, well I'm running out of time. They set the date for November. I've made a promise to myself that after tonight, if I couldn't get her to admit if she has any feelings for me, I'm giving up. And I mean it. She walks away tonight and that's it. I've gotta get on with my life."

"I wish you two luck, honey," Mrs. Baker reassured him.

Mr. Baker finally cut in, which left Joe free to head for the bar. He ordered another glass of wine, which he swore would be his last for the night, and sat down at one of the empty tables near the dance floor. The bride and bridesmaids were kicking up their heels, dancing together and having a ball. He was having a ball himself just watching them. They did a little dirty dancing, and Alex's moves were among some of the most sensual he had ever seen. Her moves were making him want to secret her off to his room and show her a few of his own moves. He needed to talk to her again before the night was over.

When Alex left the dance floor and grabbed her purse, he figured she was going to the ladies room. He seized the opportunity and followed her. Fortunately, the hallway was deserted. When Alex exited the restroom a few minutes later, she found Joe leaning on the wall opposite the door. He had removed his tie, and his shirt was open at the neck. His hands were in his front pockets and it was obvious he was waiting for her. He pushed himself off the wall and approached her.

"Are you stalking me, or are you lost?" she bantered lightly.

"I guess you could say a little of both actually. For sure I'm stalking you, and I guess I am kind of lost. At least I feel that way. You know, you were driving me crazy out on that dance floor with all your dirty dancing. You weren't by chance doing that for my benefit were you?"

Looking at him like he was out of his mind, she clucked her tongue and replied, "Of course not. I wasn't doing anything for anybody but myself. We were just having a good time. So if that's all you have to say, I'm going back to the ballroom."

As she started to walk away he reached out and grabbed her arm. "Not so fast, counselor. I want to talk to you. Come on. I found a private place."

While waiting for Alex, Joe had discovered an unlocked janitor's closet. He walked her toward it, and pulled her inside.

Unsuccessfully, she tried to wrestle away from him. "What are you doing?" she demanded. Her deliciously kissable, glossy little mouth was posed in an adorable frown. He looked into her eyes, and all coherent thought left his brain. She put her hand on her hip. "Well—I'm waiting. What do you want now?"

He gave it a moment. "What do I want? That's a loaded question Alex. I could give you a lengthy dissertation, but I'll make it brief. I want *you*. Thinking about you drives me crazy all day and night. You have no idea how much you turn me on. I want to kiss you, touch you, and make love to you everywhere with my mouth and every other part of my body. When it comes to you, I want everything. I want to take action on all the wicked thoughts about you that have ever entered my mind. And I guess I've had just enough wine to say this. I want you in my life. Forever."

Whatever she had expected him to say, this certainly was not it. "I, well, I…" She couldn't complete her thought process.

Taking advantage of her hesitation, he took both of her hands and pulled her to him. Bending his head to kiss her she tried turning her head to keep him from doing so, but he was too quick for her. He started making little kisses all over her lips, starting with her top lip and then the bottom. Then he began to suck her bottom lip, and when she moaned he took one hand and pulled her head closer so he could get a better angle. Her hair was done up with pins, but he didn't care. He had his fingers entwined in it and wasn't about to let go.

Fueled by alcohol, the pair's inhibitions fell by the wayside. He itched to touch her everywhere and began to do just that. First his palm caressed her neck, and then, as he fingered the strap of her gown, he hesitated only a moment before placing his hand on her breast. He quickly pulled down the strap, and put his hand inside. She let out a sigh of rapture, and he took that as a sign to continue. Her uninhibited pleasure rocked him to the core.

He pulled his mouth from hers. Out of breath, he groaned, "Tell me to stop Alex, and I will. Tell me. Because if you don't, I can't promise I'll be able to stop."

Pulling his head back to hers she whispered, "I don't want you to stop. I can't stop when it comes to you," and then she began to take over. She knew she wanted whatever it would take to feel satisfied. She had denied her intense desire for him for so long, she couldn't stop going for it now.

He began tugging up the bottom of her dress, and after pulling down the top of her gown, his mouth found the access it sought. When his hand traveled lower, her dampness encouraged him to continue. A skilled lover, Joe knew what would please her, as he started a pressured rhythm and Alex began to pant.

Shrugging out of one side of his jacket, while keeping his hand right where it was, he unbuckled his belt, undid the top button of his trousers, and struggled to unzip his fly.

Zzzzzz, went the zipper. What? Suddenly something in the deep recesses of Alex's mind brought her back to planet Earth. She pulled her lips away from his. "Oh, my God! We have to stop this Joe. We can't make love in a stupid cleaning closet! It's just not right."

Oh, yes they could. And it was now or never, as far as he was concerned. Joe grabbed her hand and put it on top of his briefs. How could she deny such an obvious manifestation of his desire for her?

"Joe, stop. Stop it!" She drew back her hand.

It hadn't occurred to him that she might actually take him up on his offer to stop. And now he was going to have to get his gentleman on and do as she requested.

"If we're going to do this," she explained, "it should be special, not a frenzied quickie in a stupid closet. I want you, Joe. But not like this."

He grimaced and ran his hand through his hair. Then without looking at her, Joe started shoving his shirt back in his pants, zipped his trousers, and buckled his belt. He picked up his jacket and put it on. He noticed that Alex had managed to mostly straighten herself out as well.

They stood there a moment looking at each other, still out of breath, before he stepped closer and put his forehead to hers. He took her shoulders into his hands. Through his ragged breath he apologized as best as he could. "Jesus, this got out of control too fast, and I don't know what to say. I'm sorry. I respect you Alex. We could go up to my room, but that probably wouldn't be wise. They'd notice we were missing. Besides, you don't seem to be sure about taking this to the next level."

After what seemed like an eternity he continued. "Well, no, I'm not really sorry. As much as I want it, you know I wouldn't ever force you to do anything you didn't want. Honestly, when I first thought of coming in here I had no intention of this happening. I just wanted to talk to you and say goodbye."

"What do you mean say goodbye?" She sounded nervous. "You don't mean goodbye as in goodbye *forever* do you? You sound so serious. Are you going somewhere? Or planning to do something crazy?"

Stepping back, she could see his determined expression. After pulling himself together a moment, he uttered the words she never thought she would hear. Taking a deep breath he closed his eyes and sighed, "It's over Alex." He then opened them and looked at her with genuine pain. "I told myself if tonight you didn't show me, in either words or action, that I really mean something to you, it has to be over. I'm going to get my life together and move on. Oh, I think you want me sexually, but you've never had the guts to express your true feelings. But maybe I was assuming that you felt more for me than you actually do."

Alex looked as shocked as he felt. Looking grievously disappointed, Joe opened the door and closed it behind him, leaving Alex standing confused and distraught.

Trying to understand what had just happened and what exactly he meant by goodbye, she tried to piece together a meaningful explanation. But her emotions were so jumbled and her mind so confused she couldn't think. Tears began to stream down her face as she stood there feeling that her heart would break. When she finally calmed down a bit, she concluded that stopping him had somehow conveyed to him that she didn't want him, or that she was just teasing him. In reality, she had simply been afraid. The passion between them was so intense, she didn't know what would happen if they gave into their desire. The power of their emotions was truly frightening.

Suddenly she knew it was inevitable she and Joe would become lovers, and when the time came, she wanted it to be in a comfortable bed when they had hours and hours to explore each other. Theirs was a love that shouldn't be rushed or played out in a closet.

The thought of Joe giving up on her and going away brought Alex to realize that she had decided she needed to sit down with Richard and do what was right for her. She needed to stand her ground and not let him blackmail her into marrying him.

CHAPTER 13

Two weeks after the wedding, Alex continued to be haunted by memories of Joe. The tryst in the closet was consuming her thoughts during the day and invaded her dreams at night. The newlyweds had just returned from their honeymoon, and Alex was anxious to share her anxieties with her best friend.

She wanted to find out once and for all whether Joe's feelings for her were purely sexual, or whether he wanted to have a long-term relationship. And vice versa. Maybe having sex with him was the way to find out.

The weekend that Stephanie returned from her honeymoon Alex told Stephanie her plan. Steph was a great friend and vowed to support Alex no matter how she decided to handle the situation.

Alex decided to move forward with her plan to test the relationship waters with Joe. She got the address to Joe's lakefront penthouse from Stephanie, but spent a week lingering over her exact plan. Finally, she determined that Friday she would stop by.

Thursday night found her standing in her closet looking at her wardrobe options. The following day was supposed to be a typically hot summer day. Thankfully, the firm allowed business casual dress on Fridays. After changing her mind a dozen times, she finally chose a short khaki skirt, a capped sleeve blouse made of a light fabric with a taupe and brown geometric design, and a pair of flat beaded sandals. She decided to add her Yurman earrings and the matching necklace Joe had given her

Richard was out of town on a case and wouldn't be returning until Saturday night, so this would be a perfect time to carry out her plan and talk to Joe. Her stomach was in knots all day just thinking about seeing Joe, and more than once she told herself giving in to curiosity was a very *bad* idea. She should back out before she did something she might regret. And then her heart would prevail and tell her she was doing the right thing.

Alex left the office at 5:45 and took a cab. When the cab arrived at his building, her stomach was full of butterflies. Taking one last look in the mirror, she let out a long breath, paid the driver, and approached the doorman.

"Hi. I'm here to see Mr. Baker. Mr. Joe Baker. Actually, he isn't expecting me. It's, uh, kind of a surprise. My name is Alexis Parker."

The doorman held out his hand and introduced himself as Charles. It was highly unusual for Joe to have unplanned visitors, especially a woman. Other than his family and Carolyn, females were a rare occurrence as far as visitors were concerned. Well, clearly when Mr. Baker had females over, he did it right, if this lady was any indication. "I'll let Mr. Baker know you're here," he said, dialing Joe's unit. "Mr. Baker, I have a Miss Alexis Parker here to see you."

Joe's heart missed a beat. Had someone paid off Charles to play a prank on him? That would be something Carolyn would do. But since Carolyn knew how Joe felt about Alex and how wounded he had been, he knew she would never be that cruel. What if it was actually Alex? What would bring her here? Had she finally come to her senses? "Thanks Charles, send her on up," he finally said into the intercom.

She was escorted to the private elevator leading to the penthouse. Charles inserted the key, reached inside, and pushed the button. He explained there was only one unit on the highest residential floor. She would arrive directly at his penthouse. There was no turning back now.

Joe stood on his side of the double doors. He had come home, worked out, taken a shower, opened a beer, and was set to relax. His hair was still wet, and he was shirtless and shoeless. He oozed masculine sex appeal, dressed only in a pair of faded, well-worn Levis. He had taken out his contacts and donned a pair of glasses with black rectangle frames. Holding his beer in his left hand, his thumb and forefinger holding it around the top, he waited anxiously.

Alex stood on the other side of the door trying to compose herself before she reached for the buzzer. Her heart was beating like crazy. She had a small handbag over her left shoulder and her small briefcase in her right hand. As Joe looked at the security camera aimed directly at the outside of his door, he realized with pleasure that it actually was Alex. He watched her as she stood there with her head down. He could tell she was probably thinking about what she might say, because she had that uncertain look on her face. After several seconds, she rang the bell.

Joe opened the door and stood and looked at her. He hoped to remain expressionless, trying as best he could to not give away what he was feeling.

The past two weeks he had been working on rebuilding that wall around his heart, and he really wanted to feel nothing the next time he laid eyes on her. Unfortunately, that wasn't happening.

"Hi," she said softly.

"Hi, yourself," he said, as his gaze traveled from her face down to her little toes and then back again to her face. He noticed every detail, and it seemed like forever since he had seen her.

If Alex had considered turning back, there was no chance of it now. She took in his wet hair, the way his jeans showed off his naked, muscular chest, and how his bare feet added to his sex appeal. She had mentally undressed him many times, and now she saw that everything she had ever fantasized about his body was true. His chest was perfect except for the scar on his right shoulder, which she noticed right away because its whiteness stood out against his tanned skin. The night in the closet when he had unbuttoned his shirt, the lighting was very dim so she couldn't really see him. She was surprised to see him wearing glasses, but as is usually the case with men, they just enhanced his charm. The glasses made him look extremely hot. She had never seen him in glasses—never even suspected he wore contacts. She realized then how little she really knew about him. He had a beer casually dangling from his hand and he looked good enough to eat. Oddly enough, as much as she had fantasized about this moment, somehow she felt unprepared. For some reason, she thought she might find him looking completely undesirable in a raggy t-shirt and old baggy sweatpants.

"Did I interrupt something?" she asked with uncertainty in her voice.

He cocked his head to the right and studied her. "No, why do you ask?"

She stammered. "Well, I uh, I just," she said, sweeping her hand at his body. "I mean… Your hair is wet, and you don't have on a lot of clothes. Uh, I thought that…"

"You thought what? That I had a woman here? I don't think so. But, thanks for the compliment. No. It's just you and me right now."

He took the briefcase from her and put it on the console inside the door. He took her hand. "Please come in. Welcome."

She stepped in and he closed the door behind her. "So what brings you here tonight?" he asked cheerfully. Uncomfortable seconds clicked by as they stood there.

She took a deep breath and stared at the ceiling, avoiding his eyes. "I'm here to discuss *us*." There. She had finally acknowledged to him that there was something between them. She now courageously looked him straight in the eye. "If I don't resolve my feelings soon, I'm gonna lose my freaking mind. I'm supposed to be planning a wedding... not thinking about you every moment of my life. Day and night. That's why I'm here." Joe looked like he was about to speak. Alex held her hand up. "No, let me finish before I lose my nerve. I'm here because I want to talk about making a plan for us to, you know, to be together. We need to get it out of our systems. See if we were meant to be a couple or not. We need to see whether this time we were just fooling ourselves."

She was on a roll, so she decided to tell him about Richard. "I've actually given a lot of thought to coming here today to suggest that we try this out. Richard is away on business, but when he gets back, I'm going to talk to him about canceling the wedding. I want to figure out what's between you and me. I can't possibly give myself to Richard unless I feel one hundred percent positive it's the right thing to do. I won't know what I feel for Richard, until I give you and I a chance," she confessed in a single breath.

Joe's eyes got wide. Was he hearing her right? Was she propositioning him and calling off the wedding? "Let me get this straight," he began. "You want us to be together? Does that mean spending more time together, or continuing where we left off in the closet? Or both?"

She shifted uncomfortably and took a step back. He advanced and her back was up against the door. He deposited his beer on the entry table and then planted both of his palms flat against the door above her head, trapping her against it, as he had done at her house against the refrigerator. "You're here, I'm here... There's no better time than the present," he said, in a sexy voice. He couldn't believe how his luck had suddenly changed. Their eyes were locked and, to cover her nervousness, she pushed her chin outward and defiantly countered, "Uh, I'm not prepared for this just yet. I, uh, just wanted to talk about us... see what you thought. And then in, say in a week or so, we could go on a date."

"Alex, if we wait a week, Richard will be back and you'll be all confused again. You'll cancel our date and run away again like you always do. Let's have this thing out, once and for all, right now. I told you at the wedding that I was done playing games."

She stared into his eyes. She was falling under his spell again.

Enough with the words. He would just have to take over the situation. This was his big chance to convince Alex how he felt about her and to make her understand that she belonged with him. He leaned toward her. "You drive me crazy, you know that?" he whispered in her ear. As he gently stroked her hair with his right hand, he began placing little kisses on the left side of her neck. Alex couldn't resist. He took her into his arms and kissed her urgently. There was no doubt Joe meant business. Whether she liked it or not, Alex's body responded with unrestrained passion as they worked their mouths on each other.

Suddenly he swooped her up in his arms, as her handbag slid to the floor, and he started down the hallway to his bedroom. She didn't kick up a fuss, just had her arms around his neck snuggling him close and giggled, "I just knew you were the kind of guy to sweep a girl off her feet."

Softly, Joe deposited her on his huge bed. He continued kissing her, as he gently began to remove her clothing. He noticed she had chosen sexy red lace panties and a matching bra for the occasion. He had never wanted her more than he did at this moment. The passion flowed easily as it always did. His lips left her mouth and started on her ear and down her throat. It was difficult to restrain himself and stay in control, but he wanted this to go well and he didn't want to rush her.

"Are you okay?" he asked. She nodded, and he looked at her and slid the back of his hand over her cheek. "Damn, you're a beautiful creature Alex. I've wanted to make love to you for a very long time." He kissed her cheek and then began to explore her chest. Finally, tonight, she belonged to him. He couldn't get enough of her.

His mouth traveled down her upper and then her lower abdomen. Alex felt like she would explode from excitement.

"Oh, God. Please don't stop," she begged. Her heart was pounding with excitement and tension. Delirious with pleasure, Joe worked his way skillfully toward her most intimate part. It was hard to tell who was closer to heaven as he expertly pleasured her. She tried to let herself go, but was unsuccessful, despite his urgings. "Come on baby, you can do it. Just let go," he whispered. He was as patient as he was gifted, and before long Alex felt an overwhelming wave explode over her.

Never in her life had any man taken Alex to completion that way. She just had never connected intimately enough with anyone for something like that to happen, even with Richard. "Oh, God!... Oh, Joe! I've never..." she panted.

He scooted himself up and looked into her eyes. "You've never done this before?" He couldn't believe it.

"Well, um, not like this...and not to finality," she admitted.

Joe held her tightly and stroked her hip, thoughtfully. He couldn't believe he was in bed with the woman he had pined over for so long.

He was kissing her neck and shoulder gently, waiting for her to be ready for round two. His hand brushed her cheek and came away wet. "Hey, Alex. Did I hurt you?"

She shook her head no and then sighed, with the tears continuing to run down her cheeks. "I'm okay. That was just a little overwhelming. And I'm trying to get a grip on all this. I'll be fine in a minute. Just hold me."

"Sweetheart, please don't cry. God knows I never, ever want to hurt you," he offered.

The words were music to her ears. As Alex looked into his eyes, she found tenderness and concern. She realized she had been totally wrong about this man. He actually did care about her.

"You know, I've been thinking about our making love for a very long time," she admitted. "And I was sure that if and when we did, it would be, you know, anticlimactic. Actually, I was hoping it would be awful, so that we could forget each other. But things aren't turning out that way at all," she said, still sniffling a little.

"Well, I don't know about you, but I think this turned out rather well," he joked, to lighten the mood.

"Well, certainly for me, it did. But I want to please you, too."

Yes, he wanted that, too—more than anything. And the fact that she was asking somehow made it okay. She was right. They had come this far and they needed to take it to completion.

"Okay, hold the thought. I'll be back in half a second," he told her as he zipped to the bathroom to suit up.

When he came back in the room she looked up and saw Joe in all of his manly glory. She had never wanted him more or been more sure that making love to him was the right thing to do. He was an expert at making love, and she could only imagine how amazing the main event would be.

He lowered himself beside her and took her in his arms, kissing her face, her neck, and then her upper chest. When she was ready, he rolled on top of her. They were both in heaven as Joe began a leisurely rhythm. He paced himself, hoping to please her a second time. When she tried to close her eyes and relax into the moment, Joe would have none of it. "No closing the eyes. I want you to look at me when it's time."

Passion overtook him, and it was getting tough to restrain himself. "Darlin', I can't wait much longer. Please do it again for me." The more he urged her with his hot words, the more on fire Alex felt. Finally, they were both out of control, giving in to the desire they had fought for so long. When they were both satisfied, out of breath, chests heaving, he assured her, "I feel like I've died and gone to heaven."

Alex dreamily let her eyes drift shut. Their locked gaze the entire time somehow seemed to intensify their lovemaking, and now she felt not only sated but also a bit vulnerable. Joe spooned her and stroked her arm. Before long, they drifted off to sleep.

An hour or so later, Joe woke up. Alex was still asleep. He stared at the ceiling with his mind in overdrive. *When the hell did this happen? When did I fall in love with her?*

He knew he cared for her deeply and wanted to be with her as much as possible, that he wanted to protect her and watch over her, and she was constantly on his mind. He had never thought he could fall so hard. After his divorce, he swore he would never let a woman get to him that way again. He had slowly but surely built that wall. It had taken some time, and when he met Alex he thought it was impenetrable; but somehow she had managed to put a few cracks in it. Over all the months he had known her, she had been chipping away at his veneer without his even realizing it. He could easily see himself spending the rest of his life with her. He could also envision them growing old together. He also knew in his heart that when the passion faded and they were old, he would still want to be with her. The question was, did she feel the same? If their lovemaking was any indication, he hoped so.

But would she really have the courage to break up with Richard? And not just postpone the wedding?

And if he told her he loved her? Would that make any difference? The last thing he needed was a replay of what his ex-wife had done to him. Maybe it was better to wait to share this news with Alex for a time when she seemed more receptive. Life after she broke up with Richard.

Alex was stirring. Joe embraced her and said, softly, "Are you hungry? I'm famished. You've given me one huge appetite."

She turned to him and protested. "No. I really should get going." She glanced at the clock at his bedside.

"Absolutely not. I've got a couple of chicken breasts marinating. I'll throw them on the grill and make a salad. I won't feel right if I don't feed you before I take you home. I'm holding you captive and then I'll take you home. That is, unless you want to stay here with me," he responded firmly, as he rolled out of bed and went to the bathroom to retrieve his jeans. "I'll be in the kitchen."

Watching his back as he retreated from the bedroom, she laid her head back and stared at the ceiling, thinking about what had just transpired between them and the repercussions to follow. She prayed to God that she could handle this. The problem was she wasn't sure she could just walk away from him like nothing had ever happened. She had thought she could, but she had proven herself wrong. She was also afraid that once would never be enough for either of them.

She found one of Joe's shirts that he had thoughtfully draped over one of the overstuffed chairs, in the sitting area adjacent to his bed. In her mind's eye she could see him sitting there, quietly reading a book before he retired, and watching the flames in the fireplace as he gazed out at the lake. For the first time, she realized the enormity of his bedroom suite. Like the rest of what she had seen of his home, it was comfy but masculine. Everything was done in taupe and brown, with black accents. This most obviously had been the work of an experienced and excellent decorator. Though, possibly, since Joe had possessed so many other talents, he could have chosen the décor himself.

She made her way to the bathroom, washed up, and tried to make some semblance of order to her hair. She peaked into his adjacent walk-in closet with all the built-ins. She'd never seen such an enormous, well-organized closet. *God, I'd kill for a closet like this,* she thought.

Taking one last look at the bed they had shared, with not only an incredible bout of lovemaking but also some tender moments and sleep, she walked down the hallway into the massive great room and kitchen. It, like every other room she had seen, had unrestricted views of the lake.

He turned around and smiled warmly at her. "Already helping yourself to my wardrobe?" She could see that he had set the outside table with simple everyday dishes, taupe napkins, some funky napkin rings, and delicate looking wine glasses. In the center he had placed and lit a thick square candle on a clear glass base. He was still in nothing but his jeans and had put his glasses back on.

"Can I help with anything?" she asked. He was cutting a tomato to add to the salad. "No, I'm good. The grill's fired up, the chicken is ready to go, and I've mixed the balsamic vinaigrette." She smiled as he added, "I've got a great new white wine I tried at the tasting at the Tuscan shop downstairs held last month. Want to try it?"

She raised her eyebrows; thinking of the mess wine had gotten them into at Steph's wedding. He laughed aloud. "Don't worry, I know what you're thinking. I'll only have one glass with dinner." He retrieved the wine from the bar refrigerator, grabbed the opener, and swiftly removed the cork.

"Let's go out on the patio while I put the chicken on. Would you like a little wine before dinner? I'm going to open another beer seeing as I didn't get to finish the other one. Well, you know, I did get a little sidetracked," he chuckled.

"Sure that sounds great. I'd love to see the view from outside."

Joe returned from the bar with a beer, and handed Alex the bottle of wine. "I'll get the chicken, and we'll be set to go," he said as he opened the right door of a massive stainless appliance. When they reached the patio, he pushed a button on the wall near the set of large French doors. *This place is amazing,* she thought—*everything is remote controlled.*

When they stepped out, the temperature had cooled down considerably, and there was a slight breeze off the lake. She walked over to the railing and realized that no adjacent building could see inside the unit, because basically all the windows faced the lake and had an incredible view. The entire patio could be closed in, because she could see tracks going into both sides.

She could hear Joe open and then close the grill. As he walked up behind her, he put his arm around her waist and pulled her close to him. "Do you like it?" he asked. It seemed to her he was somehow asking for her approval. "You know the floor is heated, and I have patio warmers so I can sit out here in the winter and enjoy the view of the frozen lake. Now that can really clear your head, ya know?" He seemed wistful.

"Joe, everything is beautiful."

His mouth turned up at the pleasure of her response. "I bought this place on a whim," he explained. "I'd been living in a really nice house in a good neighborhood that I loved. When I met with the contractor who was building this place to bid on the job, he showed me the plans. He said it would be a great investment for anybody *if* you could afford it—especially the penthouse. And naturally, the best time to buy is during pre-construction. I liked the location and closeness to the lake more than anything else I'd seen. After running it by my financial advisor, I put a down payment on this unit, signed the papers, and the rest is history. I'm glad you like it. It truly is my home, and I really enjoy living here. And besides, I know it has the best quality concrete money can buy," he teased.

"Do you ever get lonely, Joe? You seem to have it all. You're busy with your work and all, but surely sometimes you might think about finding yourself a partner to share all of this with?" she asked gently.

He turned to face her. He put his palm on her cheek. "Of course. I invite my closest friends and my family over. I do some formal entertaining, but not much. Alex, I want you to know I don't ever have women here—you know other than Carolyn, and of course my family. This is my home, my private place." He gently kissed her. "So, actually, you're the first."

Alex looked at him with a skeptical brow like she didn't believe him. "You ARE kidding right?"

"Nope," he said as he walked over and looked at the chicken. He went back inside to get the salads and a basket of baguette he had just cut. When he returned, he said, "So, young lady, you should feel privileged about that okay?" He poured a glass of wine for each of them. "I'd like to propose a toast. To the beautiful woman who just shared my bed and who stole my heart as well." They clinked glasses. Alex just shook her head, and then they laughed.

When they sat down, she realized just how hungry she was. "This smells wonderful." She raised her glass. "To a man true to my heart—handsome, pours the concrete for his own home, AND he can cook."

His expression intent, he held her eyes and raised his glass to hers. "To us."

It felt good to talk with Joe over dinner, and the conversation flowed easily. They laughed as they talked about their first crushes, pets, and going through puberty, about their lives and childhood experiences. Time passed quickly, and at meal's end Joe said, "I'll clean this up and then scoop up some gelato I bought at the little Italian store. Wait until you taste it. It's great—mint chocolate chip. Interested?" She nodded and got up to help him clear the table.

Later, when they had licked the last drips of gelato from their spoons, Alex said, "You know, I need to get going."

Suddenly, expression anxious, he grabbed both of her hands. "Look at me. Stay with me tonight," he said softly, his eyes searching hers. "I promise I'll take you home first thing in the morning."

She took in a deep breath. "Oh Joe, do you think that is such a good idea?" she asked with a pained look on her face. "I mean this whole thing was so risky, and spending the night might be pushing my luck. I don't know... Maybe it would be a really big mistake. Richard will be calling, and if I'm not there he'll be worried. I don't want to do that to him. Don't you think it's just best to stop it here before it goes any further, at least right now?"

He stood. "No I do *not* think we should stop it here." He began to get irritated. He wished she had already broken up with Richard. He couldn't believe he'd have to wait a little longer to really claim her. He wanted all of her—right now. There were very few times in his life when Joe Baker couldn't get or achieve what he wanted, and this was one of them. It was killing him.

Walking up behind him, she wrapped both her arms around his waist and hugged him tightly. Right now they were both vulnerable. The fact that she hadn't called off the wedding or told Richard she wanted to made things tense. All she knew for sure at the moment was that the contact of her body with Joe's made her feel like doing sinful things. She wanted more of him.

She supposed she could call Richard on her cell and tell him she would be home late and not to worry. She could talk to him again in the morning. It didn't really matter, because she had already done the unspeakable by going there to be with another man.

"Okay," she said in a near whisper. "I'll stay. But I have to get home first thing in the morning. No arguments, alright?"

When he turned around, he sighed with relief. "I promise. And just so you know, I'm a man of my word. I never break a promise. Come on." He grabbed her hand. "And if you think I'm gonna sweep you off your feet a second time, you'd be getting a little too confident sweetheart." His lips quirked in a half smile.

This time they would take it much slower, savoring every minute and doing it right without being rushed. They stood at the foot of the bed. "You're not going to regret this," he proclaimed, with hunger in his voice and eyes. "Another promise I won't break.

First, he started with soft kisses trailing down her neck and throat, and then back up to nip her ear. He took her head in both hands. He couldn't help himself, because he needed to taste her. Slamming his lips onto hers, he began to thoroughly ravish her mouth. As her breathing quickened, he removed his hands from her head. His lips never leaving hers, he slightly lifted the shirt, and put his hands on her upper abdomen and then up her sides. As she stood naked in front of him, he drank in the sight of her from head to toe. "Jesus Alex, you are gorgeous."

She just laughed. "Baker you are such a charmer. Shut up and take your pants off and let's get to it. I mean, we only have all night, right?"

When he zipped down his jeans and took them off, there was nothing under them but his manhood. "That's more like it," she said as she threw her arms around him, kissing him with little nips, before he gently pushed her down on the bed.

They took their time exploring each other's bodies until they couldn't wait any longer. They began a slow and steady rhythm that quickly turned hard and fast and out of control. "We're one—you and me Alex—we're one," he gritted his teeth and exploded inside her. When it was over, he whispered in her ear, "We're one..."

Her eyes flew open when she realized the magnitude of what he had said. It not only startled her but also scared her.

He looked at her with wild, dazed eyes as he tried to slow his breathing. When he finally focused, he looked at her with a look she had never seen before. "God," was all he said.

He felt like he could never get enough of her. She was a giving lover, no doubt about that. But, even if there were nothing physical between them, he knew he would still want to be with her. A man his age should not be feeling like a lovesick kid, but he was.

"Hey, I'm kind of tired," she said as she lay next to him and nuzzled in. She whispered in his ear, "Don't forget I need to get home early and you promised, okay?"

"Uh, huh," he said sleepily as he turned her so her back was toward him as he held her tight against himself. Before they knew, it they were both fast asleep.

Alex woke to the smell of bacon. Still groggy, she looked at the clock and saw that it was only 6:00 a.m. True to his word, Joe had them up early. The thing was, she didn't really want to be on her way. She wanted to cuddle with him and sleep some more. But reality was what it was, and she had to get home and figure out her next steps in convincing Richard it was over.

After she retrieved Joe's big white shirt, she went into his bathroom and tried to finger-comb her hair. She had black smudges under her eyes, which were puffy from sleep. She used a tissue to rub off the mess of mascara and then padded down the hall into the great room. He was whipping eggs in a steel bowl and had set the patio table again.

He looked over at her as he heard her approach, smiling slightly, and then turned his attention back to what he was doing, not looking at her. "Mornin'. I figured the smell of my culinary skills would wake you. The coffee's just done. Ground it fresh myself. It's Starbucks' Columbian Morning. One of my favorites. Want me to pour you a cup? Looks like another beautiful day. Did you sleep well? Boy, I was dead to the world and can't believe I woke up so early. But then again I told you I keep my promises, right? Do you want cream and sugar? Is a little cheese in your eggs okay? Not a lot, just a little for flavor. You can go ahead and sit outside if you want. I'll bring your coffee."

Joe had blurted out this whole speech without a single breath. Usually it was the woman who endured the morning-after nervousness. He seemed edgy, which was very unusual for him.

"It all sounds good to me. Want some help?" she asked, as she stood in front of him at the island. She bent her head down to try and look into his face as he continued looking down concentrating on his eggs. "Ya know, I think you've whipped them enough, don't you?"

He looked up at her and down again at his eggs. "Oh, yeah. You're right. Sorry 'bout that. I'll get your coffee so you can enjoy the morning air. I turned on one of the heaters. It's a little chilly yet. The lake breeze can be pretty cool in the morning."

He poured her coffee into a mug. "Breakfast'll be done shortly. The juice is already out there." After popping the toast down, he eased the eggs into the fry pan. When he finished scrambling them, he quickly buttered the toast, pulled the bacon from the oven, and made them each a plate.

Carrying the plates outside, he placed them on the table. He then sat down and settled the napkin into his lap. "Oops, forgot my coffee." He returned with his cup and a refill carafe. He lifted his mug and offered a toast. "To a beautiful lady and a beautiful day."

"Yum, delicious," Alex complimented her handsome host. "Hard to believe I could be hungry after that lovely dinner last night." *And the best sex I've ever had in my entire life*, she thought.

He nodded and just kept eating, taking an occasional glance at the lake, not really saying much of anything. They both ate in silence. It was hard to think about the fact that they were going to be apart soon. And for how long, neither one knew.

"Would you like to shower before we get going? There's shampoo, and I put out some other hair stuff. Hopefully you'll have a few things that work to do your hair. I can clean this up," he said as he stood up and turned toward the kitchen.

She had an idea what might break the stifled atmosphere. "Well, I think we'll save time if I help with the cleanup, and we shower together," she said with mock seriousness.

He stopped and looked over his shoulder. "You wanna shower together?" he asked, surprised, but delighted.

"Sure, why not? You've got a huge shower. We'll do our part for the environment."

"Of course we will," he agreed.

When they had finished cleaning up, they walked hand in hand down the hall. The two stripped down and Alex waited while Joe adjusted the temperature. When it was just right, he led her inside. They stood facing each other and then both began to laugh. He pushed the soap dispenser and started lathering her and then himself. They took turns washing each other, smiling like teenagers. Joe insisted on washing her hair and she his. She had never known how sensual it could be to wash someone else's hair or to have her lover wash her hair. Richard would never have gone for something like this.

When Alex went back to lathering his body, her hands brushed his groin. Being naked in the shower together, Joe was powerless to prevent his manhood from doing what it naturally wanted. Her touch set him on fire. "Okay, if you know what's good for you you'll stop touching me there right now, or you'll have to face the consequences."

Alex laughed and looked down at him. "Well if I don't, what's gonna happen, big guy?"

She looked back up at him with a dare expression on her face. When she looked up, his eyes had gotten dark and he had quit laughing. At that moment she knew what the consequences were. *Who the hell cares?* she thought. She was already a damned woman for what she had done, no matter if she did it again or not. No doubt she wanted him again. And he wasn't about to turn her down. He pushed her hair behind her left ear. "You sure you're in such a hurry to get home?" he murmured into her ear. His mouth captured her neck, and then moved to the front of her throat and then captured her mouth.

As she closed her eyes, she couldn't help that same feeling coming over her again. She was such a goner as far as he was concerned. Her body wanted one thing, and the sane part of her mind wanted to reject what her own body wanted. She pulled her mouth from his and smiled slightly. "I think I can spare a few minutes, if you've got a fast car," she replied.

"Deal. Can do," he remarked as he grabbed her hand and pulled her into the bedroom. They jumped back into the mussed bed. Their kisses were intense and urgent. Their lovemaking just kept getting better and better each time.

Once their pleasure ride was complete, he whispered in her ear. "Alex, we belong together."

When her cloud of desire subsided, it occurred to her that he was whispering about belonging together. She thought, *What is he saying—my God what is he feeling?* She felt panicked. They couldn't be together, at least not right now. Not yet. She knew this was the reality of their situation, but convincing him was going to be one of the biggest challenges of her life. How could she convince him that nothing was yet set in stone as far as the two of them were concerned.

Once they dressed, Joe insisted on driving her home, although all she wanted was to grab a cab and hightail it out of there. Being with Joe felt so good and so natural, but Alex was, in fact, still engaged to Richard. In her state of alarm, she needed to think and to sort through this whole mess. She was beginning to regret getting herself into such a tight spot.

Alex and Joe rode the elevator to his four-car garage on the level reserved for those few with private garages. She noticed there was some type of fancy sports car she didn't immediately recognize in one space, two spaces remained empty, and in the fourth she made out his Tahoe. To her surprise and delight, Joe was holding open the door to the passenger side of the sports car. She got in. After Joe got in on the driver's side, he hit the button and the top automatically came down.

"Wow, I'm impressed. Never seen a garage like this one," she explained as he just grinned at her.

"Glad you like it."

Once she got comfortable, she realized that the car was a BMW—a BMW 650i to be exact. Alex knew her cars. She knew this exact BMW had a price tag of around one-hundred thousand dollars. "Yeah, well I guess you need this kind of garage to keep a toy like this. I personally know that these things cost mucho buckos, like around a hundred grand."

He turned to her with a questioning look. "Yeah, give or take a few bucks. How do you know so much about cars?"

She shrugged. "Guess you could say I was kind of a gear head growing up. My dad's always been a car buff, and we never missed the Auto Show. It's still kind of a tradition for us."

"I bought it last year. When I saw it, it called my name. You know how that goes," he disclosed.

They talked about this and that, avoiding the fact that there was an elephant in the car. After they had turned off the expressway, and knowing she was running out of time, Alex bravely acknowledged it. "Joe, we aren't *one*. You know that, right? At least not right now."

Joe didn't answer. He was staring straight ahead. Finally, he responded.

"Yes Alex, I know that. You don't have to remind me." It scared her that he said this with the coldness of someone who could have been a stranger reading the weather report.

When he pulled in front of her townhouse, he killed the engine, waiting for her to say something. She knew he was waiting for her to speak, and for one of the few times in her life she was at a loss for words.

She knew she had to say something. She gently touched his arm and turned toward him. "Look at me please and listen to what I have to say." He did as she asked, looking at her mouth, afraid to look directly into her eyes.

"What we shared was incredible, and I'll never forget it. I won't regret it ever and it was the right thing for me to do—for us to do. I hope you feel the same way. This was something that needed to take place between us, or at least it was in my opinion. We finally scratched the itch. But," she hesitated for several seconds before taking a huge breath, "about marrying Richard… I just don't know yet. I'm really confused. I only want to be honest with you." She was dying inside.

"So, that's all this was about—just an 'itch'? Well it's too bad you feel that way, because I remember making love. In my book, it was more than just *fucking*. Yeah the sex was rocket-powered and unbelievable, but this was a lot more than just sex and you know it." He was seriously pissed. As he fired up the engine, his expression changed. He looked down his nose at her with an expression she'd never seen before, and said very quietly, "I knew you'd say that about him. You can get out now."

Hesitating, but not wanting to make matters worse by hanging around, with one last look into his beautiful eyes, she exited his beautiful car and walked out of his life for the moment. She never looked back but continued to walk to her front door. She knew then and there she needed to get herself together and get it together pretty darned fast.

When she closed her front door, she leaned against the inside and slid down to the floor in a heap. As tears began to sting her eyes, she started to cry her heart out.

When Joe screeched away, he ran his hand through his hair. He was driving too fast and he knew it. He had to figure out what had happened over the past fourteen hours. He couldn't come to grips with what she had said; yet he heard it come right out of her mouth. Alex had said she might still marry him. Joe felt that Alex had just given him the ultimate sucker punch. So here he was, filled with faith one minute, and sinking doubt the next. It was a good thing he hadn't told her he loved her.

Slowing down, he used his OnStar to ring Mike's cell.

Mike picked up on the second ring. "Hey, you're up early. What's up?"

"What's up? I just got the ultimate shaft that's what's up! You home? I'm coming over. I need to talk."

*What the heck*, Mike thought. He could remember only a handful of times in all the years they had known each other that Joe had gotten really riled. "Something happen at work? I thought we weren't running today."

"We aren't—it's about your wife's other half. I'll be there shortly. And get ready to hand me a beer when I come through the door."

*Whew, this is some serious stuff*, Mike thought. Just what he needed first thing on a Saturday morning. He and Steph had planned a quiet day hanging out and working in the yard. It looked like their day might not go that way.

Mike called out, "Honey, Joe will be here in a little bit. Hope you're decent."

Stephanie had just finished showering. She had on jean shorts, a tank, and had pulled her hair into a ponytail. At the mention of their impending visitor, she began to get nervous. She already knew what this little visit was about.

"So, did he say what's up?" she asked as she casually strolled into their den, trying to make her voice sound calm.

"He said he just got the shaft from your other half and I'm assuming that to be… Alex?"

Guilty and cringing she replied, "I'm assuming he's talking about the little visit she paid to his house last night. I didn't tell you about it because she begged me not to, and I promised! Please don't be angry with me. She told me she needed to clear the air and talk to him about some things. Frankly I thought it was a good idea and was hoping things would go well. Let's face it, we both know the two of them have been dancing around each other since the day they met."

Mike walked over to one of their leather recliners and sat down facing her. "That's okay, sweetie. I know you had to honor your friendship. But apparently things didn't go well, judging by the way he was ranting and raving. Has she called to give you the scoop yet?"

"No. But I guess I'd better check in with her before he arrives." At that she went back into the kitchen just as the phone rang.

Alex sat there with her head against the back of the door. She didn't know how long she'd been there when she finally pulled herself together. She picked up her briefcase and carried it upstairs to her bedroom. When she looked at herself in the bathroom mirror, her eyes were red and swollen, and she looked a heartbroken mess.

After washing her face, she checked her machine and listened to Richard telling her he had gotten home early and to call when she got in. There was no way she could talk to him right then, at least not until she composed herself and talked to Stephanie first.

When Alex dialed her number, Stephanie answered immediately.

"Alex, are you okay?" Stephanie asked.

"Oh, Steph, it was wonderful…but now he hates me," she rambled as she started to cry again.

"Well Mike knows something happened, because Joe is on his way over." Just then Steph heard the front door slam.

"Make that he's here. What the heck are we going to do with you two?"

Alex sat there as the tears continued to stream down her cheeks. "What are they saying, can you hear them? Is he giving Mike intimate details? Is he telling him he never wants to see me again?"

Peeking out, Steph took one look at Joe and knew things were not good.

Joe plunked himself into a chair, his elbows on his knees, his hands scrubbing up and down his face. Then he began to massage his forehead with his left hand like he had a massive headache. "In a nutshell," he told Mike angrily, "she showed up last night, we made love a few times, had dinner, she spent the night, we had breakfast, and then we made love again. Then I drive her home, and she tells me she might still marry *him*." He took a breath. "We finally get together, have a fantastic, no, an *unbelievable* time, and she walks away from me. Just like that!" he said, as he snapped his fingers.

Sitting down opposite him, Mike's expression was thoughtful. "You two did it how many times?"

Joe looked up with disgust. "What does it matter how many times?! That's not the point. It was amazing, and I'd bet every cent I have that it was the best three times she's ever had in her damned life!"

"Three times?"

When he nodded, Mike beamed. "Holy shit man. Three times in, how many hours?"

Joe glared at him. "You know Mike, we're not in college anymore. This isn't fun and games like it was back then. This is the real thing. I should have never told you, so just try to forget that part okay? What I'm saying is that she liked being with me. If she'd give me a chance we could have so much more, but she thinks it's only sex between us and that's all it will ever be. But that's not true. I care about her and I'm pretty sure she feels the same way."

"Well," Mike smiled. "I'd say she had to be pretty hot for you, don't you think? It's gotta be more than just sex, of course, even though she was that hot for you."

Joe was getting angrier by the minute. It seemed all his buddy wanted to talk about was what went on physically. "Will you just stop talking about that? And don't talk about her that way. It was amazing, and if she was faking it she deserves an Academy Award."

Tiptoeing into the room, cell in hand, Stephanie whispered, "Alex wants to know if you hate her. You don't hate her do you? No, you don't have to answer that because I know you don't."

His squinting, glaring eyes pretty much answered her question.

She closed the double doors and retreated back to the kitchen. "He didn't give me an answer; but he didn't say he hates you. So, I'd say you're okay. He just looks angry and confused right now. Maybe he just needs a little time."

"A little time?" she wailed. "A little time to figure out if he hates me? I can't stand this. You know, maybe I should give myself a little time. Maybe I should call off the wedding for now to think things through. You know I've tried talking to Richard. Maybe I just need to be more assertive about this whole thing."

"You better be pretty sure about this, honey. Do you want me to come over?"

"No," she wailed again. "I've got to call Richard back. He's left several messages and before you know it he'll show up at my door, and I can't see him like this. Not feeling the way I do and certainly not looking the way I do. I don't want to see him. I just want to see Joe. No, I don't want to see Joe. Oh, God. I'm so confused! I don't know what I want."

Stephanie walked out into her backyard to get some fresh air and sat down on a stone bench, hoping to think more clearly and be able to give some good advice. "Honey, right now I think you had better call Richard and try to sound as normal as possible. Ask him about his trip. Then tell him you don't feel well. Tell him you'll call him later. Go lie down for a while and then call me back. Are you *sure* you don't want me to come over?"

She rubbed her eyes. "You're right. I'm emotionally exhausted. Physically, too—and don't ask why. I'm going to lie down. First I'll call him back, and then I'll call you later. I promise. And Steph? Take care of Joe for me, okay?"

She assured Alex, "I will—we will—I promise."

When they hung up, she called Richard. She got his machine, so she left a message. Alex crawled into bed and fell asleep as soon as her head hit the pillow. She didn't sleep long and woke up in a pool of sweat. Dragging herself up, she headed toward the bathroom to wash her face. One look in the mirror told her there was no way she could see Richard that night. Plus, she didn't WANT to see Richard. Taking a deep breath to calm herself she went into the living room, plunked herself down on the sofa, and dialed his number.

After two rings Richard picked up. "Sweetheart, I've been worried. I left several messages. I was just thinking I should just drive over to see if you were okay. Is everything alright?"

She closed her eyes and shook her head to herself. "Yes, I'm sorry. I needed a nap and just woke up. I'm tired and have a dreadful headache. And, before you ask, no I didn't drink too much last night; but work this week was a challenge and I guess with all that is going on right now it caught up with me. How was your trip?" She tried to sound as light as possible, but she wasn't even convinced herself.

"The trip was successful—very successful. I'm glad to be home of course, but I'm reveling in winning the case. It was a tenuous trial but we were the victors. You should have seen them, Alexis. We put them into the ground. Father was ecstatic, as you can imagine. It was my best effort to date, and the firm will probably make the headlines. I've made myself proud. And, of course, you, too. What would you like to do tonight?"

*Okay, I can do this,* she thought. "I am so proud of you. Everyone will be talking about it on Monday. If you don't mind, how about you stop by tomorrow.

I won't be the best company tonight, as I truly feel dreadful. How about I make us a special dinner tomorrow? I'm sure I'll feel better by then."

"Honey, I've missed you, but I understand. Is there anything you need? I can just stop by. Do you want me to pick up some soup or something?"

Alex wanted to scream. "No thanks. I just want to crawl under the covers. Is it okay if I just call you later?"

He seemed reluctant. "Are you sure everything is okay? You sound funny."

"Yes. I'm okay. Truly I am. Just tired. I'll call you later, okay?" After he agreed, she quietly hung up. Who was this stranger she had just spoken to? Suddenly she felt sad and very alone.

She napped but it didn't help. She decided to distract herself. She grabbed her grocery list and made her way to the market. As she stared at the chicken breasts in the meat section, thoughts of Joe's delicious dinner the previous night came to mind. She stood there feeling like a fool.

As the day dragged on and she went through her mundane tasks, Joe kept creeping into her thoughts. She finally made a decision the only way she could sleep that night would be to call him to assure herself, and to hear it from his own mouth, that he truly did not hate her.

When Joe had finally left his friends' house, he had to resist the urge to head to her place. He decided what he needed was an unbiased female opinion on what had happened. He punched in Carolyn's number at the store. "Hi, it's me. I was wondering if you were busy tonight. If not, maybe you could come by for pizza or Chinese, whatever." And then after a huge sigh he admitted, "Well, okay, so I really need to talk to you about something. Are you free?"

"You sound stressed. What's wrong?"

"I need your advice on something that transpired last night between me and Alex. So can you make it or not?" he said.

*Something between Joe and Alex? Wow!* Carolyn thought. "Okay, I'll be over after we close. Are you sure you don't want to tell me now?"

"No, let's talk in person. I have to stop at the market to pick up a few things, and I'll grab a bottle of your favorite wine. I'll see you tonight." He hung up, thinking about Alex and just wanting to be with her.

When Carolyn arrived, Joe looked tired and seemed lightly buzzed. The stereo was blasting AC/DC, and she had to yell above the music. "Honey, you look like hell," she said, shaking her head. She walked around him, picked up the remote, and turned down the sound. He sat down in one of the recliners and put his feet back up, taking another swig of beer.

"So, have you been drinking since you called earlier?" she asked as she walked over to the bar, grabbed a wine glass from the cabinet, and poured herself a glass from the bottle he had already opened. She took a sip, sat on the sofa, and placed her glass down on the coffee table. She scooted her neck forward to try to get a better look at his face, while he stared out at the lake.

"So, are you going to talk or just sit there ignoring me?" she pressed. When he didn't respond, she stood up. "Why are you doing this to yourself?" She grabbed the beer from his hand, walked to the sink, and poured it down the drain. He made no resistance to her actions.

"I'll tell you what I told Mike. She showed up last night. We made love, had dinner, and she spent the night. When I took her home this morning, she told me she still might marry him. She wasn't sure." She could see the muscle in his jaw twitching and she knew he was seriously upset.

*Incredible*, she thought. She knew he wasn't making this up. Never in her wildest dreams would she have believed Alex had it in her to take that big a step with Joe. She took in a deep breath and shifted uncomfortably on the sofa. Slowly she exhaled. "I'm really sorry," she said empathetically. "I know how much you must be hurting, because I know you truly care for her." She held up a hand. "Now before you start denying it, think about who you're talking to. I know you. You can't deny your feelings for her. I can tell you care, because you look like crap. "

She got up and walked over to where he sat and stroked his head as she bent over him. "Do you want me to call her? Not that I think she'll talk to me. I mean I don't see why she wouldn't, but maybe she will feel free to say things to me because I'm a woman and I'm your friend. I can put in my pitch for you. I'll tell her what a wonderful man you are, and that I think she's making a mistake marrying him." She gave him a hopeful smile.

He put his head back, looking up at the ceiling not saying anything, but she could tell he was thinking about what she had just said. "No." He shook his head. "Nothing is going to change her mind—I'm pretty sure of that—at least not right now. You know what I think?" He looked straight at her. "She doesn't love the guy. She loves the idea of marrying what he represents. A dream man she had wanted for so long. Now that she's so close, she won't back down, even if she cares about me. But I think the real problem is that she thinks all there is between us is this sexual attraction thing and that's all there would ever be."

"But if she gave you a chance she would see there is so much more. For God's sake, anyone can see what's between you two. I see it, and you know Mike and Stephanie see it. Stephanie will try to talk to her. And you said you talked to Mike. What did he say?"

"I stopped there after I dropped her off. He didn't know what to say. Steph didn't know anything yet. But Alex was on the phone with Stephanie while I was there, and she wanted to know if I hated her. Of course I don't hate her," he said impatiently, " I lo..." he said heatedly and then stopped before he said the L word.

He gave her a dopey grin. "I didn't say the L word—I didn't, so don't look at me that way and don't go thinking I was going to say it, because I wasn't. Anyway, right now I don't know what I'm feeling okay?"

She picked up her glass and took another sip of her wine. "So the wedding isn't until November, right? We've got some time. It's not like its next week or anything, so you've got time to work on her and change her mind. But you've really got to want this. You've really got to put forth the effort, because if you don't, for sure you're gonna lose her," his friend counseled.

Joe got up to grab himself another beer and turned to her. "Right now you're trying to offer comfort and I appreciate that, but I'm not going to change her mind. She's got to be the one to figure out what *she* wants. Nothing I do is going to *make* her not marry him."

She nodded. "Okay, but at least give it some thought. Think about it for a while and don't dismiss it entirely, because there is always hope. Anyway, I'm going to order dinner."

What she had said made him feel a little better that at least there was hope. He guessed that without that, you had nothing. Suddenly things didn't look so bad.

An hour later the doorbell rang. Carolyn had set the table inside, because Joe couldn't bear to sit on the terrace. He didn't want any memories of the meals he had just shared with Alex. As he was paying the delivery person for the dinner Carolyn ordered, the phone rang.

He called out, "Hey, can you get that? I'll be there in a minute."

Alex couldn't stand being miserable a minute longer and had decided to call him. She didn't really know what she planned to say, but she just had to hear his voice and then hopefully the words would flow. She would tell him she would promise to give the whole wedding thing some serious, immediate thought. And she needed to know he didn't hate her.

Carolyn picked up Joe's phone. "Hello."

Alex was surprised. It sounded like Carolyn, but she couldn't be sure. Why would Carolyn be answering Joe's phone, she wondered.

"Hello?" Carolyn repeated. After several seconds, Alex clicked the off button and felt her heart might break.

Joe deposited dinner on the table. "Who was that?"

"I don't know. I said hello twice and they hung up. Must have been a wrong number. The caller ID looked like it was blocked."

"Huh…" he said as he took his seat and helped himself to some fried rice. "Good thing I had you to force dinner on me. I haven't eaten since breakfast early this morning. Drinking the beers on an empty stomach probably wasn't a good idea, especially being as upset as I was."

She gave him a skeptical look. "It's going to take some time. Just remember things may or may not turn out like you want them to, but you've got a very good chance at winning her over. Whatever the outcome, you need to start preparing yourself for what that outcome might be, okay?"

Joe realized how lucky he was to have a friend like Carolyn. Just bouncing the situation off her and gathering ideas was helpful.

Alex was sitting alone feeling nauseous. How could he have a woman in his house already? And what had he told her about bringing female guests up there? And even if it *was* Carolyn, did that make it right? Maybe it was one of Joe's sisters. Hopefully he was as miserable as she was and had asked his sister to answer the phone for him. She double-checked and knew she hadn't misdialed. What no one knew at the moment was that Joe's caller ID wasn't working.

Then Alex pondered calling Steph. But then Steph would tell Mike, and Mike would tell Joe. Besides, the problem was hers to iron out and no one could make the decision for her. With her brain on overload, she gave up for the night and went to sleep.

The following day, Alex knew she couldn't avoid Richard anymore. She had spent every waking minute going back and forth over what she should do. She had even tried making a list of pluses and minuses to compare each man's traits. But, when it came down to a final decision, none of that mattered. What mattered was what she felt in her heart. Previously, she had been all about thinking with her head, which had made it easy for Richard to argue her back into his plans. Now she allowed her heart to take the lead. She had changed her mind. Never in her wildest dreams did she think she would give up Richard for another man. Now she was facing the horrendous task of officially backing out of their engagement and figuring out how to gently break the news to him. *I have to do this. I just have to,* she thought.

Naturally, Richard threw a fit when she told him. However, Alex had not foreseen the magnitude of the tirade. Apparently, they had been down this road too many times, and he was tired of it. He wanted an end to her waffling. Now. He had unleashed a side of himself she had never seen. In no uncertain terms he had told her she had made a verbal contract. And a verbal contract was as legal as one that was written. They had not yet signed the marriage license, but they were as good as wed, right now. Then he started in on the guilt trip and the shame of backing out on plans that had been months in the making. How would this make their friends and families feel? Not to mention how Richard and Alex themselves would feel. Yes, Richard was a partner in a prestigious law firm for a reason. He was good. Very good at argumentation.

Alex drew on all the skills she had learned in law school, but as she was not a litigator, she couldn't defend her decision as well as she had hoped. He ripped her testimony to shreds as she tried, weakly, to make her case.

Finally, several hours later, after threatening her with defamation of character, breaking a contract, and threatening to have her fired, she relented. Then he apologized, kissed her, and left.

The moment she closed the door behind him, she fell apart sobbing. Two days of this emotional roller coaster was more than she could bear. Why was it that Richard always managed to win in the end? Feeling helpless, she vowed to forget Joe Baker and go on with her life as originally planned. She spent the remainder of the night lying awake trying to convince herself that all she and Joe really had was a purely physical attraction. And she'd just have to get over him.

CHAPTER 14

The next couple of months went by quickly. Even though she was moving forward with her wedding plans, not a day went by that she didn't think about Joe. She kept telling herself everything would be fine, and she relied on faith to make it so. Unfortunately, as a good friend of Mike and Steph's, Joe would always be a part of her life, which was going to be difficult. Once he got over his wounded pride over her choosing Richard even after their night of passion, he was civil to her at best. Always the gentleman, he did his best to avoid her at mutual friends' gatherings and spoke to her politely, only when necessary. The situation was hard on them both. Feeling guilty, Alex went out of her way to be extra nice.

Deciding on a final wedding invitee list, Alex had toyed with the idea of inviting Joe. The bond that had developed between the two of them in the past year and a half was something that had to be addressed. Maybe the best thing would be for Joe to be a part of the celebration and realize the finality of it because she was, in fact, going to be Mrs. Richard Churchfield. Not knowing how he would feel about being invited, she decided the best approach would be to just ask him. If they were to continue being friends, she felt it was necessary he be invited. But the fact was, she really *wanted* him there. Her head wanted him there of course, but secretly her heart wanted him to show up, stop the wedding and carry her off in the sunset. It was her life, but she was still so confused she wanted someone else to make that decision for her. More than anything, she feared the wrath of her co-workers and some of her friends if she didn't go through with marrying Richard.

Waiting until the eleventh hour to mail the invitation, she nervously dialed his cell. He answered promptly. "Baker."

She hesitated. "Uh, hi. It's me. I'm sorry to bother you at work, but I need to ask you a question. But first, how are you?"

He wasn't expecting to hear from her, given the few short weeks until the wedding. He was counting the days, hoping she would call the whole thing off, not that he would admit that to another living soul. He wasn't sure what she was up to. "Is that the question? You're calling to see how I am? Fine, just fine. Busy as usual. Yeah, sure, fine. And you?"

She closed her eyes, and then blurted it out. "Would you come to the wedding if I invited you?"

He wasn't sure he heard her correctly. "Come again?"

She impatiently replied, "I asked you if you would come to the wedding on the seventeenth. The invitations are going out, and I wasn't sure how you would feel about it. I'd like to have you there but only if you want to be. We've hashed everything over and both agreed to go forward as friends. And, friends do attend each other's weddings."

He was shocked. Well actually not shocked he supposed, but he wasn't sure he could sit there and watch her marry another man. "I don't know, Alex. Do you think that's such a good idea?"

Joe mulled it over a few more seconds. No, he did not want to be there when they were pronounced man and wife. But if he declined, it would look like he was uncomfortable with the idea and that wouldn't be good either, especially if they were to remain friends and see each other at least those few times a year that it couldn't be avoided. Friendship. What a joke that was. This would certainly be a big first step. A few seconds later, he sucked in his breath and let it out. "Alex, I honestly don't know how I feel about it."

She thought it over. "Okay, I guess I understand. No pressure. I'll just leave it up to you. Thanks for being honest."

After saying goodbye, he clicked off the phone and slowly exhaled. It would take all of his emotional strength to get through something like this. But, on the other hand, maybe seeing her become Richard's wife would finally get him to give up and move on. All he knew was he'd better have a pretty guarded attitude about his attendance or he'd end up a basket case.

Alex told her friend about their conversation. Stephanie couldn't believe she had actually invited him. For some reason it irritated her. Probably because she was afraid being there would bruise Joe's heart even more than it already was. "Frankly, I think it will be hard on him. Are you sure you aren't secretly hoping he'll voice his objections during the ceremony?"

"What are you talking about? Of course not. We've decided we can be friends, and this will be a wonderful step in the right direction."

"Well, it is your day and you're entitled to have anyone there that you choose."

She received her answer the next week when Joe called Alex to say he would be at the ceremony to wish her well, but he preferred to skip the reception.

Alex's wedding day arrived; a crisp, clear, sunny November morning. In the back of her mind, she again secretly fantasized that maybe Joe would rescue her from her fate when the priest asked whether anyone objected. Then she scolded herself: what a terrible thing to be considering on the most important day of her life. Richard did not deserve that.

Joe had consulted with Carolyn regarding the purchase of a new suit for the occasion. Together, they chose one of dark charcoal that fit his physique to perfection. They picked a fine striped shirt and striped tie with white, gray, black and a blue that matched his eyes. Carolyn had talked him into buying some new, expensive tie shoes to finish the look. She wanted him to look perfect that day. He could have been a model walking the runway. She wanted Alex to take one look at him and realize what she'd be missing. Well maybe that wasn't nice, but she loved Joe with all her heart and wanted him to be happy.

When Joe arrived at the church, he sat with Mike in the third row on the bride's side. Quietly, Mike asked him, "You okay?" Joe nodded.

When the groom stepped out, Joe could see him scanning the crowd. When he saw Joe, his eyes locked on him. *God I hate him*, Joe thought. His resentment was simmering but he knew he had to cool it. Richard looked like a rooster with his puffed out chest and triumph in his eyes. *How mature,* Joe thought.

As the music began, the four couples in the wedding party made their way down the aisle toward the altar. Stephanie was the last, accompanied by the best man. Mike was beaming at her as they walked slowly forward. She was a vision of beauty in her deep purple silk dress and her hair decorated with flowers.

Alex stood at the back, hanging on to her father's arm, butterflies doing a hectic flip flop in her stomach. She couldn't believe she was standing here, finally, after all the years of waiting to be Richard's wife. Despite their obstacles to get to this point, Alex believed they could get through their issues and be happy.

She was a vision in her simple, form-fitting ivory gown. She had her hair styled in an up-do, which her stylist laced with flowers to match the ones in her bouquet. When the guests stood and turned to look as the bride began to make her way to the front of the church, they saw a beautiful and confident woman. Joe couldn't take his eyes off of her. He had never seen her look more beautiful. He had loved the way she looked that morning she woke up in his bed all sleepy and tousled. He was thinking she could have looked this way for him, and it could have been him waiting as her groom. When their eyes met, she caught her breath and faltered a second. *God he looks handsome,* she thought, and it brought a smile to her face. In those scant few seconds, she noticed he had had his hair trimmed and was dressed impeccably.

When the Parkers reached the altar, Alex's father handed his daughter over to her groom and then took his seat next to his wife in the front pew.

Alex gave Richard a slow smile as they faced each other and Father Paul began the ceremony and nuptials. She thought she was in complete control of her emotions as they began to proceed. But while he was reminding them of the obligations and sanctity of marriage, her mind began to wander into its more dangerous recesses, and she couldn't focus on what he was saying.

Mike glanced over at his friend and saw that he kept glancing at the ceiling or appeared to be looking at the stained glass windows. He was looking anywhere he could, so he didn't have to be looking directly at the woman he loved and her husband-to-be facing each other. He was dying inside and couldn't watch as she slipped away from him. His right knee was bouncing up and down, and his jaw was twitching. At that moment, sensing Joe's anxiety, Mike could not for the life of him understand why Alex had asked Joe to be here or why Joe would subject himself to such an emotional ordeal. *He deeply cares for her, that's why,* he thought. In a very uncharacteristic move, he grabbed Joe's hand, quickly squeezed it and released it.

As the ceremony progressed, Father Paul began to relate how Alex and Richard had met. He talked about love. And then he came to the part where he noted that there should be no objection by anyone to such a glorious union before he proceeded. He paused; glanced from one side of the room to the other, front to back. Satisfied, he continued. "Alright then—we shall proceed with the vows and exchange of rings."

Alex stood frozen—waiting. Waiting for him to speak up. *Please*, she thought. *Help me...*

Father Paul was addressing her, but his voice came out garbled to Alex's ears. She wasn't hearing what he was saying. Although looking elsewhere, Joe had been listening. When Father Paul said they would next be exchanging rings, Joe focused his attention back to the front. She glanced over and looked into her mother's eyes, and then her eyes looked behind her mother as they locked with the eyes of the man she loved more than anything. He cocked his head and studied her a moment and held her gaze. He saw desperation in them, and panic, and he wanted to pull her into his arms and tell her everything was going to be okay.

Father Paul cleared his throat. "Alexis?"

She looked up at the priest, God's representative here on Earth, desperate, like a doe in headlights. Seconds seemed like hours. Finally, she shook her head and blurted out, "I can't do this. I just can't." Her chest started to heave, and she began to hyperventilate. "I'm sorry," She huffed out. Then she looked at Richard. "I'm truly sorry," she burst into tears. "I can't do this." Her timing was certainly not the best, but it was now or never.

She looked at her parents and then her eyes swept the room. "I'm sorry everyone," she cried, on the verge of hysteria. Mike turned to Joe with a huge grin on his face. "Holy shit..." That about summed things up.

Then Alex silently asked for God's forgiveness as she walked as quickly as the huge dress would allow to the bride's room. She could hear the murmurs of shock.

"*YOU BITCH!*" Richard yelled. Alex momentarily stopped her retreat, realizing what he had just said and letting the impact of his words sink in. She then began to run away from Richard and the disastrous situation she had caused.

Joe jumped up and started for Richard. Mike pushed him back in his seat. "What, are you crazy? Don't make this any worse than it already is. You just sit there," he pointed at him. "Do you understand me?"

Richard started for Joe as his groomsmen held him back. "You." He pointed at Joe. "You bastard, this is all your fault. I'll get you for this. I promise you, I'll ruin you!" he yelled.

Joe was wise enough to not say a word. Words weren't necessary because his eyes shooting daggers said it all.

The groomsmen pulled Richard away, and the remainder of the crowd that had until then remained seated began to stand. Mr. Churchfield was shocked at his son's behavior. After all, he was a Churchfield, and Churchfields conducted themselves appropriately—at *all* times. He would have to have a serious talk with his son after this debacle was over.

Mr. Parker stood and tried to get the attention of the guests. "Everyone, please sit down a moment." He tried to compose himself and get his thoughts together. "I think this has come as a surprise to us all. But since you have all taken the time to join us today, my wife and I would still like you to be our dinner guests. So please join us at the Club as planned. We'll just go ahead and celebrate life, family, and friendship."

Joe felt his stomach churn as he sat down, put his elbows on his knees and his head into his hands. *What the hell have I done?* he thought.

Stephanie had quickly followed Alex to the back of the church, with the rest of the bridesmaids following. Alex flung off her veil and plunked down in a chair. She was hysterical. Steph threw her arms around her best friend and did her best to comfort the distraught woman. "Honey, honey, please stop crying. It's going to be okay. I mean it's over and done with, and you did the right thing. You did what was right for you and that's what's important."

There was a loud knock at the door. "Let me in. Alex, please let me in. I have to talk to you," Joe said, his voice full of desperation. He had to hold her and tell her how he felt.

"No, go away!" she cried. "Please just go away."

Turning to Mike, who had also followed, he directed with desperation in his voice, "Tell Stephanie you need to see her and then go in there and plead my case, okay? Just get me in there. I've got to talk to her."

He did what his friend asked and knocked softly. "Stephanie honey, it's me. Unlock the door so I can come in. Joe will stay outside." Without hesitating, she unlocked the door, opened it and let her husband in, closing it behind him. Alex had quieted down a bit but looked a mess.

"I *do not* want to see him right now."

He stood with his hands on his hips. "Look, he only wants two minutes.

Two lousy minutes. You can give him that can't you?"

"No, I cannot. If you want to do something useful, please go get my mother," she said, as she got all weepy again.

Joe paced back and forth in front of the door waiting for Mike to say it was okay for him to go in. He stopped, ran his hand through his hair, and then started pacing again. He looked up to see Mrs. Parker making her way toward him and the closed door.

She gave him a gentle smile. "Hello, Joe. Well this certainly has been quite a change of events hasn't it? I'm assuming she refuses to see you?" At that he nodded. "I'm not surprised. Just give her some time to sort this through and, no, I had absolutely no idea she was contemplating backing out. But to be honest with you, I'm quite relieved. She wears her feelings on her sleeve, and she certainly wears her feelings for you way out there. The first time I saw the two of you together I knew there was a huge connection. She just wouldn't admit it, not even to me."

She lowered her voice and continued. "You know for so many years she had a thing for Richard. And when he finally paid some attention to her, she thought that her dreams had come true. But in reality, I knew that wasn't the case. When you want something for so long, and when you finally get that something, you don't have the ability to realize that it could be wrong or may be a mistake even if it's right in front of you. She always thought he was perfect. When they finally got together she kept thinking the same, even though there were so many obvious times that showed he has flaws just like all of us. She just didn't recognize them, or should I say in her heart she refused to recognize them. God knows I tried to talk to her about it many times, and she kept telling me to basically mind my own business. Her father even tried talking to her from a man's perspective, but nothing seemed to phase her so we had no choice but to let her make her own choice."

He shoved his hands deep into his pant pockets and said, "Then you won't be surprised when I tell you that the last thing I wanted her to do was to go through with this, just like you. But I couldn't stop her. It was a choice she had to make, and now she has made that choice. I thought maybe it was because of me, or at least had a little to do with me, but apparently it doesn't because she doesn't even want to see me. Certainly you know I'm very happy right now, but at the same time I'm sad for her. If I'm confused, I can't imagine what she is feeling. I truly care for her Mrs. Parker. But then you already knew that."

She patted his cheek. "Of course I do dear. She won't be happy that I'm telling you this but…" She took a deep breath. "Several months ago she told Richard she wanted to end the engagement." Joe looked at her in shock. "Yes, she did. It was a nasty scene at first, and then there were a multitude of other times she tried talking to him and he would have none of it. He is a very strong individual and can be very manipulative. Much of his life as an attorney crosses over into his personal life. Way too much, if you ask me. As far as I'm concerned, he treated her like one of his opponents. He won his case by making her believe no one would like her anymore if she pulled out, and that her step up in partnership level would be compromised." Tears had appeared in her eyes as Joe reached out and hugged her tightly. When she pulled away she tried to comfort him. "You just hang in there. I'll see what I can do."

As he nodded his assent, she looked into a pair of very sad eyes. She opened the door and closed it behind her.

Alex looked up and then threw herself at her mother. "Oh, Mother! I'm so sorry. I just couldn't go through with it. I'm so confused, and I'm sure Richard is heartbroken. Do you think he'll ever forgive me? And my God, Mr. Churchfield will certainly fire me. We can't continue working together after this mess."

Mrs. Parker hugged her, trying to comfort her and assuring her everything would be all right. "Sweetheart, right now things are very upsetting. But in a few days you'll look back on this and know that you did the right thing. If you had felt this marriage was the right thing to do, you would have proceeded with it. Apparently you didn't." She patted her cheek. "Why don't you go on home and rest. I'll be happy to come with you or find one of your friends to come with you, if you want company. Daddy is going to go ahead and host the guests for dinner at the club. Don't worry about anything."

Mrs. Parker took a deep breath and continued. "I spoke with Joe before I came in here. Dear, he is very distraught right now. He wants to comfort you just like all of us do. I think you should just give him a few minutes once you get yourself settled down." She held her away from her, taking her two arms into her hands. "You look a mess. Let's get you cleaned up a bit, and then I suggest the two of you have a private moment together."

As she let her mother steer her into the adjoining bathroom, she began to think of the repercussions that would follow. *My God this wedding cost a fortune*, she thought. She would have to return dozens of gifts and personally apologize to dozens of people. She would not be able to face anyone at the firm, and what about the honeymoon?

When they finished Mrs. Parker whispered, "I'm going to send him in, but I'll be right outside if you need me." Alex nodded.

She opened the door and motioned Joe into the room, quietly closing it behind her. When Alex looked at him with sad, defeated and reddened eyes, all he wanted to do was hold her, stroke her face and whisper to her that everything would be okay. Instead he remained standing where he was, silent, gazing into her eyes and waiting for her to speak. He wanted her to tell him how much she wanted him in her life.

Looking at him, with that defiant upturned chin, she shook her head with disgust. "Well, I've made a mess of it haven't I? And don't say I told you so or you knew I wouldn't go through with it, because I was going to go through with it. I'll confess that I thought you would speak up. Speak up and say you knew this was a mistake I'd be making and stop the wedding. But NO, you didn't, did you?" she accused. "You could have stopped it, but you didn't. Why didn't you?!"

He started pacing, hands thrust into his pockets. He turned to her and carefully replied. "Don't you see? You were the only one who could decide if you wanted to marry him—or not. I couldn't decide that for you. You had to decide for yourself. If I had said something and interfered, and if it wasn't what you had wanted, you would hate me. I made known to you in no uncertain terms I thought you were making a mistake. I told you this as not only someone who wants to be with you, but also as your friend. But no matter what you decided, I would have gotten used to the fact that you were married to another man—because I would have had no choice."

Alex jumped up and poked at his chest. "No. You could have stopped it. It was your chance and you didn't. So obviously you don't care as much as you profess." She stopped and then hung her head.

"Cut the crap, Alex." He took a step toward her, grabbed her and pulled her to him. "Why are you doing this and saying these things? Why are you trying to justify what you did by blaming it on me? You don't know what I feel. You can't answer for me either." He was becoming frustrated and angry. He crushed his mouth to hers and pulled her against the length of him, forcing her mouth open so he could slide his tongue inside and taste her like he had craved to do for months. But she didn't kiss him back, and her body remained rigid. He released her and paced the floor again, running his hands through his hair. "I care for you deeply. You know that because I've told you. But what do you expect from me? Do you think I could just lay my feelings on the table when you had a wedding planned with another man? Maybe I was the one that forced this friendship from the beginning, but you were just as much at fault. You wanted it as much as I did and you were the one," he pointed his finger at her, "that said we could be friends and invited me to this damned wedding to begin with." He was right and she knew it.

Alex thought about what Stephanie had confidentially told her a while back. Mike had told Stephanie that Joe was scared to death to meet a woman and settle down. Joe had also confided to him that he really wanted that more than anything, as afraid as he was. She had replied to Stephanie, "Then why hasn't he?" Her friend's response was that Joe just didn't let people get close very often. It was that fear that kept him from making that connection. She knew in reality this made sense, but her heart just didn't understand.

Knowing this was a lost cause, he stepped back. He accepted defeat, at least for the moment. He took a deep breath and let it out slowly, closing his eyes. He opened them and stepped closer to her, turning her chin up, and forcing her to look him in the eye. "Look, you're confused and in shock. Nothing I say right now will help or matter anyway, so I'm not going to waste my breath. When you have everything sorted out, maybe you can see things clearer and give us a chance. He looked at her with pleading eyes and gently kissed her on the cheek. "When that time comes, you know where to find me."

He opened the door, closed it and walked out of her life, at least he hoped only for the time being. He was scared to death she would permanently reject him. As he closed the door, tears were beginning to sting his eyes.

Following the wedding catastrophe, more than two weeks went by and she hadn't called. Each time his cell rang, or his home phone, he picked up the call with bated breath hoping to hear from her. Every night when he got home he checked and rechecked his messages, but still nothing. As always, not a day went by that he didn't think about her, or a night either for that matter. Mike had assured him that everything was going as well as could be expected.

She had taken a short leave of absence from the firm. There had yet to be any talk of her leaving the firm or of them letting her go. The first day back in the office would be hell, having to face everyone.

Richard had not even tried to contact her, nor had Joe. She expected better of Richard. She knew Joe was giving her the space she needed. She knew he would wait and let her call him. It was amazing how well she knew him sometimes. Much better than she knew Richard, anyway.

The rumor mill at the office, according to Stephanie, was still in overdrive. Word held that Alex had fallen hard for another man and called off the wedding because of him. But no one knew with certainty what was really going on, not even the man that she supposedly had fallen for. Only Alex knew the real reasons, and the more she thought about them the clearer they became. How could she have been blind to so many things?

Maybe meeting Joe hadn't been entirely to blame for all that had transpired. He had been a catalyst. He was in the right place at the right time. Beneath it all, she realized she was ignoring Richard's faults. Being with Joe, especially that one powerful night, put it all into perspective.

CHAPTER 15

Mr. Churchfield acknowledged she was a valued partner, and this small bump in the road because of cancelled nuptials to his son would soon be forgotten. However, he did feel it best that she left the firm, and he would do his best to assist her in finding employment at another firm. He acknowledged it would be too awkward if she remained at Churchfield and Bryant.

Christmas came and went, and Joe, though heartbroken, finally gave up hope that Alex would call him. Alex and Stephanie very seldom discussed him. New Year's Eve was upon them, and she was looking forward to a quiet evening with friends. That year Mike had decided to forego his annual skiing trip with Joe and their buddies, in order to ring in the New Year with his new wife in their new home. Alex recalled Joe telling her their ski trip tradition. It was a major event for Joe, Mike, and their crew.

Mike and Stephanie urged Alex to join them for an early dinner New Year's Eve, but she declined. Snow was expected, and even though she could have spent the night at the Murphy household, she decided to make herself a nice dinner, enjoy the festivities on television, and go to bed early. She needed the rest. She promised to join them for dinner the following day, weather permitting.

Across the country, some twelve hundred miles and a time zone away, Joe was hitting the slopes, drinking, and living it up. He'd been doing the latter a little too much lately. He promised himself that the significant amount of drinking he'd been doing was only temporary. Once he had gotten over Alex, he'd be fine again. He was doing his best to move on.

New Year's in Aspen was celebrated a couple of hours behind New York and one behind Chicago, so Joe and his friends had agreed to meet at a bar at nine for drinks and to toast the New Year together. Normally they would have done a little night skiing, but the runs were closing early that night. Two of his buddies were now married, and those guys would call it a day and be back in their rooms by eleven to call home before midnight. Joe wasn't really feeling up to another night of ski bunnies.

By 9:15, heavy drinking had ensued, and a good time was being had by all.

Yet Joe couldn't manage to drink Alex out of his mind. He couldn't stop from wondering what she was doing. Did she have a date? Was she toasting to the New Year with Mike and Steph, or with her family? Somehow he got it into his head that knowing what her plans were would make him at least feel a little better. He was pretty sure she would remember that he was skiing. But then again, maybe she didn't care.

He felt miserable. The more miserable he felt the more he drank, figuring at least being numb was better than hurting. Several of the "bunnies" had asked him to dance. He bought them drinks, but no way was he going to bed any of them. He felt like he'd never, ever, be in the mood again. The fact that they were playing some stupid melancholy songs that night didn't help matters. When he had walked in the door, they were playing Dan Fogelberg's "Same Old Lang Syne." He had always disliked that particular song and thought it was damned depressing. The song was about two people who should have been together, but something has interfered causing their lives to take different paths. Perfect. Just what he did NOT want to hear.

Shortly before eleven, thinking it would soon be midnight in Chicago, on a whim he grabbed his coat, slipped his headband over his ears and headed toward the outdoor terrace to be alone with his thoughts. The air was frigid, but the night was clear. Light snow was falling, and the moon lit up the runs making for some beautiful scenery. A couple of patio warmers had been turned on for anyone wishing to enjoy the evening outside, but the place was deserted. He made himself comfortable on one of the reclining lounges under the eaves and crossed his feet, putting his hands behind his head. Staring at the sky and breathing in the fresh air helped clear his mind of some of the booze. The outside speakers barked out the same music that was being played inside.

He had debated calling Alex on Christmas day but felt he probably shouldn't. It took all he could do to not pick up the phone and dial her number. He was going through the same uncertainty right now. He wanted to call her. Badly. His resolve dissolved when suddenly he heard them playing the Fogelberg song again. Listening to the song made him crazy. Glancing at his watch, he saw it was just a few minutes before midnight in Chicago. He whipped the headband from his head, grabbed his cell from his pocket, and hit the speed dial. He had no idea if she would even answer, but he had to give it a try. Maybe it was the alcohol affecting him. Or maybe it was the damned song. He didn't know. All he did know was that he needed to hear her voice.

Alex picked up on the third ring. "Hello?" She sounded disoriented, as if she had been sleeping. Dozing on and off, she had finally succumbed to slumber while lounging on the couch and waiting for the big ball to drop. Joe was happily surprised she answered and hoped she was alone.

"Happy New Year."

When she heard Joe's voice she thought she was having a dream. Several seconds passed and she didn't respond.

"Alex?" Joe thought he had lost the connection.

She hesitated, finally realizing it wasn't a dream. "Hi. Um, aren't you in Colorado?"

*God it's good to hear your voice!* he thought. "Yeah, it's only eleven here. I don't know. I just—I just wanted to call you that's all. To wish you a Happy New Year." Alex thought he sounded funny—maybe a little drunk. She wasn't sure what to think or to say. After what seemed an eternity to him, she finally spoke. "Oh. Oh yeah, the time difference and all that. I've got the TV on, and it's midnight here."

He glanced skyward for God's direction. "I hope I didn't interrupt anything. It's just that they were playing this damn Fogelberg song, and it made me think of you so I just decided to call. I'm glad you're there, Alex. I'm really glad you answered. How's everything going? You been okay?" *Jesus Joe, get your shit together*, he thought.

She grabbed for the TV remote to turn down the volume. "Yes, I've been fine. We've gotten a lot of snow here, so I decided to stay home rather than going by Stephanie's tonight. I'm going over there tomorrow. How about you?"

"Yeah, I'm good. It's snowing here too. Actually I'm outside on the terrace by myself looking at the runs in the moonlight. It's really beautiful." He hesitated. "I wish you were here with me," he said softly.

Alex didn't know what made her sadder, the fact that he sounded so alone, or that he wished she was there. "I'm glad you have a nice view," she said, pretending she hadn't heard the last part, even though she knew he knew she had heard him. "How's the skiing been?"

*I don't want to talk about skiing. I want to talk about us*, he thought. "It's been good. It's been good being with the guys. We're all beginning to slow down a bit. You know—we're more careful than we used to be."

"I'm glad you're being careful…"

At that moment, during the break in the conversation, each of them were thinking what it would have been like if Alex had given him a chance. They'd have been together right then putting the happy into the new year.

The conversation, albeit brief, had begun to drag. Neither of them really knew what to say. Joe figured since he had initiated the call he should be the one to end it. "Uh, well, I'd better let you go. Here's wishing you a good new year. Give my best to Mike and Steph, just in case I don't reach them tomorrow, okay?"

That same old pain stabbed at Alex's heart, and she had to stifle the beginnings of a sob. She didn't want him to hear her cry. Instead, she cleared her throat. "You have a good one, too. Thanks for calling."

"Sure," he responded. "Bye, Alex."

"Bye," she whispered, and clicked off the phone as the tears began to run down her face. After she pulled herself together, she found her old disc of Dan's *Greatest Hits*, popping it in to play "Same Old Lang Syne."

CHAPTER 16

For the past several years Mike had hosted an annual Super Bowl party, and the event was now something of a tradition. This would be his first year hosting the party in his new home with Stephanie, and she was excited to have all the guys over. There really was no need for her to plan a menu, because years had dictated standard fare. Mike's famous Super Bowl chili was the *piece de resistance* in the center of the usual heart-attack-on-a-plate munchies. Alex was invited, but originally declined, figuring that Joe would be there. She was doing everything she could to avoid him, not that it had been hard. After the wedding fiasco, the holidays quickly came and went. She visited with her friends when she knew Joe wouldn't be there. The last time she had spoken to him was New Year's Eve. She had heard that after Aspen, he'd come back to Chicago, then done a turnaround and left for his house in Long Boat Key.

Stephanie had assured her he would not be back in time for the game this year, as he was planning to spend more time than usual at his place in Florida. He had reported to Mike the weather in Florida was magnificent, so he decided there was no rush returning home to winter. When Alex was informed he would not be in attendance, she decided the football party might be fun. For sure it was better than staying home and watching the game alone. Stephanie had said that as she was currently the only female, she needed Alex's company.

After the first of the year, Alex had kept her New Year's resolution to get a makeover, which she felt she desperately needed. She believed that a new hairdo and a makeover would give her a much-need lift after the disappointments of the previous year. She decided just a little shorter and shaggier around her face would be good—a new look but not anything drastic. But the stylist convinced Alex that highlights and lowlights were just the thing, and Alex was quite pleased with the effect. The stress of the past few months had caused her to lose some weight, and she had stepped up her workout program and was really getting toned. Alex knew she was looking good.

Informed there would be several eligible men at the party who Stephanie thought might be a good match for her, she dressed in what she thought would show off her figure without revealing too much. She wore her newest jeans, along with a fitted black turtleneck and her short spiky black boots.

Knowing that several of the attendees were from Baker Concrete, Mike agreed to introduce everyone to her and let her know if he was a co-worker or friend to Joe. That way he could let Alex know if she should avoid anyone who was too closely connected. She just couldn't see herself dating anyone who was one of his employees or close friends. Mike assured her there would be a single guy from their neighborhood and a couple guys from his auto club, so there would be plenty of non-Baker employees to choose from, if she was so inclined.

"Hey, can I help with anything?" Alex asked as she peeked her head into the kitchen and saw Stephanie removing some wings and egg rolls from the oven.

Her friend took off her oven mitts and walked over to embrace her. "Hi. I'm so glad you decided to come." She waved her hands. "Besides, look at all this food. There's enough here to feed an army, even though my dear husband insists it will all be consumed by the hungry bears. All the guys were assembling in the great room in front of the sixty-inch flat screen. "We plan to serve the chili at half time. What are you drinking? Mike is making cosmos if you want one," she said as she lifted hers and took a long swig. "I'm glad I decided to take a vacation day tomorrow, because a couple of these and I'll really be ready to party," she chuckled.

They walked into the great room, each carrying a tray full of food to place on the massive built-in bar that reminded her of the one at Joe's place.

"Alex, how about the drink of the day? I've only gotten a couple of the guys to try one, so I need another volunteer," Mike grinned. She agreed. As he was mixing her drink, she took in the couple dozen guys of various ages yelling as they watched the kickoff, swigging beer and other drinks and stuffing their faces at the same time.

Mike looked at her, studying her face and hair. "Hey, you've changed something. You look fantastic. I mean, not that you didn't look fantastic before, just different. New hair, right?"

Alex laughed. Men could be so oblivious and didn't usually notice if a woman had changed her hairstyle or color. "Yup, I had a makeover. I'm glad you noticed. What do you think?" she said as she twirled around for him. "I'm trying for the sexy mama look. Do you think this qualifies?" she teased.

"Honey, you look terrific. I'll probably have to protect you from the guys who will be trying to crawl all over you. But I'll make sure your virtue is not compromised so no need to worry. Besides, my wife would never forgive me if someone manhandled you in our home." They both laughed and turned to the television because one of the teams had just scored a touchdown. The room suddenly was in an uproar of cheers and boos.

At the end of the first quarter, Alex stood idly leaning against the bar sipping her cosmo while her friend was in the kitchen refilling the food trays. A somewhat familiar looking guy approached her. He was cute, with a nice smile. She had seen him before but couldn't quite place him.

"Hey," he extended his right hand to her. "Brady Gifford. You probably don't remember me. I met you briefly at the wedding and remember you from the uh," he whispered conspiratorially, "day you stepped in our pour and sent the boss into a rampage."

*That's where I know him—from the wedding. So he works for Joe*, she thought. She blushed and nodded, looking down, thinking of an appropriate response. "Oh yes, I knew I had seen you before. I apologize. I just couldn't quite place you." When she looked back up at him, she could see the guy was definitely a hunk. She pegged him as in his late 30s or early 40s. Definitely younger than she was. He was tall and buff, his muscles evident from the tight Henley he had tucked into his Levis. His eyes were very dark, and when she looked into them they sucked her in like a vortex. But it was his hair that gave him that edge and made him so attractive. His sandy hair was cut short, spiked up, and very trendy.

"Can I get you another drink?" he asked. "I'm getting another beer before the second quarter." She accepted his offer, and he took her arm and led her to the other end of the bar.

Looking up as they approached, and seeing the two of them together, Mike scowled. It would figure that stud muffin, as the guys called him, would take the lead in hitting on the only other woman at the party.

"Brady, I see you've met Alex." He made it a point to add, "Brady works with us at Baker, right Brady?" She knew he was trying to be subtle in pointing that out to her to stay away from him because of the connection. The martini had given her the courage to not care what Joe would have thought had he been there. She was going to do what she wanted. This guy *was* pretty cute, and he was giving plenty of attention.

"What can I get you? The same?" Mike asked.

Brady nodded. Alex said, "Great cosmo. Think I'll have one more, but that will have to be it because I have to drive myself home. Unlike some of you, I have to work tomorrow."

After accepting their drinks, they drifted off to the far end of the room, a little away from the crowd that had gathered to watch the second quarter. Brady seemed to lose interest in the game and stayed near Alex to talk to her.

He had asked her all the right questions about herself, and then she turned the tables and started asking him about himself. He proceeded to tell her he was a foreman at Baker and had worked for the company eight years. He lived in a small condo in an old converted building in the city. He volunteered that his status at the time was unmarried and "looking." She of course had not asked for that information, but he seemed anxious to share it with her. He seemed to be a reasonably sincere guy.

"Say, would you like to have dinner with me one evening when you're free? There's a new Greek place on Rush that I've heard is great. Maybe we could check it out together."

This was not quite what she had in mind. Flirting for an evening was one thing, but going to dinner with him? Well that would be kind of like a date, and it probably would not be a good thing to "date" one of Joe's guys, *especially* one of his foremen. But on the other hand Joe didn't own her, and he didn't own his men, so she should be able to do what she wanted and so should Brady. Ever since the first of the year, she thought she needed to get back into the dating scene. She truly wanted someone to do things with, even if he ended up being just a friend. She wasn't ready for any type of commitment quite yet anyway. She wouldn't mind getting married, but this time to the right guy, not to someone she idolized but didn't truly love. Maybe he would be just the start she needed.

She smiled at him demurely. "You know, Brady, I think I'd like that. When were you thinking of going?"

He looked pleased. "Well, how about next Saturday around seven? Give me your address and cell number. I'll swing by and pick you up."

"Okay, before I leave tonight, I'll give it to you," she agreed. Then they turned their attention back to the game.

It was nearly halftime when Joe arrived. He had decided staying in Florida would be nice, but he didn't want to miss this annual event. It was probably time to head back home anyway. Half of him was convincing himself he didn't want to miss the game because it was tradition. His subconscious, however, was telling him that there just might be a chance that Alex would be there.

He hadn't called Mike, figuring it was no big deal if he just showed up. When he turned into the neighborhood, there were a lot of cars and he had quite a walk to get to the house. It had started to snow lightly, and his boots crunched as he made his way up the street. He was glad to be home. Florida had been a good time, but he was ready to get back to the reality of everyday life.

When she answered the door, Stephanie was surprised to see him.

"Joe! Honey, this is a surprise! I thought you were still in Florida."

He leaned over to give her a hug and kiss her on the cheek.

"How's my favorite sister-in-law?" he asked as he smiled at her. "I decided it was time to get back to the real world, so I was lucky enough to book a last-minute flight. Figured if I made part of the game it was better than none. Didn't want to miss the famous halftime chili."

When she shut the door behind them she took his coat. "Well, you know the drill. If Mike's not at the bar he could be in the kitchen, so help yourself to a beer. I'll put your coat in the bedroom."

For some reason she looked nervous. Was it his imagination? He wasn't sure. When he walked into the great room there were still several minutes on the clock for the second quarter. He walked over to Mike who was mixing up some concoction, opened the fridge and grabbed himself a beer.

Mike looked up, just as surprised to see him.

"Hey, bud. Welcome back. I thought you were staying another week or so."

*What the hell? Why do they both look so nervous?* he thought.

"Oh, I got tired of all that sunny weather and all the beautiful women in bikinis," he teased. He took a long swig of his beer. "Actually I missed you guys and was hungry for some good football grub. How are things?"

Mike shrugged his shoulders. "Good. I finished the engine this week and she's coming together. The car's going to really be sweet, and Jason and I are getting excited to get it finished."

Joe glanced around the room, nodding to a couple of guys he knew who caught his eye, but most were engrossed in the game.

Toward one side of the room, he noticed Brady smiling and laughing with a woman whose back was turned to Joe. At first glance he thought it could be Alex, but the hair was too short and too light. The woman seemed a little thinner, too. He was pretty sure it wasn't her. Even though he would have loved to see her, he actually breathed a sigh of relief. Maybe he wasn't really ready to see her after all.

Mike realized Joe had seen her. "Wanna come down to the basement and see my progress? The remodel is really coming together." He was trying to get him away from Alex. The last thing he wanted was a disaster in the midst of his Super Bowl party. The guys would *not* understand.

"Nah, maybe after the game." He finished his beer and grabbed another. He kept staring at the backside of the woman talking to Brady, slowly drinking his beer. When the quarter ended, the usual cheers ensued by those rooting for the winning team.

The woman turned around. She was still laughing with Brady when he recognized her, and it reminded him of the time she was laughing in his shower. Then their eyes connected. Hers became large, registering shock at seeing him. Instantly she turned her back to him, looking nervously at Brady who couldn't figure out why she had such a peculiar look on her face.

Joe leaned back against the bar, continuing to study them both as he downed his beer. He and Mike looked at each other for several seconds, Mike's unspoken words telling him to cool his jets. Joe grabbed another beer, twisted off the top, drank at least half and strode over to where Alex and Brady were standing.

Alex could feel his breath on her neck and she turned around. With apprehension on her face, she looked at him and then he saw what he thought was fear. She said nothing.

Continuing to only look at Alex he calmly said, "Brady, get lost."

"Huh?" Brady was confused. "Hey, boss, we didn't expect you back so soon. How was Florida?"

"I *said*, get lost."

Brady looked at Alex with confusion on his face. Alex was still staring at Joe as he continued to scowl at her.

"Joe," she said softly, "Brady and I were having a conversation. He does not have to get lost."

He seethed. "Yes, he does if he knows what's good for him, if he values his job and if he wants to keep making a damned good living," he said without taking a breath. He was extremely irritated at the moment and needed to get Alex to himself so he could talk to her. Glaring at Brady, he grabbed Alex's arm. "Okay, so don't get lost. Alex and I need to have a little chat so we'll get lost. *You* stay here." Brady's eyebrows drew together but he didn't say anything.

He practically dragged her from the room, Mike taking in the entire scene, as they made their way down the hallway toward one of the guest rooms with Joe towing Alex behind him. Beer in one hand and Alex's slim arm in the other, he pushed open one of the guest bedroom doors and kicked it shut.

He grabbed both of her arms, never putting down the beer. "Damn it, Alex! What the hell are you doing with Brady? He's one of the biggest players in the whole damned city of Chicago. He'll break your heart like it's a toy. He trolls the clubs just about every night looking for an easy hit." Suddenly, he stopped. His eyes rolled down her body and then back up again. "Of course you'd be an easy target because you're the only other woman here."

Now it was her turn to get mad. "Take your hands off me and quit yelling. You don't own me you know." He could see she was more than angry with him. She was furious.

"Of course he would hit on me. After all, I'm the only other woman here," she mocked him. "Thanks for the compliment." She yanked her arms away from him.

He gave her a look that said, "Don't mess with me," but when she started for the door he grabbed her again and pulled her close. She struggled against him but he succeeded in pulling her even closer. "I've missed you," he said, seriously.

She pushed him away and looked at him, taking in his overall appearance. "Joe, you look like hell." She noticed the dark circles under his eyes. He looked like he had been partying too much and sleeping too little. His five o' clock shadow made him look even more tired.

"What have you been doing to yourself while you've been gone? I heard it through the grapevine," she spat out at him "you said you were going to Florida to drink, party, and get laid. Looks like you succeeded."

He ran his hand down his face and he sighed. "You know, there was not one day or night I didn't think about you. You once cared about me. Why can't we have that again?" He sat down in an upholstered chair. After finishing his beer he put the bottle on an adjacent table, put his head down and his hands on his knees. Then he shook his head and rubbed his eyes. When he looked up she could swear the brightness she saw in them might be tears beginning to form.

Alex sat down on the bed. "Look, I didn't know you would be at the party, and I certainly didn't intend to get Brady's attention." Then she took a deep breath and let it out. "You should know that I agreed to go on a date with him next Saturday. But I certainly have no intention of going to bed with him. It's just dinner. You needn't be so upset about this."

"You're damned right you're not going to bed with him! He's been with every twenty- and thirty-something babe in the city. I don't want you catching something from him. He does a good job at work, so his personal life is his business and not mine. But I won't stand still watching the two of you get involved. I simply won't have it."

Knowing he better cool down, Joe closed his eyes. He knew showing his anger wouldn't get him anywhere. He couldn't control the one lone tear that slid down his cheek. Joe quickly wiped it away hoping she wouldn't notice. He wished he hadn't had so much beer on an empty stomach. He suddenly felt very vulnerable.

She actually felt sorry for him. "You and I will never be. I have to go on with my life. So do you, which I'm sure you did while you were in Florida." Then her jealousy got the best of her. "Tell me Joe, how many women did you sleep with this past month? Five, six? Ten? I'm just curious."

He sighed. "Why would you even care if, since as you say, *we* will never be?"

She was biting her bottom lip to keep it from quivering. The last thing she wanted to hear was that he had been sleeping with another woman, but she would never admit it. She was the one who had asked the question. Her feelings for him ran so deep, but she kept trying to deny them and keep them buried. He looked up at her again, his eyes tired.

He studied her as if seeing her for the first time since his arrival. He cocked his head. "You look really hot, Parker. A little scrawny," as he studied her body, "but definitely hot." She gave him a look that said she didn't understand what he was trying to say.

*Hell, Baker, this isn't coming out the way you want it to,* he thought. "What I mean is, I loved the way you looked before, and I love the way you look now too, it's just…"

*Did he just say "love"? I've never, ever, heard him use that word. I didn't think it was in his vocabulary.*

"What's with you Baker? You never use that word."

He looked at her without a clue. "What word?"

"You just said 'love' twice in the same sentence."

"Oh, I just meant it figuratively. You know what I mean…"

Alex just shook her head. "Yeah. Yeah, I do know what you mean." She'd been through this how many times in her head. As many times as he told her he cared for her, he never once came close to saying he loved her. That would have made a difference to her, but, then again, she never told him she loved him either. But she knew why she had never said it. Because she figured he would never be able to return those feelings. He knew what she was thinking and reached out to her, but she backed away.

"I know. I know," he continued. "You want me to declare my undying love for you. Why does it have to be that way? Why can't we just care about each other without all that other crap?"

"Oh Joe," she replied. "What are we doing to each other? This has got to stop—this stupid volleying back and forth."

He put his hands gently on her cheeks. "Alex, look into my eyes. Tell me you don't feel anything for me."

He had his arms wrapped around her instantly before she could even react. "Kiss me, Alex, and tell me you don't feel *anything*." She didn't move, so he kissed her. Their lips gave away their emotions. They were two people who cared deeply for each other. When he pulled away, he could see regret in her eyes for everything they had put each other through these past few months.

He took a deep breath. He could see she was being incredibly stubborn. He wasn't going to win this round. Finally he said, "Okay, you go out with Brady. Let him wine and dine you, but I'd be surprised if it lasted a month. Besides, why would you agree to go out with him, when you won't agree to go out with someone who cares so much for you? In fact, I've got a proposal. You can date both of us and then make a comparison. I'll guarantee you'll pick me in the end."

At that she smiled. "Cocky as ever, aren't you Baker?" It was hard not to look into those beautiful eyes and not want the man. There had never been any denying her physical attraction to him. And there was no denying she cared about him. She just wasn't sure he could give her what she needed—a lifetime commitment. From what she'd heard, his painful divorce had ruined him for other women.

"Look, I think we better get back to the party because people are going to start talking. God knows Stephanie is probably a nervous wreck wondering what's going on in here."

After hitching her determined chin up just a tad, she said, "I'm going to date Brady for a bit and see how things go. I hope you can accept that."

He then held her chin and looked her straight in the eye. "Promise me you won't go to bed with him."

She couldn't make that promise to him, could she? "Okay, I promise. At least for now."

He grabbed both of her hands in his, "That's all I can ask I guess. I don't think it will take you long to realize he's not for you. Good luck with that."

"I'm a big girl Joe. I can take care of myself, and I think I'm quite capable of making my own decisions who I want to spend time with."

Joe slowly shook his head back and forth. She'd have to learn the hard way. Again.

When they returned to the party, Mike and Stephanie were standing by the bar. Stephanie looked relieved they had surfaced, but Mike looked annoyed. He was upset they had worried his wife. Brady eyed them, but kept his distance. His eyes shot questions at Alex, but she quickly averted his gaze.

"Michael my dear, I think I'll have another one of those famous concoctions of yours." She smiled at her hosts like nothing was wrong. Joe opened the fridge, grabbed another beer, and strode toward the TV.

"What the hell is going on?" Stephanie grabbed her friend's arm and pulled her to the side. "I was worried about you. Did you clear the air? He looked seriously pissed when he got here and saw that you were flirting with Brady."

Alex looked tired. "Yes, he was pissed I was talking to Brady, and he's pissed that I don't want to see him. And, well, he's generally pissed at me about everything. He won't get it into his thick head that I'm not interested in him right now, and I want to get back into dating, just not with him."

Stephanie sighed. "He doesn't look very good to me. He's lost weight and looks like he's been partying too much. You know he cares very deeply for you and just can't take the rejection. Heck, no one's ever rejected the man. I think you're the first. Well, other that his ex of course. He could have just about anyone he wants. He wants you but you don't feel the same way, and it's killing him." She just shook her head. "You know, I can't understand why you won't at least give it a try. I mean you've been together sexually and you know that worked. Quite well, I might add. He's a wonderful guy with everything to offer. Maybe you should go on a few dates with him. You guys really started off on the wrong foot—literally," she laughed at her own joke. "Why are you so opposed to doing that?"

Alex snapped at her. "Because if he wanted me, if he really wanted me, he would have stopped me from going ahead with the wedding. But did he? No, of course not. I don't see a lasting relationship with him. I don't think he can commit to me. I don't think he could commit to anyone."

"Rumors, Alex. Rumors. Oh, and you think Brady Gifford is a guy who can commit? Honey, you have no idea what that guy is about. He's all about fun, fun, fun."

Alex snapped again. "I'm not looking for a commitment from him! He's cute and I want to go out with him, just to get the hang of dating again. We're just going to dinner."

Joe made his way back to the bar to get another beer. *This is not good,* Stephanie thought. He was looking even angrier as he glared at Alex when he slammed the refrigerator door. She voiced her concern to Alex. "I think he's starting to get trashed. Now I've got to worry about him driving home, and you better call it quits too since you've gotta drive."

Alex threw the rest of her drink into the sink as she watched Joe walk back to the TV. Brady stayed in the corner minding his own business. Some time before she left she'd have to give him her address and phone number.

Brady and Joe managed to stay away from each other the remainder of the game. Alex managed to stay away from both of them. She watched as Joe chugged beer after beer, drowning his sorrows.

It was getting late. Mike was handing out jackets, as the guys slowly made their way to the door, thanking their host and hostess for a good time.

Alex looked anxious. "Mike, I think you should convince Joe to spend the night. I think he's had way too much to drink. Frankly, in the mood he's in, I'm worried about him driving. Can't you talk him into staying?"

He shrugged. "I'll try. He probably won't listen, but I'll try."

Brady had retrieved his coat and approached Alex when he thought Joe wasn't looking. "Just in case you forgot, and I know things did get awkward, but you were supposed to give me your number. Here," he said, putting his card into her palm, "is my info so you can call me. Why don't you let me walk you to your car? It could be slippery out there and we can talk a minute." He put on his jacket.

She took his card and put it into her jean pocket. "I'm fine. You don't need..." Joe was suddenly between them finishing her sentence, "to walk her to her car. I'll be doing that."

Brady scowled at him and Joe scowled right back getting into his face, his blue eyes getting dark and ominous.

"Look, I can walk *myself* to my car. There's no need for either of you to do that. It's not like this isn't a safe neighborhood."

Joe called out, "Mike, can you get mine and Alex's coats? We're gonna get going, and I'm going to walk her to her car."

Conceding defeat, and not wanting to cause another scene, Alex turned to Brady. "I'll be fine. You go on." *Please*, her eyes implored.

Hesitating, he looked at Joe and then Alex. She smiled. "Really, I'll be fine." Brady shrugged, went out the door, and headed for his car.

After he had left, Alex looked at Joe. "Hey, can I talk to you a few minutes before we leave?" She motioned him down the hallway back toward the guest room. Joe didn't hesitate to follow her. When she got to the guest room she opened the door, motioned him in and closed it.

"Look, I know this has been a difficult evening for both of us to say the least. I don't want us to be enemies, Joe. We will be a part of each other's lives for a very long time, so we need to just make the best of it. I really would like you to not drive home tonight. So, I want you to give me your keys and promise me you'll spend the night here."

"I'm fine. Look, it's late. You've got work tomorrow and we better get going. Come on, we're both tired and now is not the time to discuss this any further."

He kissed her gently on the cheek. "Come on, I'll walk you to your car." He grabbed the doorknob and proceeded out the door with Alex following him.

When they made their way to the foyer their friends were waiting for them, coats in hand. Stephanie was the first to speak. "Joe, I think it would be a good idea if you spent the night. You've got a much longer drive, and the roads may be starting to get bad. Since I'm not working tomorrow, I'll make my famous grand-slam breakfast. Alex, you can stay too. I'm sure I have something you could wear to the office. What do you guys think?"

She knew her friend probably wouldn't go for it; but if keeping Joe from driving home meant having her also spend the night, then it would be mission accomplished.   "I can't. As much as I'd love one of your breakfasts, I've got an early meeting. But, Joe, like I said before, I think you should stay. Please?" she implored with a look of worry.

Joe took her coat from Mike's hands and put it on her, zipping it up, and then put on his coat. "You guys, this was great. Sorry I sort of crashed the party, but it was lots of fun as usual. Really, I'm fine. Gonna walk Alex to her car, and brush off the snow, and then I'm off. It's been a long day with the travel and all." He hugged Stephanie and Mike. "Come on Alex, we better get going so you can get your beauty sleep."

When they walked outside, it was snowing again. Joe wasn't worried about her driving. She was only a few miles away and had her all-wheel drive. Besides, she was probably as cautious with her driving as she was with the rest of her life. Knowing his drive was longer didn't worry him. His Tahoe was good in the snow too.

"Give me your snow brush and I'll clean the car off for you," Joe said. It seemed the fresh air had cleared his head because he seemed more normal. Alex still wasn't totally convinced that he should be driving home, especially to the city. She did as he said. As he brushed off her car, she continued to try to convince him to stay.

She thought about what tactic would work, because she would never forgive herself if something happened to him. If he were distracted thinking about what had transpired with the whole Brady thing, then it would be a really bad thing. *Okay Alex, you're a smart woman. What would a smart woman do?* she thought. Concede of course. She was an attorney. She knew the value of bargaining power. Tonight she had to use her bargaining power and her expertise as a lawyer, even if it meant conceding.

When he finished and put the brush into her back seat, she squared her shoulders. "Okay I'll make a deal with you. You give me your keys and spend the night here and I'll... Okay, I'll go on a date with you."

He wasn't sure he had heard her right. "What?"

"I said, you give me your keys, we go back to the house and you spend the night and I'll go on that date with you." She looked at the ground and shook her head slowly. *Some attorney you are. You just lost this case,* she thought.

He just chuckled. "Let me make sure I understand correctly. If I stay here and sleep it off, as you think I need to do, I get a date with you? What else are you throwing in with this deal?" He was getting turned on just thinking about it. "I'm assuming you still intend to go on that date with Brady?"

She was exasperated. "Of course I am. I just agreed that I would go out with you too. So what is it? Deal, or no deal?"

He stepped closer and grabbed her hips, bringing them against his. "Okay. Deal. So I don't win money like on TV, but I might win you so I think that's a really good deal." He was still buzzed.

When she gazed into his eyes she felt all hot and bothered, like she usually did when she was close to him. Knowing this was not a good thing, she pulled away. "Ya know, Joe, it seems like you always win the argument, but damn, I'm the attorney and I'm losing all the time. What is *that* all about?" She did a semi-laugh. "But I want you to know I expect a really fantastic date from you. You'll take me to some ridiculously expensive restaurant, and we'll have some outrageously expensive wine. And maybe you'll jet me to New York with first-row seats to the latest Broadway play, or do a quick trip to Vegas where I'll gamble away a bunch of your money. But whatever it is, it better be over the top, out of the ordinary, and exotic, okay?"

"What you're saying, then, is that it's not over with us?" He put his hand into his pocket and withdrew his keys, slapping them into her palm. "You win, counselor. But you're gonna lose in the long run, you know that don't you?"

She grabbed his arm. "Honey, you've just won this case against the best counselor you will ever know. Come on. We're going back to the house, and I'm giving Mike your keys. I, on the other hand, am going to drive home and get up early for a meeting while the three of you enjoy that great breakfast." She laughed and dragged him back to the house to ring the doorbell.

Driving home gave Alex time to think. She had been fighting the attraction for how many months? Maybe having a real date with him wouldn't be such a bad thing. Maybe, just maybe, it would be a disaster and everything would finally be settled. But then again she had thought having sex with him would be a disaster, and that certainly hadn't turned out as expected. No, that had certainly not been what she had expected at all.

CHAPTER 17

Not wanting to seem too anxious, she waited until Thursday night to call Brady. Joe hadn't called her about the date card he was holding, so she figured she'd go ahead and get things going with Brady. Frankly, she was surprised that Joe hadn't called. He had always been so insistent. Maybe he was getting tired of chasing her or maybe, because she had agreed to the date, the challenge was no longer there.

When Brady answered, she was a little nervous. "Uh, hi, Brady. It's Alex. Did I get you at a bad time?"

"Hey, I've been anxiously awaiting your call and, nope, this is a good time. I'm going out in a bit, but always have time for you."

*Okay, he is going out. Wasn't that what Joe had said—that he went out a lot, even during the week?* she thought.

"Great. So, um, when do you want to get together?

"Well how about Saturday night, like we discussed. If so, ya wanna hit that Greek place I was telling you about? I'll see if I can get a reservation for 7:30, if that sounds okay. After that we can go to a club if you want."

Before she had time to back out she agreed. "Sounds good to me."

"Okay, great! I've got your number from Caller ID, so how about I get back to you tomorrow with a set time and then you can give me your address."

"Okay, I'll look forward to it," she replied, wondering if she was doing the right thing.

"Alright. Well, I've got to run. Have a nice night." He hung up, anxious to get to his favorite club.

At least he wasn't one of those guys that wanted to chat. But then, maybe he was just in a hurry to get to his partying. Alex realized she was letting what Joe, Mike, and Steph said about his party habits form judgments, which wasn't really fair. She was a big girl and could form her own opinion of the guy.

Joe finally called the next morning. When Heather buzzed to tell Alex he was holding on the line, she figured he was going to ask her out for Saturday night. A little rude to be asking only one night in advance, she thought. Besides, Brady had already beaten him to it.

"Hi. How are you?" she asked.

"I'm good. Uh, since I'm holding my one date card, I figured I better redeem it before it expires," he teased.

She just shook her head. "Frankly, Baker, I'm surprised you waited this long to call. I'm busy tomorrow night."

"Well, so am I, actually. I was thinking about getting together a few weeks from now. I wanted to be sure to get on your calendar. It might take me a little time to come up with something absolutely spectacular and ridiculously expensive for our date. I don't know how I could possibly top the experience at the pier. You have to admit that was pretty good. What does three weeks from tomorrow look like? "

He had thought of all kinds of exotic things to do like she had jokingly demanded. Borrow his friend Pat's jet and fly to Frisco for dinner? Maybe go to Vegas for a show like she suggested? Nah, that would be too over the top, and she'd think he was trying to impress her too much if he followed through with something like that. No, he would go right for the heart strings. What could be more spectacular than a truly simple-but-romantic evening? He thought he knew something that would please Alex, and get to her heart, much more than throwing a pile of money at the situation. She probably didn't even realize how much better this strategy would be.

So Joe concluded that dinner at a little Italian restaurant in the old neighborhood would be the perfect start to their evening. It was one of his favorite places, and he went there often enough that the family who ran it knew him well. He had never taken a woman there, but Alex was different. He was thinking maybe take in a movie, maybe a comedy or romance, something he figured she would like. Then maybe find a place for ice cream. An old-fashioned date. The kind that always worked. That got the girl.

So far she was free, unless of course she and Brady became an item, which by all accounts seemed unlikely.

"Okay, that date works for me right now. Just casual you said?"

"Yup. You know, jeans and a sweater or something like that. Is 6:30 too early to pick you up? I thought we could go out for a while after dinner."

Alex wondered what on earth he had in mind. 6:30 and casual? It would be just like Joe to try to impress her with something off the wall.

Alex was determined to treat this as a date between two friends and nothing more, at least for now. She hoped he would not try to get physical to distract her from being objective about their relationship. They needed to cool down physically so they could work on their mental connection. So they could figure out whether they had any substance.

"Sure. That works for me. Give me a call if there's a change in plans, okay?"

"Will do. I'll look forward to it. So… take it easy and I'll see you soon," he said, clicking off.

She thought he was being very cool and calm. Maybe he had decided his strong come-on approach was not the way to go. In the meantime, she would enjoy her time with Brady and see where that relationship took her.

Brady picked Alex up Saturday night in one of those big pickups with the extended cab that looked like it was on steroids. She should have expected this. After all, the man worked in construction, he was younger, and that was probably his thing at the moment. Brady looked as cute as she remembered, with his moussed up spiky blond hair, standing in her doorway. He had topped his designer jeans with a bulky red sweater, under his three-quarters-length brown leather coat. He had on very masculine brown boots. Hiking boots, maybe?

Alex had chosen a pair of her better jeans and a patterned bulky sweater. She was relieved to find that she was neither overdressed nor underdressed by Brady's standards for the evening.

"Hello, Beautiful." He kissed her on the cheek. "Ready to go?"

"I am. Just let me get my coat. You have any trouble getting here? Were my directions good?" she asked, looking back at him.

He stood in her foyer looking at what he could see of her condo. "No problem at all. Nice place. I heard that Jason is renting Stephanie's place next door. I hope he's a good neighbor."

"Well, he's certainly a quiet neighbor. He's rarely home. But when he is, it's kind of nice knowing he's there in case I need him for anything. He's a great kid." She returned to the foyer. "Okay, I'm ready."

On the way to the restaurant they chatted easily about how they were both already tired of winter and ready for spring. Brady explained how busy spring and summer were for the business. They had some big jobs coming up, one of them being a large repave at O'Hare. Alex decided that he was an intelligent guy who knew his stuff and was easy to talk to. He obviously enjoyed his work, which was evident in the pride he showed when talking about Joe's company.

Once they arrived at the restaurant, there was no lack of conversation and she felt very at ease. He ordered her a glass of Greek wine that had been recommended and himself a beer as they began to discuss the menu. He seemed to like that she asked for his guidance.

The evening was going well, and he told her a lot about himself and she the same. He seemed to be quite impressed with her profession and confessed that he had dated a lot of women but never an attorney. She had to give the guy credit. He didn't try to hide the fact that he had played the field a lot and was just enjoying all that life brought his way.

"I was thinking maybe after we leave here we could stop at one of my favorite clubs and do a little dancing. Does that suit you? Or is there something else you would like to do?"

Alex was not much of a clubber, but it might have been fun with Brady. She hadn't danced since Mike and Steph's wedding. Thinking back to then brought up all kinds of memories, and she couldn't help but think about Joe. Richard had been ticked off at the attention she was receiving from Joe. And she was getting plenty of it, that's for sure.

"Sounds good to me. I don't think I've danced since last summer." She laughed. "I may be a bit rusty, so you'll have to be patient and take pity on me. These old bones aren't what they used to be."

He smiled at her. "Alex your bones aren't old, or is what you're really meaning to say is that it's been awhile since someone actually jumped them."

Looking surprised but appearing very cool in her comeback she responded, "The status of my bones being jumped is of no concern to you, at least not yet. Give me a break. This is only our first date." She laughed.

"Well if and when the time comes that you want me to take care of your *bones*, I'll be more than happy to oblige." He was flirting with her, and it was actually kind of fun.

"I'll take that under advisement," she said, in a formal tone.

After they finished their meal, they walked out into the crisp night air. "I'm thinking we should go to Vertigo. It's a happening place but doesn't get too crazy, especially on Saturday nights because that's date night. They play a mix of everything. That okay with you?"

She didn't have a clue what Vertigo was, so she'd just have to trust his judgment.

"That's fine with me. It's been awhile since I've been to one of the downtown clubs."

Alex actually had a great time. They danced a lot, laughed a lot, and he introduced her to all of his friends. She could tell by their expressions that a couple of the females looked like they wanted to scratch her eyes out because she was with him.

At the end of the evening, when he walked her to her door, he asked if he could see her the following weekend. When she agreed, he told her he would call during the week to set things up. Taking it slow was a good thing.

He kissed her on the cheek, thanked her for the evening, and said he looked forward to seeing her again.

She called Steph the next day to tell her all about the date with Brady. Stephanie sounded like she couldn't have cared less and that hurt Alex. Humph. As usual, Steph was probably siding with Joe. Alex made a mental note not to mention future dates with Brady until inquiries were made.

To her surprise, Brady called Alex twice during the week just to say hello and see how she was doing. They agreed he would pick her up the following Saturday and that it was her turn to pick the restaurant and make a reservation.

When Saturday rolled around, Brady and Alex headed down to one of her favorite Italian spots in the Loop. After enjoying a great dinner and sharing a bottle of Chianti, they decided to go back to Vertigo.

They had another wonderful evening, and this time when he walked her to her door she asked him if he would like to come in for coffee or a nightcap. He eagerly accepted. While he turned on the gas fireplace, she retrieved two snifters and poured them each a brandy. They sat on the sofa facing the fire while Alex rested her head on his shoulder. *Maybe this dating thing isn't so bad after all,* she thought. So far he hadn't made any overt moves of the physical kind, and she was enjoying the close contact of her head on his shoulder and his arm around her as they stared at the fire.

Brady declined a second brandy. After she retrieved his coat, they both stood silent in the foyer looking at each other. "Do you mind if I kiss you?" he asked. Wow, unlike Joe, who jumped right in, Brady was actually asking permission. Alex was touched and pleased.

She leaned her head to the side and smiled. "I think I'd like that."

Given her consent, he leaned in and very lightly kissed her, using the five-second rule for new daters—not too long, not too short, and no tongue. Alex promised herself that if she kissed him, she would be open to the experience. She vowed to remain judgment free, to refrain from comparisons, and to just enjoy it.

As much as she *wanted* to enjoy her first kiss with Brady, no bells rang for her. She thought he was very cute and very buff, but she felt no chemistry. Although she had said she wouldn't compare, he was no Joe.

When he broke contact, Brady was grinning. He gave her a bear hug and thanked her again. "I had another wonderful evening with you, Alex." Then he winked at her. "I'll call you this week." As he made his way down the front steps, she quietly closed the door behind her. *What am I doing?* she thought.

Brady called her the next day to ask if she wanted to come to his house and just "hang out." Alex declined since she had to prepare for an important meeting Monday morning. He told her he understood. No pressure, he had said. That's what she liked about the guy. They talked again on Wednesday, and Brady said on Saturday he wanted to cook dinner for her at his place and then he had some fun planned for them. Alex wasn't so sure about going to his place. Her radar was going off. Usually when a man cooked for a woman at his place, he had something physical planned. Yet, she decided to take her chances.

Brady's home in Lincoln Park was very nice. He owned a condominium in a one-hundred-plus-year-old building within walking distance of restaurants, bars, and some great shops. Brady admitted that his culinary skills were somewhat limited, but he had managed to whip up a pretty decent pot of chili.

Thus far, Brady had been a gentleman throughout dinner. As they were cleaning up the dishes, he asked, "Hey, ever been to Dave and Buster's?"

She hadn't, but had heard of it. Wasn't it a place for kids? But if he was suggesting it, maybe it was fun for adults, too.

"Nope, but I've heard of it. It's a bunch of video games and stuff like that, with a restaurant and bar, right?"

He nodded. "Yeah. I thought it would be fun. We can play some games and have a few beers. It's usually good for a couple of chuckles."

Alex shrugged. "Sure, I'm up for a new adventure."

On Friday, a couple of guys from Baker told Joe they were planning on hitting Clark Street Saturday night for a little fun and frivolity. They hadn't been to Dave and Buster's in ages and invited Joe to join them. Joe thought he was getting too old for that kind of stuff, but he did like to be a boss who supported his guys by hanging out with them socially. He had nothing more interesting or urgent to do, so he agreed.

He thought about Alex and wondered if she had a date with Brady. Brady had been silent, but he heard it through the grapevine they had gone out a couple of times. It pissed him off, but there wasn't anything he could do about it. He couldn't imagine that they would, but if Brady and Alex did end up in a serious relationship, he just couldn't see keeping Brady on as an employee. Joe didn't want to be constantly angry every time he looked at the guy.

Joe arrived at the venue around nine. He ordered a Miller Lite and took a stroll around the place, getting reacquainted with the layout.

"I am so bad at this! I suck!" she laughed. He heard her voice before he saw her.

"It takes some time and a little practice, so just keep trying. Don't be a quitter, Alex," Joe heard Brady's voice.

When Joe looked in their direction, he saw the two of them at side-by-side Nascar simulators. Alex was squealing with delight. "How do you keep the stupid car on the road?"

Brady just laughed and took his left hand off the wheel and patted her back encouragingly. It looked like the two of them were having a fine time together. Joe should have walked away right then and there, but his feet wouldn't move from the spot. He took a long swig of his beer and just watched them. They were concentrating on their games, oblivious to his presence. Mostly his eyes were fixed on Alex. After a while, she could feel someone watching her. She looked around. She nearly fell out of her seat when she saw that it was Joe looking at her. Joe seemed upset. His jaw was twitching. He stood there locking eyes with her, the beer dangling from his hand.

Brady's focus had not wandered from his game.

Joe bit his lip and looked down to the floor, finally pulling his eyes away from hers. He swallowed hard, trying to quell his temper. After taking a deep breath, he finally looked back up at her. She continued sitting still, looking at him and ignoring the screen with the crashing racecars. Brady was so into his game he didn't even notice that Alex had stopped playing. Joe took one last glance at Brady and then Alex, holding her gaze a moment longer. He turned away from her, deposited his beer on the nearest table and walked out. He knew Brady wasn't Alex's type, but it still hurt to see them together, to see a player like that with a woman who deserved so much better.

She watched him walk away until she could no longer see him. Her heart was beating wildly and she sat there staring at the screen, unable to focus.

Finally Brady realized she no longer had her hands on the wheel. "Hey, why'd you quit?" He looked at her a moment then turned his attention back to his screen.

She made an excuse. "Uh, my arms are just tired. I'm going to the ladies room."

When she got there, she put her forehead against the cool tile in the stall hoping her racing heart would slow down. Seeing Joe had unnerved her. She just wanted to go home and end the evening with Brady.

After, she told him she would like him to take her home because she suddenly wasn't feeling well. She sat in silence on the ride home, except for when she needed to respond to Brady's questions. She kept insisting she would be fine. She just needed to go home and lay down for a bit.

When they arrived at her house, she pulled out her keys, unlocked the door, and did not ask him in. When he told her he hoped she would be feeling better the next Saturday, he was surprised to hear that she had other plans.

Brady was wracking his brain trying to figure out what he could possibly have done wrong between dinner and the game place to have Alex suddenly blowing him off this way. He couldn't think of anything he had said or done. Had he been too focused on the games? What could have made her cool off like this?

"What is this, a kiss-off?" he asked trying to control the anger in his voice.

Alex shook her head. "Of course not. It's just something I've had planned for a while. That's all. We'll see each other again. That is, if you still want to."

"Yeah, whatever." He started to walk away.

Clearly she had hurt his feelings. "Look, I'm sorry you're upset, but I can't change next Saturday's arrangements. I'm not blowing you off. I'll call you this week," she assured him.

He smirked. "Yeah, right. See ya around." He knew what this kind of chick was about. They were done.

She threw her coat on the hall chair and strode into her family room, plunking down on the sofa. She exhaled with relief. Tilting her head back on the sofa ledge, she realized that he really wasn't her type. If the guy was going to be such a hothead about taking her home early, and jumping to conclusions, she didn't want anything more to do with him.

Her thoughts wandered toward Joe. He wouldn't have behaved like Brady. Ever. He had looked so angry, and then hurt when he saw her with Brady. Never had she meant to play with his emotions the way she had. She felt badly about all of their ups and downs, suddenly understanding how much he cared.

The week following the Dave and Buster's fiasco, Alex barely had time to think about the fact Brady had not called. And she had not bothered to call him. Joe called on Thursday to follow up about their date for Saturday night. When Saturday evening came, her stomach was in knots. She had tried on at least a dozen combinations of sweaters, jeans, shoes, and boots and they were all over her bedroom. Nothing seemed quite right, she thought in dismay. Every sweater was either too boring or too provocative. She didn't want Joe to think she was boring or get the wrong idea that she was coming on to him if she showed too much. The purpose of this date was to test the waters of a relationship and to go out as friends. After nearly losing her mind, she grabbed her handbag and headed out to her favorite new boutique to ask for Carolyn's advice. Alex didn't try to hide the fact that she had a date with Joe and asked her advice on the look she was trying to achieve.

With Carolyn's help, Alex came away delighted with a new pair of the latest trend in jeans and a kick-ass peach sweater. She could finally relax, knowing she had achieved the perfect look. The jeans fit her perfectly and the sweater showed some skin but not too much. With her light leather coat and her short, black spiked boots, she was set.

Joe, always prompt, rang her doorbell at exactly 6:30.

There were at least a dozen butterflies doing gymnastics in her stomach as she opened the door.

He looked good—delicious. Joe had on nice jeans, cowboy boots, and a black leather coat she hadn't seen before. A white shirt, and that killer smile of his completed his outfit. When he smiled even wider and quietly said "Hi," she nearly passed out. Thankfully Joe didn't notice her swoon.

He thrust a bouquet of pink roses at her. She put a hand to her stomach. Pink roses meant happiness, as well as admiration. They were off on the right foot, at least.

She smiled warmly and took the flowers. Then she thanked him, gently brushing his cheek, suddenly wanting some physical contact with him, even if so slight.

"It's good to see you. Nice coat. Looks imported," she said as she felt the smooth leather.

"Yeah, just a little something Mom picked up for me on their last trip to Florence. Glad you like it."

"It's good to see you. I've really been looking forward to tonight." He took a step back to distance himself from her so he could look her over. "You look fantastic as always." Noting the sweater he said, "That's a good color for you. I like it."

At his compliment, her face turned red. "I'm glad you like it. Actually Carolyn picked it out. She told me it was my color."

"Ah, so you bought a new sweater just for little ol' me?" he teased, secretly pleased.

"Don't flatter yourself, Baker. I needed something new anyway. You know, that ego of yours could come down a notch or two."

He grinned. "Yeah, and you're just the one to do that, aren't you."

"You know it, buddy," she bantered back.

The conversation with Joe felt so natural that Alex found herself wanting to grab him and feel his lips on hers again. Knowing her thoughts were going in an entirely wayward direction, and that her face might reveal her thoughts, she pulled back even further to widen the distance between them. Tonight was all about discovering whether they had substance, staying power. It was a chance to start off slowly.

"Let me get my coat, and we can be on our way. I'm hoping you've picked a killer dinner spot. I'm prepared to be impressed. Is it Paris? Milan? What?" she teased.

He spoke to her as she got her coat. "Well, I thought friends should probably go somewhere a little more low-key. Besides, it's a long trip back if you decide to throw your escargot at me in disgust and dump me. So," he continued, "I thought I'd take you to one of my favorite Italian place outside of Milan. There are decent restaurants in Chicago, you know."

"Well, I'm sure if it's one of your favorites, then I'll like it, too," she replied, her curiosity piqued.

Joe followed her out of the townhouse and then stopped on the porch while she locked the door. Holding her elbow, they proceeded down the stairs, and then he opened and closed the passenger side door for her.

They rode in comfortable silence for a few minutes, both lost in their own thoughts. He was the first to speak, giving her the movie options and telling her he thought the comedy would be a good choice. He wanted something fun and light, just like he wanted their evening to be. When he said that, Alex was a bit surprised.

"So, you want our evening to be fun and light? Why is that?"

Joe had decided to take the "friend" route after seeing her with Brady. He didn't want to get his hopes up, and he didn't want her to think of their evening in any way other than just hanging out together. "Well, isn't that the kind of evening friends normally have? I mean this is what we are striving for, so at first it will take a little effort that's all. Remember you want me to think of you in a non-romantic way, so since that's what the colonel ordered that's what the colonel is going to get."

Alex was surprised at what he said. She thought he wanted a "date" with her and for her to give him a chance. She took that to mean something romantic. She frowned and turned in her seat toward him. "Look Joe, I'm sorry you're looking at it that way. Can't we just try to be ourselves and then see what happens? And I never said I wanted you to think of me or treat me in a non-romantic way."

"You don't want me to be myself around you," he said softly, " because if I were, then I'd be in trouble. We've been down *that* road. It's not my fault I want to ravage your body all the time. I'm a guy. It's just normal." He chuckled. "I'm trying to be on good behavior here on our date night."

Because she didn't say anything, he glanced over at her. She was staring straight ahead, absorbing his words and looking serious.

He grabbed her hand. "Look, I'm just kidding around. I only want to ravage your body some of the time, not all the time," he joked.

When she looked over at him, she couldn't help but smile. And then he agreed, "Okay, let's just be ourselves."

Facing ahead, she shook her head up and down. "That sounds like a perfect plan."

The conversation flowed easily the rest of the way to the restaurant. Alex, of course, left out any reference to Brady, and Joe left out any reference to anyone he might have been seeing. Alex had finally begun to relax a bit, and she was aware of how much she enjoyed being with him.

As they turned into a long-established Italian neighborhood, Joe was happy to locate a parking space nearly instantly. There were several charming restaurants, but Joe steered Alex toward a small restaurant with a narrow awning made in Italy's colors of red, green, and white. "Maria's Ristorante," it proclaimed.

Joe opened the restaurant door for Alex. Inside the cozy foyer, a woman Alex thought must be Maria herself bustled toward them.

The lady kissed Joe on each cheek and gave him a motherly hug. "Joseph, it is so good to see you. Why do you stay away so long?" she scolded. "You haven't been here for weeks!"

He laughed. "You know I can't eat your fantastic pasta and drink your fabulous wine, every week. I have to watch my girlish figure."

With that Maria laughed and patted his stomach. "You are a good boy, Joey, but you could use a few pounds, eh?"

*Joey? She called him Joey?* Alex thought. She had to suppress a giggle. Joe was no more a Joey than he was a Joseph. When she thought of the name Joey, she thought of a cute little boy; and when she thought of Joseph, she thought of a saint. Joe was no little boy, nor was he a saint, that was for sure. He was, however, a cute boy—a very cute "big" boy with looks that could turn any woman's head no matter what age.

Joe grabbed Alex's hand and pulled her close to him. With a big smile on his face he said, "Maria, this is my good friend Alex. Alex, meet Maria. She runs the joint."

Alex extended her hand. "Maria, pleased to meet you. Joe told me all about you on our way over. I can't wait to taste your cooking. I *love* Italian food."

"Any friend of Joey's is a friend of mine," she said with gusto, gathering Alex into a bear hug. Maria looked her over, looked at Joe, and then back again at Alex.

"Bellissima!" she announced, clearly satisfied. "Joey, your Alex is very beautiful. You make a good couple. She is almost prettier than you."

Joe looked a bit embarrassed.

"You must be very special. I wait how long for him to bring a woman here and does he? No. Always either alone or with his men friends, but he never brings a lady. So I know you must be the special one. Am I right?"

Alex blushed, as did Joe, who spoke first. "Yes, she is very special. That's why I brought her here. But no more questions right now, okay? We want to eat!"

"Don't worry! I'm a gonna make you something very special!" Maria assured him.

The blush continued to creep up to his ears as Maria studied him. "You know Joseph, you have the look. I saw the look on my Nico's face when we first fell in love. I see it on your face, too."

Maria turned to Alex. "You will meet my Nico in a just a minute. He is busy in the kitchen. Such a handsome man …He took me away from Joey's father many years ago. You met Joey's father yet? Such a handsome, nice man too." She laughed. "And he married his"—she motioned toward Joe with her thumb— "beautiful mother Kathryn after I broke his heart." Then she laughed again. "But still, Joey, he is like my own son." She stopped talking and admired him proudly, then kissed both his cheeks. Finally, she continued, "You two lovers, what table you want? How about I put you in the back corner? Then you have more privacy for smooching."

Joe rolled his eyes and laughed. "Thank you, Maria. That would be nice."

She grabbed Alex's arm and hugged her to her side and whispered, "My Joseph, he's-a good man. You cannot do any better. You two take care of each other and be happy!" she advised, squeezing Alex again.

With her eyes shining, aglow with joy for Joe, this second mother led the couple to a table in the back corner, and then disappeared into the kitchen.

A tall, handsome, elderly man emerged from the kitchen, just as Alex and Joe were sitting down.

When he approached, Joe stood to greet him. The fatherly man kissed Joe on both cheeks, and then wrapped his arms around Joe, slapping him on the back. "Joseph, my son! I've missed you! It's good to see you!"

The man turned to Alex. "And-a who is this Bellissima? Finally, you bring a lady for dinner. Must be serious," he observed, studying Alex.

Then Nico took Alex's hand, kissed the back of it, and welcomed her to his restaurant. "I am Nico. Joseph, he's like my own son," he said proudly. "Now what can I get you to drink? I send over my best waiter to take care of you. But I take care of your drinks myself. You want a cocktail, or do you want some of my best homemade wine?"

Joe turned to Alex, brows raised in question. When she just looked at him with no response, he turned to his host. "A bottle of your special Chianti sounds good to me. What do you think Alex?"

"Sure, that sounds great."

Nico's nod expressed his pleasure that Joe had ordered one of his homemade concoctions. "I'll be right back! Half a minute!" Nico said, as he walked away to the area that housed a small bar.

Shortly thereafter, a waiter brought them menus. Joe and Alex studied the specials. Alex might as well have been looking at blank pages, because she couldn't concentrate. She found it interesting that Joe never brought women to his penthouse, and he also had never brought a woman here. Clearly, he must really value her. Alex didn't know whether to be flattered or nervous by this realization.

When he looked up to ask what she thought looked good, he could see she was staring at the menu. He was hoping his friends had not overwhelmed her. He didn't think they would react the way they had to his bringing a woman for the first time. Maybe the whole thing was a really, really bad idea. The last thing he wanted her to feel was uncomfortable. She seemed fine with the overtures extended to her at first, but now he wasn't so sure.

"So what looks good to you, my sweet friend?" he asked. When she didn't respond he inquired, "Alex, you with me?"

When she looked up, a bit startled, she replied, "Gosh, everything sounds great. They make their own pasta, right? What do you recommend?"

Smiling softly he replied, "Well, everything here is fantastic. But I'm a sucker for Maria's lasagna. I'm practically addicted to their bruschetta. And the fish is always a winner. So my choice usually depends on what I've eaten for lunch. I like the lasagna, if I'm hungry. You did say you were hungry, so how about this: we'll get Nick's bruschetta, a salad with house dressing, and then Maria's lasagna. Sound good?"

Nodding, Alex agreed. "Sounds great."

Nico arrived with a decanter of his wine creation. He poured some in each of their glasses, and poured less than an inch in the glass he had brought for himself. As they brought their glasses up, Nick proposed a toast. "To my good friend, his beautiful lady, and to a beautiful couple. May we share many glasses of wine together."

Alex smiled, thanked Nico and took a sip of her wine, nodding in appreciation. The old Italian's gesture added a warm glow to what was shaping up to be a truly memorable evening. The Italians, they definitely knew about love and romance. Alex was beginning to feel very comfortable.

"Hey, thanks Nick. I hope we have many more together, too," he said as he took a sip. "Bellisimo. The best, as usual."

Their host drained his small glass and motioned for the waiter to take their order.

After Joe had placed their order, they sat in silence as Alex gazed into her glass, thinking, and then suddenly drained it. "Great stuff. Can I have more?" Joe gave her a questioning look and then poured more into her glass.

Then he chuckled. "You know I am not so good with wine, so I am going to wait to give myself a refill when dinner comes." His face went distant for a moment, and then he continued, "Remember that time in Las Vegas? I pretty much made a fool of myself kissing you like I did. I must have looked like a real idiot. That's why I limit my consumption when it comes to wine. It makes me stupid."

The wine had begun to warm her, and her thoughts began to flow in rapid succession. *God, he makes me happy. I'm so comfortable around him. He is the hottest man I have ever met, plus possibly the kindest. He's always looking out for me and trying to protect me. He's the perfect combination of everything that I love in a man. Why didn't I see this before?* After her epiphany, Alex was determined to enjoy every bit of this night together.

The atmosphere of Maria's Ristorante was the perfect setting for both Joe and Alex to feel comfortable really getting to know each other for the first time. Joe talked a bit about the restaurant and his youth. Alex discussed her family and how it was growing up on the North Shore—very different from Joe's upbringing in the city, they soon discovered. Neither of them was trying to impress, pull back, push, or do anything unnatural. There were no pretenses or games. Tonight they were successfully being themselves.

Suddenly, Alex had a clear image of the remainder of her life unfolding, with Joe by her side. Suddenly, being with Joe made perfect sense to her. She knew, right then, that she needed to give this relationship a real chance. She was willing to risk a broken heart. He, she felt, would be worth dealing with devastation, if necessary.

"Hey, I can see smoke coming out of your ears. What's cooking in that busy little mind of yours?"

Smiling thoughtfully, Alex replied, looking into those stunning azure pools she had grown to love, "Thank you for bringing me here. I finally realized something important."

He gave her a quizzical look. "Are you going to share this epiphany, or wait until the *National Enquirer* offers you a million dollars for it?"

She gave him a courteous laugh, but then her face grew serious again. She wanted this to come out right.

"I really, genuinely, like you. I guess I always have. I don't know why I always second-guessed my feelings and questioned your intentions. I can see now that I've been wrong. Oh, Joe—I'm so sorry."

His baby blues were focused intently on her face. "Darlin', you have nothing to be sorry about. You didn't do anything wrong, so there's no need to apologize. We both know you can't make someone care about you. It has to come from in here," he said, as he fisted his left hand to the center of his chest. Then, gently touching her face, he stared into her eyes. "I really like you too, but then I'm sure I don't need to tell you that, do I? I think I always have told you, or at least shown you, haven't I?"

Just when things were getting a bit too serious, the waiter interrupted them by laying down a beautiful tray of bruschetta and saying, "Buon appetito!" He bowed and walked away.

Alex had suddenly lost her appetite as they looked at each other again. She could feel the intensity between them. *Good Lord... I think I've fallen in love with him.*

Picking up his wine glass, Joe proposed another toast. "To Alex's new revelation. May it be only the beginning of good things to come." They clinked glasses and smiled. For a man who wasn't easy on smiles or laughter, he sure was different tonight.

The meal was a feast for the senses. Having regained her appetite after his toast, she nearly inhaled the appetizer, tasty salad, and wonderful lasagna. After they finished their second glass of wine, both were content to just sit and make small talk and discover something new about each other. Looking at his watch, Joe informed her that if they were going to catch the movie, they had better think about finishing up.

"We can have a little dessert after the movie, if you like," he offered. Then he added, "But only if you're a good girl and behave."

Joe settled up the bill, but noticed Maria and Nico were not around. So, he pulled Alex into the kitchen in search of the two hosts, just like it was his own.

Maria was chopping onions on a side counter. She wiped her hands on her apron and approached them. "You are leaving us so soon? Everything was perfecto tonight?" She turned to Alex. "Bella, how was the lasagna?"

Smiling warmly, she replied that it was the best she had ever had and hoped Joe would bring her back soon.

"Of course he will bring you back! Maybe next week, right?" She gave Joe a "you'd better" look. Nico approached, and he and Maria each kissed both of them on the cheeks and followed with a round of hugs.

Maria, having to have the last say, ordered Joe to please not wait so long to come back and that he must bring Alex with him.

Alex felt her heart glowing as they got back into the car and drove to the movie.

The movie was romantic and funny. The characters were star-crossed lovers who, as expected, ended up together. She couldn't help wondering if Joe specifically picked this movie because of its parallels with their own relationship. They snuggled and held hands, as they enjoyed laughing together at the twists and turns to the plot. To Alex it seemed like it was the most perfect thing for the two of them to be doing.

It was shortly before eleven and the evening was still young, so Joe suggested they stop for ice cream. The night had remained mild, and they were able to take a short stroll around the neighborhood to enjoy their dessert. Alex felt like a kid, licking her ice cream and walking hand in hand with Joe. She really hated knowing that eventually the date would come to an end. Never in a million years would she have dreamed that the night would have turned out the way it had.

Walking back toward his car, he turned to her. "Ready to go? It's getting late and I think it's time to get Cinderella home." He had remained a perfect gentleman all evening.

She shrugged. "It's up to you. I'm fine if you want to take me home now. I suppose by the time we get back to my place, and you make the trip back to the city, it will be pretty late."

Both were lost in their individual thoughts, saying very little. Alex teased him about not having designed an over-the-top adventure, as she had insisted. And he bantered back. They both knew it had been a wonderful evening without any ostentation or pretense. Clearly simplicity was the key to connecting hearts.

When they arrived at Alex's place, Joe cut the engine and came around to her side to help her out. When they reached the landing, she inserted the key into the lock, opened the door, and then turned to him. They stared at each other a few moments.

Finally, Alex spoke. "I had a great time." She looked down, and then up into his eyes. "You know, I was pretty nervous about tonight. But the evening turned out to be perfect, and I did have a wonderful time." She cupped her hand to his cheek, and he then reached up to put his hand on top of hers. Alex closed her eyes a moment before placing her lips on his. She seemed to act on instinct. Kissing Joe seemed perfectly natural. They both felt the connection. Their lips met, warmly and tenderly at first, but the intensity quickly grew. Pulling his head toward her to increase the pressure of the kiss, she began to run her hands through his hair. She just couldn't help herself. She wanted to devour him.

Finally, as the two of them became breathless, Joe pulled her hands away from his head and backed her away from him. His voice was thick with desire. "Alex, don't start anything unless you're one-hundred percent sure you're willing to finish it. You can't play with me like this. I won't allow it anymore." He didn't know where she stood with Brady.

She looked disappointed but what he said made sense, even in her sexually fogged state.

"Do you want to finish this right now? If not, then I'm saying good night."

Thinking about it for several seconds, she closed her eyes and took a deep breath. He was right of course. Jumping into the sack on their first "date" was probably a bad idea and one they might both regret. Weren't they trying to start fresh, with a clean slate? She had to give him credit for having so much more control than she did.

She agreed. "You're right. I'm sorry. I got a little carried away. We need to take it slowly, that is, if you want to see me again." Suddenly, she felt vulnerable and unsure of herself, a place she had not often been. The better part of her entire life she had been so self-assured. Since meeting Joe, that had all changed.

Stepping back toward her he put his forehead to hers and whispered, "Of course I want to see you again, are you kidding me?" They stayed that way for a few moments when Joe finally backed up. "I'm glad you enjoyed the evening. I did too. Very much. So let's do it again soon. Okay?" He didn't want Alex to feel pressured about exactly when next time would be.

"I'd like that very much."

He nodded and started down the stairs. As he was about to reach his car she called out, "Joe, wait!" He turned around as she ran down the steps, and when she reached him she threw her arms around him and held him tight. When she looked up into his face it greeted her with a warm smile. He kissed her gently on the cheek. "Good night, Alex. Sweet dreams, darlin'." He swatted her rear end and then watched as she ran back up the stairs. At the top, she looked back at him one last time, gave him Stephanie's flirty little wave, and closed the door.

As Joe drove away, his face broke into an enormous grin. What an incredible evening it had been, even though they'd only been to Little Italy, rather than real Italy. It was wonderful to see Alex enjoying herself, feeling comfortable with him and not resisting her own instincts. Joe felt happy for the first time in a very long time. He thanked God for allowing him and Alex to finally find happiness together. Even just for one evening.

After he drove off, Alex made sure the house was locked up tight. She walked into her living room and turned on the stereo. Curling up on her sofa, she grabbed her throw and wrapped it around herself. She put her feet up on the ottoman and ran the events of the evening through her head.

Enraptured, she replayed every moment, from the time Joe had arrived at her door to pick her up to their goodnight kiss. Things had gone so much better than she had expected. She had to admit she had been skeptical and nervous at first. But things had all fallen into place so naturally. Tonight was like spending the night with a best friend—fun, easy, relaxing. The more time she spent with Joe, the stronger the physical attraction became. But now, there was much more than that. What had started out as only a sexual connection was ripening into something deep and meaningful. The thought of sleeping with Joe no longer scared her. Somehow, it seemed right, now.

For the first time, Alex let herself think about being with him on a regular basis. Tonight had given her a glimpse of what it would be like to spend her life with him, and the concept was very appealing. It seemed like Joe felt the same way, and had for a long time. But she wanted to be sure. She intended to find out, even if the heart she was so preciously protecting ended up broken. The light had finally gone off in her head. Tonight the bulb shone brightly, and she knew in her heart, and finally accepted the fact, that she was in love with Joe Baker. She had been for a very long time.

Alex slept like a baby that night, the burden of uncertainly finally lifted. When she woke up, she immediately thought of Joe. The morning was hers to relish. At long last, she felt confident about the direction she was heading. She called Stephanie to fill her in. Joe had already called Mike to report on their evening. Stephanie said Mike told her he hadn't heard Joe so upbeat in a long time. Alex felt pretty upbeat herself.

"It was... How can I put it? I don't know—amazing! And new. Yet very comfortable at the same time. Gosh, for the first time ever I felt really at ease around him. I was totally myself and didn't put up any walls or hold back. We had a wonderful time and I'm so glad he feels the same way. I just don't know what the next step is, ya know? I feel like a teenager instead of a grown woman."

Her friend sighed. "The next step will come naturally. I mean that's how it was with Mike and me. As you know, I wasn't so sure at first, either. But my gut tells me that when Joe sets his mind to something he goes after it. And you do, too. I think things are going to turn out just fine."

"Do you think I should call him, or wait for him to call me? Maybe I should put myself out first, since I've always held back, and he's always been the one forging ahead. What do you think?"

"What do *you* want to do? What are you feeling, Alex?" Steph coached.

She couldn't admit her feelings for him to her friend, at least not yet. It wouldn't be fair for Stephanie to know she finally figured out she loved Joe without telling him first.

"Well, I feel good about him. I'm just not sure who should call first. I don't want to mess this up," she acknowledged.

"Take your time and think things through, because this is a pretty important decision. You have to be fair to him and be absolutely certain. Let's face it, it's no news to any of us that he's crazy about you."

Alex shook her head and smiled. "Yeah, I think I finally figured that out. Okay, so I needed to be hit over the head," she laughed. "So you're sure Mike said Joe sounded happy? Like he had a great time?"

"Of course I'm sure!" she replied. "Mike said he sounded *very* happy. Do the two of us have to talk for each of you? Do you want me to tell him you love him, and do you want Mike to tell you he loves you or can you two do it yourselves? Maybe you two *are* kids."

Alex was incredulous. "I didn't *say* I loved him!"

"Well not in so many words, but listening to you, it's pretty freakin' obvious. It's me, Steph. Remember? Who do you think you're kidding?"

Alex screwed up her mouth. "Hmmm. It's that obvious, huh? Okay. Well, if and when I do tell him, you'll be the first to know." She paused a minute, then she added, "I think I'll wait to see if he calls. If he doesn't, then maybe I'll call him tomorrow to thank him for the lovely evening. I've gotta get some things done now, though, so I'll see ya tomorrow morning," she told her best friend. It was delicious thinking about her next conversation with the man she… loved. *Yes, that's right*, she reminded herself. Loved.

For his part, Joe was also uncertain whether to call Alex or wait for her to decide when it was time for them to talk. After calling Mike to report on the previous evening, Joe had worked out, showered, and made himself something to eat. He wondered what Alex was doing. He didn't want to push the relationship. He thought maybe that evening, after dinner, he'd give her a quick call to remind her what a great time he'd had last night. He knew they both wanted to take things slowly.

When Joe hadn't heard from Alex, he called her that evening. They laughed a lot, and Joe thought she sounded happy. He didn't bring up seeing her again. Their next date had to be on her terms. Alex was disappointed that Joe didn't bring up the topic. She didn't realize he was waiting for her to make the next move.

Chapter 18

When Monday rolled around and Alex returned to work, she had a hard time concentrating. Feeling antsy all the time was unusual for her. Her thoughts constantly drifted toward Joe.

When she got home from work Wednesday night, she was listening to "Far Away" and realized what her next move should be. Steph had said things would evolve naturally, and she saw now that Steph was right. Alex retrieved a recordable CD and popped it in her burner, where she recorded Donna Lewis's "I Love You Always Forever." The lyrics described exactly how she felt. This was exactly how Joe had conveyed his feelings for her at Navy Pier. She knew he would understand. He really did have the most "stumbling blue eyes" she had ever seen, and she did "love him always, forever." All she had to lose was her heart, but she had to take this where she hoped it might go.

Thursday morning she retrieved an overnight envelope from the office mailroom, put the CD and case into a protective mailer, and put it into the envelope for Friday next-day-delivery to the penthouse on Lake Shore Drive. Then she filled out the return address on the air bill. Feeling no note of explanation was necessary, she sealed the envelope and dropped it into the mail bin.

She felt giddy as she waited for him to receive this message and imagined Joe's expression when he played the CD.

When Joe came home Friday, Charles had put his mail at his door as usual. He was curious about the overnight envelope and at first didn't look at the return address. He took off his work boots and socks at the front door, carried them in, and deposited them on the marble entry floor. He hung up his coat and sat down in the great room. He glanced at the few other pieces of mail and threw them on the coffee table. Then he reached for the cardboard envelope. The sender section had Alex's name and address on it.

After ripping the pull-tab, he reached inside and pulled out the padded mailer with the CD. Looking in the envelope he saw there was no note and nothing written on the CD. He was confused for a moment and then figured he was supposed to play it. He walked over to his stereo, powered it on, and popped in the disc.

The song was one he was familiar with. He stood in front of the player, listening. When the song ended, he waited. Would there be a spoken message? More songs? No, just silence. He hit the rewind button and listened to the song again, this time paying more attention to the words. He stood rooted to the spot staring at the player as the singer talked about stumbling blue eyes and love, always and forever. As he began to play it a third time, he questioned himself, thinking he had misread the return label. He turned and grabbed it from the table and read the name again. *Yes, it says Alexis Parker,* he thought.

It couldn't be a joke. That would be the ultimate cruelty. And if it wasn't… He could scarcely contain himself at the meaning. He listened again. Was this really from Alex? Was she really trying to tell him something important? Did she have trouble putting her feelings into words, the way he did?

Joe found his heart pounding wildly. She thought he had amazing blue eyes? She would love him always and forever? Overcome with joy, he pulled out his cell phone and started to call her. No. Something this important needed to be dealt with face to face. He cranked up the volume as he played it again and went to the bathroom, took a swig of mouthwash, and struggled into his topsiders. He grabbed the CD and slipped it into his coat pocket. Then he ran into the bedroom, withdrew a small silk drawstring bag from his nightstand, and shoved it into the front pocket of his jeans.

He could hardly concentrate on the road he was so excited. He continued to play the song, listening carefully to the words, on his way to her house.

Alex was nervous waiting for Joe to discover her message. She didn't know what time he would be home and wasn't even sure if the CD would arrive that day. Sometimes overnight services screwed up and things didn't get delivered on time. Deciding to forego making dinner because her stomach was a mass of flutters, she poured herself a glass of wine and curled up on the sofa, tensely waiting for the phone to ring.

The ringing of the doorbell snapped her out of her trance. Whoever it was didn't have much patience, because the bell rang incessantly. Putting down her wine and making her way to the door, she glanced through one of the side clear stained-glass windows and made out Joe's features. He looked serious, deep in thought.

She opened the door and took in his appearance. He still had on his work clothes, as evidenced by the Baker Concrete shirt under his unzipped bomber jacket. His hair looked like he had been running his hands through it, and his five o' clock shadow made a strong presence. He had changed out of his work boots, but failed to put on a pair of socks. It was obvious he had been in a hurry.

He held the CD in front of her face. "Did you send this to me? You better not be playing with me again, because if you are I've had it. I can't take any more games." She looked into his eyes with a seriousness she hadn't seen before. But his eyes were that stormy color she was so familiar with.

Not wanting to cause a ruckus in front of the neighbors, she pulled him inside the townhouse. "No, Joe. It's not a joke. Did you listen to the song?"

His jaw was twitching. He was scared that she was toying with him again.

Alex knew that from past experience he had a reason not to trust her. It was obvious he didn't have a clue what was going on. She'd just have to spell it out for him. This wasn't quite how she had pictured the situation playing out. In her fantasies, he swept her off her feet and told her he loved her, too. But maybe this could still be salvaged.

"Here, let me take your coat and then let's go sit down." He relinquished his jacket, still not letting go of the CD, looking at her skeptically. He reluctantly sat on the sofa.

"Here, give it to me," she said. He handed it to her, and she popped it into the player and sat next to him on the sofa. When the song started playing, he took a quick look at her out of the corner of his eyes and then began to stare at the floor.

"Okay, now listen to the words," she demanded.

Having spent months hoping she would someday want him in her life, he felt like he was somewhere on some other planet instead of sitting in her living room. The past few days had seemed surreal. When he looked over at her, he read tenderness on Alex's face.

Overcome with emotion, he pulled her face closer to his. "Alex, I need to hear it from your own lips… are you trying to tell me you love me?" he asked softly, tears beginning to sting his eyes. He blinked a couple of times to keep them from spilling down his cheeks, as they clung to his thick dark lashes.

"Because if you love me and you say it there's no turning back. You can't take it back. I won't let you. I've waited for you for a very long time."

Alex stared back into his beautiful eyes. Taking his cheeks in her two hands she replied, "I love you, Joe Baker. I love you with all my heart. I have for a long time. I've just been a fool to not realize it or admit it to anyone, especially myself."

What a relief. She had finally admitted it. Out loud. To the person who most needed to hear it.

She dropped her hands, cocked her head, and gently smiled at him. "It finally hit me after Saturday night, especially when I spent every waking minute after that thinking about how it felt being with you. There was never a time when we were together from the very beginning that I ever felt I didn't care about you, even from that ill-fated day at the job site when I messed with your concrete. You invaded my dreams all the time, but I thought it was a passing fancy. Gheesh, I sound like I'm fifteen. But I figured you could have anyone you wanted, and of course for a long time I had convinced myself I was in love with Richard." She shook her head. "Can you imagine if I had actually married him? What a disaster it would have been. You saved me."

Looking at her questioningly, he asked, "So maybe that's why you think you love me—because I saved you from Richard?"

"No, you just opened my eyes, that's all. I was so afraid that you wouldn't love me back that I kept denying my feelings."

With that she stopped. "Oh, I guess you didn't say you loved me, did you." She bit her lip and looked down. *Oh, crap!* she thought.

He gave a loving smile, tears welling up in his eyes again. "Alexis Parker," he said with deep emotion, "I love you with every inch of my being. I have for a very long time."

Alex was on the verge of tears herself.

She didn't speak, so he continued. "Sitting in that hospital after your car accident, thinking I might lose you, that's when I knew. I knew my life would shatter if something had happened and I lost you. I didn't care when I found out about Richard. Nothing mattered but you getting through that whole thing and the chance that someday you and I might be together."

Thinking about it, she leaned back on the sofa and put her hands behind her head looking to the ceiling. "Yeah, me too—I mean the part about maybe being together someday. But do you want to know what the clincher was with me?"

"There's a clincher?" he asked with an amused look on his face. He did the same, putting his hands behind his head, leaning back, and looking at the ceiling. Putting his feet up he asked, "Was it when we made love?"

"Oh, Baker. Stop being so full of yourself again. No it wasn't then, although I have to say that was pretty incredible. But don't go getting your ego in a tizzy. Actually, from the moment you pulled me from the concrete and cleaned up my Jimmy Choos, you've protected me and watched over me. No man has ever cared for me that much or treated me that way—except my father, of course."

He looked at her, searching her face. "So you're admitting you like macho, protective men like me?" He wasn't teasing. He was asking her for an honest answer, so she gave it to him.

"Well, usually that's not my gig. But then I met you and I kind of liked it. You overdo it, sometimes, of course." She got a fake indignant look at her face and then laughed at him. "Okay so I guess since meeting you it's become my gig."

He laughed too. "Okay, so where do you think we go from here?"

"How do I know? We've done a complete about-face in the past week. How does one go from denying the obvious to embracing it completely?" she asked. Joe's eyes began to twinkle. He wasn't going to let her get away again. Ever. He would have liked to do something much more romantic and memorable, but all that could wait. He wasn't going to miss this opportunity.

"Hmmm. I think I just might have an idea," he said, putting his finger to his lips and pretended to ponder it. "I think we should just go for it."

She looked at him and raised her eyebrows. "Go for it?"

Her eyes got wide, as he got off the couch and dug into the front right pocket of his jeans, pulling out a tiny silk drawstring bag. Getting down on one knee, untying the two strings and pulling open the bag, he pulled out an impressive diamond ring. It had to be at least three karats, though it was still tasteful and elegant. The style was exactly what she would have chosen for herself.

Alex was shocked. "Do you normally walk around with large diamond rings in your pocket?" she said, nervously, to break the intensity of the situation.

"Of course not. I had more of a romance-novel situation in mind. But I didn't want to wait. Just in case you changed your mind. I'm not letting you get away again. Ever," he confessed.

"And now," he said, sliding the stunner onto the fourth finger of her left hand, "Alexis Parker, will you marry me?"

The ring fit perfectly. Joe had actually made the purchase the week after Alex had walked away from Richard, figuring when the time was right he wanted to have it on a moment's notice. He had consulted Stephanie on what Alex would want and entrusted her with his plans. Though the secret was difficult to keep, Stephanie had not broken his trust.

The look on Joe's face was one she would never forget her entire life. He was very serious. Although she found apprehension and uncertainty there, above all she saw unconditional love. She felt like her heart would burst.

"Yes, Joseph Baker. Of course I'll marry you. What sane woman would say no to a wonderful, tender man who is loving too, not to mention very, very hot, if I must say so myself."

It took a moment for her response to register in his brain, which at the moment was fogged with emotion. When it finally dawned on him she had accepted his proposal, he sighed with relief and hung his head trying to control those emotions. When he looked back up at her, his eyes were bright again.

Seeing him like that she completely lost it and started crying. He grabbed her and started placing short, happy kisses all over her face. They both began to laugh, and when their laughter subsided he pulled her against him and started to devour her mouth. "You're mine now," he murmured against her lips, "and don't you ever forget it." He stood, lifted her and began to carry her. "Point me in the right direction, darlin'. I can't wait to see your bedroom."

They made love with a passion that went well beyond the previous time. They had finally connected mentally, and it showed in their physical union. Neither of them thought anything could rival that first time, but they were both very wrong. This time, their intimate expression was a complete joining of two hearts, minds, and souls.

When they were both exhausted, Joe held her close and stroked her hair. "God, you have no idea how much I've been dreaming about being with you again."

"Well, let's face it. You've absolutely ruined me for any other man," she teased.

More than an hour had gone by while they cuddled and talked about their future. They were in their own little world. Then it occurred to them that the rest of the planet existed. They needed to get the word out. So, Alex grabbed the phone and rang the Murphys. Joe took the line and spoke first. "Hey, there's big news. I wanted you guys to be the first to know that there's going to be another wedding. Yes, I'm finally getting married." He smiled. "And, yes, you know her."

Alex had to laugh at the sound of his words. She yelled so that her friends could hear, "Finally!"

Joe put the phone back into its cradle and pulled her close. "Finally. You're all mine, and I'll never let you go." He nuzzled her neck, taking in all that was Alex. Then, just for fun, he said, "So, are we inviting Jimmy Choo to the wedding?"

# ABOUT THE AUTHOR

Dani Burke has always been an avid fan of women's fiction. She finally decided it was time to try her hand at a little story-telling of her own. Having resided in the Chicago area the better part of her life, it seemed appropriate to use this location as the setting for *Highway to Love*. Dani has spent her career with various legal teams in several real estate industry–related companies. Currently she is a Legal Administrative Assistant for a Chicago real estate developer and resides with the love of her life in the Chicago suburbs.

You can follow Dani Burke on her blog:
**www.daniburke.com**